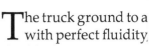

The truck ground to a with perfect fluidity, the blockage in steps too synchronized for anything natural. Aaron watched until that thing stood at the foot of the rocky barricade, and then he finally dared to breathe deeply, feeling like a giant weight had been momentarily lifted. The very presence of that thing scared him.

The creature was making quick work of the rock slide, shoveling aside the boulders as if they were Styrofoam. Its arms were a blur as they tossed aside rocks in a cascade of rubble, resembling darkened streaks that were shooting tan-colored torrents of debris. Rubble pounded the roadsides, the resonating thunderclap booming like dueling jackhammers. The mechanical preciseness made Aaron think about how that thing must have handled the soldiers at the blockade. And probably the cabin, too. He felt his internal temperature rising, his body hair stood on end, and he decided he had to get away from that monster as soon as possible. He uncoiled his legs and stretched them over the edge of the seat. Inching forward until they were just shy of reaching the floor, he dropped, trying to make as little noise as possible. The pounding of rocks drowned out everything, but it would be just his luck that the monster would pause at the wrong instant.

THE END
OF THE
WORLD

BY DAN HENK

DEDICATION

To my late wife Monica, who always believed in me

PROLOGUE

The mighty U.S. had fallen, the once great superpower fragmenting into a maelstrom of feuding territories and warring factions. An unpopular president and his socialist agenda had proved the last straw, the states breaking away as rioting and anarchy descended on the land.

Terrified local communities clustered together, more than a few of them instituting a makeshift police state as a shell government clung to power, trying to rebuild something from the ashes. Yet for a select few, this chaotic pandemonium would prove to be a bittersweet escape.

In the time before the government collapsed, a federal minion by the name of Dave, buried in the lower echelons of a government lab, had stumbled across something incredible. While working for a clandestine agency attempting to reverse engineer the recovered wreckage of a craft of unknown origin, he came across an enigmatic object, a stylized humanoid "spacesuit" strangely lacking in design details and whose full-face helmet showed no facial features except for the eyes, which resembled camera lenses. The strange surface patterns on the suit suggested muscle contours, and it was constructed of an unknown matte black material resistant to penetration by even the sharpest and hardest points they applied. Dave had developed the theory that it was intended for exploratory purposes. It was found in a chamber together with an unidentifiable apparatus, and he concluded the suit was inhabited through a transfer of consciousness before it was dropped into an inhospitable environment. His co-workers disagreed, and as his insular attitude and irritability built up, he was eventually transferred off the project.

A year later he returned, and in a bloody coup he proved the merit of his theory. He managed to possess the suit and dispense with his human form, and fled a government that was now in hot pursuit.

He retreated to a cabin up north, hoping the heat would die down before he ventured below the border and disappeared into the rainforests there. Only that proved to coincide with the fall of the government, rendering his flight to Mexico a boorish nightmare of violence and confusion. It was during a lull in his struggles, while tramping through the jungle, that he stumbled across the remains of an ancient alien outpost. It had been built by the very aliens who originated the suit, and his accidental summoning of them proved another bane in his plight. They drew him into a cosmic political game that flung him across the galaxy before eventually dropping him back into the jungle they took him from.

On another continent, a young man named Aaron was busy dealing with his share of stress, for not only was he a teenager and something of a punk rock outcast, but in a development he didn't come close to understanding, he had begun hearing the voices of dead people. Even worse, just going down a familiar trail might send him off into another world. The weirdness had started when he was an Army brat living on a base in North Carolina, and it had intensified when his family moved to Northern Virginia and he entered the throes of adolescence. Unplanned and unwelcome, the misery was compounded by having religious parents and the appearance of adults that seemed to know far too much.

The incidents increased over time, and on his last trip he ended up in an alternate reality that was like something straight out of a B movie. The freakish environment infused in him a boldness and courage that he had never possessed at home, empowering him to sexual and battlefield conquests in the midst of a full-on alien invasion. It was like a dream, which in fact was what Aaron thought was the most likely scenario. But as is the case with dreams, he stumbled back into his real life—only it wasn't the reality he was familiar with. The D.C. he returned to was an unruly tumult of anarchy and violence, courtesy of a now-failing government.

He made his way to friend's house in Northern Virginia, and the two of them fled south to a band house in Richmond. Only nowhere was safe now, and the fall of civilization was merely a precursor to what was to come.

The Sum of All Our Fears

It starts, as it often does, in space. Tensile strings of vapor whirl away in a miasma of cloudy mist emanating from the craft. Resembling more than anything an armor-plated black beetle, it descends toward an icy planet, one of several worlds the Al'lak call home.

Descent towards on icy planet, one of several the Al'lak call home

They are an ancient species, the Al'lak, eclipsing the relatively upstart race of man, which composes a faint blip in a cosmic timeline that measures its years in the billions. Passive and subsisting largely by community, the sheer efficiency of the Al'lak has worked to their advantage, allowing them to spread their ind across the universe. The more volatile species are predisposed to individualistic tendencies, and as a result they typically are easily manipulated by the Al'lak. Warlike and emotional ones, like the humans, usually wipe themselves out before they venture far beyond their own cosmic backyard. There are millions of such tiny blips scattered throughout the universe, geniuses on the verge of attaining interstellar travel. Most of those that do succeed quickly annihilate themselves soon thereafter or are annihilated in their infancy, which is largely taken to be for the good of the rest of the universe.

Ah, except for the humans, who have stumbled onto something that far surpasses their comprehension. There are so many worlds—millions in this universe alone, and beyond that a whole multiverse to contend with, some hosts to a living nightmare. But the real issue in this universe is the fact a human sentience now occupies an Al'lak suit, something akin to a Neanderthal manning the controls of an M1 Abrams tank.

A vexing experiment, on its last legs support-wise, the suit simply fell into their hands. One completely unintended aspect of the suit was that the human constitution seemed able to survive within its strictures, something that had as yet proved too much for any Al'lak. And once in, there was no extraction plan. So far the Al'lak had used terse communication and bluffing to address the problem. But being Al'lak, deception is not in their nature, and if the suit's true capacity were ever realized by its human occupant, the entire universe could be at risk. In a cruel twist of fate, the only beings capable of developing such a technology are not equipped to use it. And in what might be an even crueler twist of fate, the only beings devious enough to extract a human from the suit are members of that very same race.

The First to Go

Ben's head hurt, and it was way too early for that sort of thing. At least he had gotten some solid rest last night, even if it had been way too short. His friend Suzie had smuggled him in through the rear sliding glass door and into her basement days ago, leaving the door unlocked thereafter whenever she could. He tried not to abuse the privilege and crashed in her basement only when he had nowhere else to go.

A worn, forest-green sleeping bag was nestled next to the descending stairwell. Constructed of raw wooden planks, the place resembled an unfinished basement. The staircase itself was also made up of similarly unfinished boards, although the basement floor was carpeted, even if it was with inexpensive low-pile industrial carpeting. Some lawn care supplies occupied one corner—a lawnmower, weed whacker, and boxes packed with a variety of typical suburban gardening tools. There was plenty of open space, with a beanbag being the only other thing in the room. Ben lodged there with the fear that Suzie's parents might come down any minute and discover him. He was also sure she had a sibling or two, and he debated what would happen if anyone but Suzie found him. Given the opportunity, he would flee out the back. A skinny punk rocker, replete with a spiked leather jacket, leather pants, combat boots, and a red-tinged black Mohawk, would draw plenty of attention in this neighborhood. It was the South after all, and the suburbs accordingly were an enclave of the well-to-do and small minded. Middle-class housewives would be on their phones in seconds notifying the police, and he would stick out like a sore thumb. Suzie had asked him to leave in the morning by 6:00, only he had been out drinking with friends at the mobile home they rented from the local university as a form of cheap student housing, and he had stopped counting his drinks long before he stopped consuming them. It all combined to make the cocoon of sleep that much harder to leave.

One of the guys at the trailer was an old-school punk rocker. His appearance was more mainstream now, and it was out of nostalgia for the good old days that he had brought Ben in, a move the others seemed to tolerate just fine. Sometimes he crashed there. Only last night, Suzie had shown up at the trailer, and he'd ended up hanging out with her across town. They had gone skinny dipping in the local pool, and he had contemplated making a move on her. He wasn't even sure he wanted to fuck her, and if nothing worked out, there went one of his two crash pads. Many of his friends had left for college, and those who remained lived with parents who, once they found out he was homeless, refused to let him stay. He had spent a few uncomfortable nights in the woods using a rock as a pillow, making the hospitality offered by Suzy a rare find.

Ben was a skinny misfit who mainly got laid as a result of drunken hookups, and fortunately for him he was drunk half the time. Alcohol gave him courage, naturally enough, and the confidence to be himself, whatever that meant. All the same, he remained sensitive to boundaries and was nervous about crossing them.

He had no job, and the few places he'd approached denied him flat out. Having a Mohawk certainly didn't help. Friends had loaned him some nicer clothing, and he'd halfheartedly tried a few places: Subway, Staples, Walmart—it wasn't like he aimed high. But he was only met with headshakes. Many told him they weren't hiring before he even finished speaking. He had a telemarketing job for about a week, for a police ball, no less, and he'd already blown that money on Mad Dog 20/20, Wild Irish Rose, and Thunderbird—all tricks of the trade, and the first thing to gobble up funds. Cigarettes were a close second, but he could always bum those. He needed to eat as well, and he'd bought a sack of rice from the local supermarket. It was all of two dollars and would last him well over a week.

He'd cook it up in a plastic cup at the microwave in his friend's trailer, add a little salt and pepper from the packets he stole from McDonald's, and finish it off using a plastic spoon also courtesy of McDonald's. He was in there daily, bathing in their restroom sinks and using their paper towels to dry off. Mainly he looked after his face and his hair. He really didn't sweat that much, and only had one set of clothing besides. It was enough—and everything else was free.

Sometimes the college guys at John's trailer would kick him their fast food leftovers. They seemed to find him amusing, if nothing else. Even though they mostly had the look of straight-laced all-American kids, they were far from jocks. Even John looked a bit like them, if a little taller and stockier. He had the face of a young Mickey Rourke, his perma-grin hinting that he wasn't quite playing with a full deck. The other punks in town, the few there were, would stop by some nights. They were congenial, though distant. No one had much money, so everyone was down to hang as long as it didn't cost them anything.

Ben let none of this bother him. He was 19, his parents had kicked him out, and sooner or later he would get something going. There was plenty of time. What he wanted most to do was move. Not to Memphis or Nashville, where it was still the mediocre South. His sites were set on NYC. A hotbed of punk rock activity. But he didn't know anyone there, had no money, and knew how big cities could be cruel to newbies. That was assuming he could even get there in the first place.

His friend Tim had moved to another town. It was still in Tennessee, but at least it was somewhere else, not to mention a little closer to NYC. Maybe he could crash with him and figure out what to do from there. True, Tim had spent two years in prison. For shooting a cop no less. He was 16 when he did it, and it had been an accident—even the officer had testified to that—but them's the breaks.

Tim lived in a row house in the ghetto of Nashville with his stripper girlfriend. Ben had gone to visit him a few months earlier with his friend Chris. They had hung out with Tim and his short, red-headed girlfriend. A few cases of Mickey's Big Mouth had taken the edge off, and that night they crashed on the cold, bare wood floors in the threadbare sleeping bags Tim had provided. Ben was left with the impression the place had once been a church or other communal building back in the day. It was old, decrepit, and pretty depressing.

As Ben drunkenly gawked at the ceiling, he realized that, perhaps for the first time in his life, he was truly scared. This was the dark, depressing dreariness of reality. Of not making it. When he was a kid he imagined being and doing so many different and interesting things. The world had been filled with wonder and endless possibilities. Now he was homeless, with nothing to call his own. He couldn't get a job—he couldn't even get a break. He had to do something. He refused to let it end like this.

He reflected on how jail had changed Tim. He was still on the skinny side, only now he was covered in a sheen of wiry muscle. His boyish face and curly, dark brown Mohawk made him look less serious, only the Mohawk was fading now that his hair had grown in on the sides. His voice had deepened, his thin cheeks had filled out, and he had gone from looking like Johnny Depp to looking more like some grizzled young adult that Ben barely knew. It was also disturbing that he never quite met your gaze. Instead his eyes were occupied by a faraway look, like he was only halfway there, even at the best of times. Still, he talked the old game, and they had been friends once. All Ben really needed was a fresh start. A place to stay for a night or two, and advice from someone who apparently knew the trick to beginning again with no support. His dad, a stereotypical Navy man, had disowned him after the jail thing. The single mom he lived with was now in jail, and his closest friends had been misfit punk rockers who all went a bit strange following the lockup. They never visited or wrote him, with the exception of Chris, and two years later when he got out of juvie it must have been a nightmare. Only Tim didn't give up, and in time he had prevailed.

Ben decided his best move would be to figure out how to get Tim to open up. It was already fall, and he had spent the previous winter homeless. A few nights he had ended up with no place to stay, not even a friend's car to crash in, and had to wander the streets all night in an attempt not to freeze to death. He really needed to get something going before winter came around again.

People he once thought were friends had shown their true colors, and he had been jumped and beaten up by skinheads twice already. He knew he was too smart for this "piece of human garbage" bit. He had done well in school, at least until the last two years. The down-in-the-dumps thing was a transitory twist of fate that he'd turn around. All he needed was to get somewhere better. Somewhere that wasn't so 9 to 5. *Ha, nine to five, you're not alive...* he thought. He just had to figure out how to get to Tim's again, and then how to approach the guy. They barely knew each other anymore, and it wasn't like they were best friends to begin with.

He stayed late at John's trailer, pounding the cheap beer they always managed to scrounge up. It was the first time Ben had seen a beer bong, and a few months later he was a master at it. He must have put away twenty-five beers that night, which, considering that he only weighed 135 pounds, was a real feat. Chris had shown up, and he had talked to him about visiting Tim again.

Chris was a tall, skinny blond, with an epic purple Mohawk that he remembered from high school. His girlfriend would be by later, and even though the car was hers, Chris said it shouldn't be a problem.

Around 2:30 in the morning, with everyone either passed out or on the verge of it, this guy Mike had given Ben a ride to Suzie's house. It was all a blurry trip through darkened suburbs, but fortunately Mike had been there before since Ben was way too wasted to give good directions. He had hoped to stay at John's place, only it didn't work out that way, and the roommates had given him some excuse that his drunken cognition had understood simply as "not tonight."

They stopped down the street from the house, and Ben slunk up the concrete pathway. The darkness and the cover from the overhanging trees were probably enough for him to evade scrutiny, but he hunkered down and tried to keep a low profile regardless. He took a deep breath and realized that the cold of fall was starting to settle in. The smell of burning wood filled his nostrils as more and more fireplaces returned to use. He made out the silhouette of Suzie's house and stumbled onto the grassy lawn, waded through a swell of blades slick with dew, assessed the coast was clear by means of his peripheral vision, and cut around back. Fortunately Suzie had left the sliding door unlocked and he slipped inside. In his drunken haze he had nearly failed to slide close the rear door, but he remembered at the last moment and gave it a gasping push. He tried to be quiet, fishing through the dark with his arms outstretched until they alighted on metal. It occurred to him that he was so drunk he couldn't detect the ever-present smell of mold. Tripping forward, he fell into the sleeping bag in a wasted stupor. Trying his best to be quiet about it, he lifted up the back end and fumbled around for the opening. He'd left the bag mostly closed up, hoping to avoid drawing unwanted attention, and he was close to passing out curled atop the bag when a chill ran through him and he decided to pull it open. The minute he was inside, he was out.

The bright light of day woke him. He shielded his eyes and groaned as he tried to right himself. A sudden idea burst through his hazy mind and his eyes flew open. Frantically he tried to figure out what time it was. If he'd overslept, it could be really bad! He had never met Suzie's parents! If they spied him, they might assume he was a homeless bum who had wandered in, and they might call the police. As a matter of fact, they could have already stumbled upon him, and the police might be on the way right now!

Then he reasoned that it was probably early afternoon at the latest, and they should be at work. He might not need to stay there much longer, but he really didn't want to fuck this up at the last minute. Then he froze, and all the blood drained from his face. There were voices upstairs, and a scurry of movement. Worse still, the voices he could make out sounded strained, as if they were upset. He couldn't decipher the words, but he assumed a woman was shouting at a man. Perhaps not so much shouting since her voice was lowered, more like throwing out words in a stressed tone. He debated if they were discussing him, and a horrifying thought crossed his mind. *What if they saw me and are waiting on the cops?*

He threw open the sleeping bag and scampered upright. Fortunately, he hadn't unlaced his boots or even taken off his jacket. He must have been wrecked last night!

He kicked loose the last remnants of the sleeping bag and edged out from the stairwell. No time to even try to hide the sleeping bag now. He arced his head around the staircase wall and peered upward. The door to the basement was closed, the alcove harboring it still dark. He was pretty sure it led to the kitchen, and light was streaming from a crack under the door. Beyond it, sharp voices were exchanging angry words. Ben had a real bad feeling about this. He looked back and darted for the rear glass door.

Sliding it open, he popped out into the backyard. Right underneath the awning was drenched in shade, but everything else was visible in the sun-bleached patch of grass that spread out to a line of trees that ran along the backside of the fence. Although the leafy branches offered shade, they were widely spaced and he could see all the houses beyond. He could swear that people that were staring directly at him through all those windows. The structures were all so prim and conservative looking in the light of day, all softly colored paneling and white framework, windows with neatly drawn curtains that were open just enough for any nosy housewife to see him in all his glory. God, he hated this neighborhood. All it would take was one look and he'd be screwed.

He edged around to the side of Suzie's house, where the corridor between houses afforded visibility of him only from a few windows. Everything looked abandoned in the intense midday sun. The light was oppressive, and he felt weak and exposed. The alcohol still in his system was making him feel nauseated, and the burning smell of fall commingled with that of the freshly cut grass wasn't helping. Hunched over, he made it out onto the sidewalk and started shuffling down the path. He felt like he was in enemy territory here, only every time he picked up the pace he was overcome with a surge of nausea and had to slow down again. All he needed was to make it out to a main street. Maybe he could crash in the woods again, sleep off the rest of this hangover. The forest was nearby, and he had crashed there before.

A siren sounded, and Ben doubled over and froze in his tracks. Waves of heat flushed his skin, fighting with the liquid sickness racking his body. He tried to straighten up.

"Halt! Stop where you are!"

Ben didn't need this. He had a record. It was mostly made up charges. Well, the public intoxication *was* his fault, although the rest just made him look bad. Even the drunkenness charge would have been dismissed if he were a frat boy.

A bald, overweight cop had exited his car and was walking quickly in his direction. The midday sun shone off the policeman's oily forehead, his eyes hidden behind generic sunglasses. Ben tilted his head upright and stared. All he could make out was a blur of dark blue, the metal on him gleaming in brilliant flashes. Their jiggling glimmer induced another wave of nausea. The officer's head and hands were barely visible, the midday sun bleaching out features that were already a blur of motion.

"What are you doing here? What's your name?"

In a flash, he was instantly much closer, as if time had twisted in some weird way. It was not a figment of his imagination. An instant ago that guy had been much farther away. Pale blue eyes burned down at him from a chubby face that bespoke one too many beers.

"Ben... Ben Michaels..."

It was too hot. Ben's jacket was stifling, his tight leather jeans were plastered to his legs, and his feet felt swollen in their sock-swaddled and combat boot-wrapped cocoons. Perspiration beaded at the base of his hairline and was starting to run down his forehead. It had the effect of anchoring strands of his Mohawk to his forehead. His mouth hung open, saliva pooling in the depths. He knew he looked like a hot mess, and he had a strong suspicion this wouldn't end well for him.

"Ben Michaels."

The cop tilted his head and called to his partner, "Yep, he's one."

The other cop was still in the passenger seat of a white police sedan, the blue flashing lights rotating in silence. Their aura combined with the blazing midday sun, rendering the windshield a semi-opaque slab of brilliance.

"You know, it's a new world order. Society doesn't have a place for you anymore."

Ben had no idea what he was talking about. These types were always on his back. His dad, the counselors in school, all the uptight squares—they all had a perpetual stick up their ass. Indecent, non-Christian hordes consisting of people like him were out to ruin their *Little House on the Prairie* lifestyle, and by golly they had to *do* something.

Even though the cop's eyes were indistinguishable he seemed to harbor a smug look of disgust. It was a look Ben had seen directed at him countless times.

"I would say it's a shame, but that would be a lie. Truth is, I've always wanted to do this."

Now Ben was thoroughly confused. Was this a threat? Was the cop going to rough him up? Everything he ever said to anyone was always misconstrued and ridiculed. He was used to that, only he'd get contempt and penalties, not some raw end of state-sanctioned violence. Then again, they had beat up Tim. Of course, he *had* shot a cop. Ben hadn't done anything nearly so hardcore.

Come to think of it, he wasn't even sure if they knew he'd done anything at all.

"I...I..."

He was trying to think on the fly, trying to come up with a workable story. An excuse, some lie that could explain why he was in this neighborhood. Something that didn't sound too ridiculous. If only he could get out of this with the usual slap on the wrist. He needed to get a hold of Chris ASAP. He was done with all of this. He'd go to Tim and start a new life, get everything straight. He tried in vain to open his eyes fully. Tried to straighten up and give the cop a steady look.

As he raised his head he saw that the cop had gripped his .357. Pulling it from its black leather holster, he fired a round as Ben was rising. Blood erupted out the back of his head, the crimson torrent intertwined with the pulp of brain matter. Ben collapsed backward, his right leg folding under the left and his arms drifting out as he fell, giving his limp form a crucified look. Dead eyes stared at an indifferent sky. The officer squinted, looked around, and nonchalantly headed back, holstering his gun as he approached the cruiser.

Pulling it from his black leather holster, he fired a round

BACK TO THE U. S. OF A.

It's been weeks. The lush jungles in the lower reaches of Mexico were at times smothering, and although I was sure the feeling stemmed from a vestigial human instinct that hadn't completely faded, it put a slight edge on the environs all the same. Overgrown foliage contorted into an entangling web of roots and leaves. Rocky, uneven ground was prone to hidden drops into nets of constraining foliage. Hairy brown spiders the size of small dogs wandered languidly through leaves, stopping short of my head and examining me through a multitude of beady black eyes. Hand-sized beetles covered in golden shells crawled about my feet on shiny black legs that resembled melted plastic. Garishly colored frogs darted into view atop the moldering remains of fallen tree trunks, their gullets pumping furiously as their glassy eyes viewed me with edgy distrust. Giant armor-plated lizards strutted among the buried roots and boulders on the ground like pint-sized dinosaurs that owned the jungle. Centipedes the length of a man's forearm slithered through the underbrush, more than one attempting to bite me. Even though they couldn't penetrate my skin, they elicited a knee-jerk reaction. I didn't physically respond, but some lingering humanity in me experienced revulsion.

This terrestrial world was as alien as anything in space. Even more so perhaps as it twisted my tamer view of North American woodlands into a reality beyond my realm of experience. It was so foreign from anything I had seen before that I felt misplaced, like I was intruding on a world I had no place in. Strange, because this suit was built for exploration. At least that is the assumption I'm going on.

The human mind likes to store pernicious presuppositions, and I'd noticed that not all neuroses were associated with biological input. There were plenty of scientists who scoffed at the notion of free will, instead reasoning that all reactions essentially boil down to a very complex butterfly effect, the chemical component of our body being merely one factor at play. Our responses to input might be based as much on what we had for breakfast ten years ago as anything.

Just when I was growing accustomed to the intensity of the rainforest, the jungle opened up into the arid savannahs of northwest Mexico, and the change of scenery harbingered yet another step into an alien world. A smothering diversity of life had dissipated into the scarce flora of sandy grasslands. A dusty landscape bespeckled with Saguaro cacti and a multitude of spindly desert shrubs, the occasional tree jutting timidly through the sparse vegetation. Internal sensors broadcast an external temperature of 120 degrees Fahrenheit, the reading likely a concession to my human and Western sense of temperature gradients.

I also realized that time was becoming less and less relevant, my mind recording the cycle of each day more out of habit than anything. Every input was stored in my memory warehouse, and I could retrieve data on anything I experienced with the absolute clarity of a machine. Which brings me to a theory I developed on why the creatures that created this form couldn't survive in it. They were too literal. They focused on and analyzed the minutia until it drove them mad. Humans, on the other hand, had a more complex mental wiring. I wouldn't say it was better, just different. Through a long process of evolution and natural selection, Homo sapiens built up mental barriers that allowed them to disregard details when their train of focus was concentrated on a particular agenda. Although that trait ran the danger of heading down all sorts of paths having deadly consequences, like suicide cults and Nazism, it also led to some of our brightest points of light, as seen in scientists who can't function socially but are brilliant in the lab. I'd be willing to wager that explained both religion and most other supernatural occurrences as well.

Previously I would have included unsubstantiated occurrences like UFO sightings in that group, only now I knew there might be something behind that after all. It could be the case that the alien abduction phenomenon was tied to repressed memories from birth. Plenty of scientists favored such a theory. Big eyes, a tunnel of light, helplessness, the whole bit—parallels could be drawn to all these as things experienced by a fetus first coming into contact with the world. Yet that didn't mean it all was bunk. Often the problem with any unorthodox theory was the nutcases associated with some extension of it, which tended to discredit the theory lock, stock, and barrel.

Assuming alien visitations were occurring, how far had it all gone? What was factual and what was attributable to hysteria and hyperbole? And who knew more about the grand scheme than they were letting on?

The creatures I'd met told me only enough to accomplish some agenda, and I was sure there was a complex backstory at play, even if I had no idea how to access any of the details. There were structures built in ancient pre-history, such as those in Egypt and Peru, that could only have been built using some preternatural, advanced technology. Three-hundred-ton blocks of stone cut so precisely that not even a binding agent was needed to connect them. Did aliens have a hand in this? Were people like Graham Hancock right, with their theories of a long-lost civilization that pre-dated known history? The powers in play on Earth appeared to be more interested in gains in the immediate present. They reaped the side benefits of things like the space race, but that was motivated more by Cold War rivalry than any real urge to explore. Maybe that's why no one visits the Earth intentionally or gives me a direct answer. Denizens of this planet haven't exactly proven to be a haven of logical or rational thinking.

I know I've been spotted on my journey through the wilds of rural Mexico, but unless mankind interferes with me, I don't interact. It's as if me and the natives are different species, two creatures observing each other from afar.

The few locals I did come close to fled instantly in horror, disappearing into the trees as they mumbled in a dialect similar to Spanish. Scrolling through my language database, I couldn't find an exact match, although two words were often repeated: *chupacabra* and *viracocha*. I'm not versed in the local mythology, although I understand both terms could be interpreted to mean various things. I think the first Europeans to arrive in this area were mistaken for them, and look how that worked out. Although it's likely many natives observed me from a distance, it's not surprising they chose not to engage. No doubt word of my presence has spread, feeding the rumor mill and exciting old superstitions. All the better if it clears my path.

Initially, I had tried to disappear into the wild. Having obtained what I always desired, I had no farther-reaching plans. I thought I could negate any pursuit of me by melding into the Amazonian jungle and mull through my future plans while I explored the terrain. I had always been interested in delving into the heart of darkness and probing its hidden truths, only I never dreamed that I would find a story beyond my wildest imaginings. For every answer, two more questions would arise, and everything pointed toward theories that were never taken seriously. Contact from beyond this word, and ancient structures that defied their supposedly primitive origins. I would like to have explored more, to have learned some answers, only the web of intrigue ended up extending far beyond my reach. Secrets were guarded, technology from beyond this word dwarfed anything I had expected, and I just might have ignited a cosmic war.

I fled the northeast in a hasty attempt to escape the government, one that doesn't even exist in the same sense any more, and although I'm not sure what sparked the fall, it appears to have passed the point of a quick recovery. I'm not sure where that leaves the federal infrastructure, although I do recall something about the military maintaining a facility up in Maine that those at the higher echelons of power were very interested in. The military was using reverse-engineered alien technology to get something functional that struck me as way too farfetched to work. There was always an air of danger surrounding it, although hysteria might account for that, like when people speculated the Hadron Supercollider would create black holes that could devour the Earth. But such was my thinking back in my days at Fort Bragg and I've learned so much since then. I've seen hidden extraterrestrial outposts that were centuries, maybe millennia, old, buried beneath ancient structures that might have been oblivious to their presence. I've been through the eye of a wormhole, seen and interacted with alien creatures firsthand. They treated me as a primitive barely worthy of their time, but it does prove a point: that all this government conspiracy talk might hold a kernel of truth.

The facility in Maine is a country away from where I am, but it holds a strange appeal. I can't just hide in obscurity after all I've seen. And this might be my best chance of getting back into something beyond a planet that now strikes me as primitive and boring. On the plus side, I made it into Mexico with no idea of what I was doing. This time I have a more comprehensive outlook, and my return trip should be much easier, although that all depends on how far the United States has fallen... and what has risen in its place.

Even Through the Worst of Times

Before the U.S. fell apart, Jack was ready. He had all the apocalyptic necessities: Life Straw, waterproof matches, fishing line kit complete with hooks and bait, compass, gas-mask (German issue and recent, no less), and even a backup carbon filter. He had binoculars, Mylar emergency thermal blankets, microfiber towels, magnesium fire starter, nylon parachute cord, and mini torch. He had a Gerber multi-tool, eight rifles, two pistols, various knives, two machetes, and even a crossbow. All these goodies were sealed in his bugout bag, nestled in his closet next to his olive green Eureka Assault tent, inflatable air mattress, and Teton sleeping bag. Nine five-gallon jugs of water and a two-month supply of Wise emergency food rounded out the inventory.

Even with all this, it was still a surprise when that day came.

Ensconced beneath a harbor of venerable trees, his sprawling ranch home sat a good one hundred feet from the road, allowing him a prime view of any approaching threat. The front yard was a sunken morass of sand and tall grass, the chaotic expanse overtaken by a network of shadow courtesy of the overarching network of branches. Wild spurts of flora manifested in uneven outbreaks across a shifting field of sand and rock. The greenery finally swarmed into abundance as it escaped the gloomy shade and broke out onto the edge of the roadway, where it erupted in a flurry of green blades. Beyond a two-lane road of bleached asphalt and faded yellow lines, the pavement dropped abruptly into a short, sandy strip that was overtaken immediately by the upward surge of mammoth granite cliffs. Scaling a hundred feet, cracked shelves of weather-stained rock broke out into a level peak. Thick green grass carpeted it, the occasional squat tree struggling into view.

Dressed in black jeans, olive Vans, and a Pantera T-shirt (embroidered with the snake from The Great Southern Trendkill), Jack slapped on a light brown baseball cap that read "Lucky Gunner" and stepped outside into the early morn. Shafts of light filtered through the trees in his yard, descending through the branches in a network of lazy streams. Everything held the dewy scent of early morning, and there was still a slight chill to the air, that lingering nighttime nip that had yet to be burned away by the rising of the sun.

He stepped through the uneven thrusts of yellowed grass, marred and entangled by weeds he never cut, and out onto the bare soil of his driveway. Sitting in the spotty light of the parted oaks was his pride and joy, a silver 1975 FJ40. With Thornberg tires on black Cragar 15" rims, it sported a Warn 8,000-pound winch, a snorkel, a full roll cage, and a rebuilt Toyota inline 6. He swung open the double barn doors at the rear of the vehicle, lifted the window of the soft-top, and stuffed in his tent and sleeping bag. A few more trips to the house, and he carried out nine of the five-gallon jugs of water.

Manhandling them two at a time, his forehead beaded with sweat under the effort. Heading back in, he pulled out his supply of emergency food and an army duffel bag that held his collection of knives. He scooped his rifle and pistol cases into the growing pile in the center of his room, a 1911 Springfield .45 and M1 Garand prized among them. It took three trips to get all that into the back of the FJ and quite a few more trips to load in all the ammo. Even with the stiff suspension, the rear end sagged underneath the weight. Last up was the bugout bag, and he searched his now-bare closet for anything else.

Grabbing a few more sets of clothes and a pair of brown hiking shoes, he decided the sooner he headed out, the better. He had a brief debate with himself on whether to lock the door, and finally decided there was no harm in doing so.

The engine fired right up, and he adjusted the idle, letting it warm up at 1500 rpms for a good ten minutes. Hitting the gas, he edged out of the woodsy shelter and into the scorching late May heat. Even though the car had no a/c, he didn't feel he needed it in a convertible. Unfortunately, even with the doors off and the canvas bikini top blocking the solar glare, it was still uncomfortably hot. Beads of sweat dotted his arms, coalescing the black arm hairs into dark striations that crisscrossed the old school dagger tattoo that took up most of his left forearm. His boss at Desert Engineering always took verbal jabs at that, throwing in a few comments about his wild dark hair and ragged stubble while he was at it. Jack looked a bit like Matt Damon, fresh from a hard night of partying, something his co-workers were not shy about pointing out.

His wit, good looks, and bratty intelligence had earned him a string of hot girlfriends. A few had even moved in and lasted a few years. Only in the end his peculiarities always made him question and eventually distance himself from them. It started with a sense he was a bit smarter than whoever he was with, and that was always the beginning of the end, even if it took years.

When he broke it down, it became clear he wasn't ready to dedicate his life to anyone he viewed as subpar. More than one girl had referred to him as "cold" and "unavailable" and it was just as well, since he really didn't have the time to deal with their petty issues.

As his teenage awkwardness subsided, he grew a little smoother at the social game. The beauty of the girls increased, but in an almost sliding scale their intelligence decreased. He shifted from one girl to the next, until he stumbled onto "the one"—a witty, and quite beautiful, Italian girl with long black hair, thick, expressive eyebrows, and curves in all the right places. She also had a slightly tomboy fashion sense that rubbed him the right way. The latest in a line of girlfriends for him, the accolades on her side built up and he grew to look at her as someone special. He opened up more when he realized this was a person he *could* spend the rest of his life with, even if he wasn't ready to tell her as much. They had a few good years before the indiscretions of his past came back to haunt him. His initial indifference to these drove a wedge between them, and despite the change, she always held it against him. He was oblivious. Everything appeared to him to be going well until one day she announced it was all over. He was in shock. Heartbroken, he begged her to stay. She made some concessions, and they even attended a couple's therapy session, which she had suggested long ago, but now it was too late. One session in had made that plain to see. Everything had built up in her head, and even though he didn't fathom all the intricacies, the deal was done.

He'd been on a downward spiral ever since, panning through girls, his aloofness worse than ever. In his mind they could never compare to his lost love, and that eventually drove every one of them away. The key difference was that now *they* left *him*, usually to the accompaniment of a few choice words and via a bitter breakup. His last steady girl, a cute Mexican in her thirties, had grown so exacerbated that she cursed him out and blocked him from her social media. All of this prompted him to re-imagine his life's course. He edged toward isolation and a survivalist mentality crept in. The end of the world was a blessing. A call to action stirring up the malaise his life had become.

He had barely noticed the initial stages. It started with a slight intensifying of the tensions that had always existed. Squabbling and distrust among warring sides; politicians on one hand calling for "more humanity" and an extension of rights for the working class, while those on the other side kept shucking for the mega-corporations. Playing off their nepotism as true democracy, they continued to convert the country into an oligarchy. Even though those in power didn't say as much, it was pretty clear what was going on. Houses and vacations were awarded to politicians who played along, and they were voted into office with the help of the crooked machine that had become the election process. They usually promised to raise the personal wealth of all, with the usual result of a new offshore bank account, and raises for a select few.

Bills passed that only increased the wealth of the 1%, while strangling the free market. The knee-jerk reaction of the opposite side only hastened the downfall. Mass socialism on a stifling scale not seen since Stalin. Social justice warriors directing their outcry at whatever new cause the media focused on. The Republicans lost their majority long enough for a massive social spending bill to pass. It proved to be a short-lived speed bump in the living standard and was immediately followed by a steady downhill slide. Various parties sprang up, some pitching themselves to select groups, harping on narrow issues. Some were more Libertarian or anarchist, others merely the Trojan horses of hidden interests. People argued vehemently with one another in front of anyone that would listen. YouTube and Facebook bristled with the anger of the masses. Minorities and special interest groups were blamed, and each flipped it back on the other. States threatened to secede.

Then President Manley was elected. A slick, well-dressed New Yorker, he had barely won a contentious election. Even putting that aside, there was quite a bit of controversy about how he won. It wasn't a majority by any means, and he only got in through one of the much-touted shortfalls in the Electoral College process. His first step was to pass a socialist agenda that eclipsed even the one at the end of the Great Depression. He raised taxes on the rich to 90% and eliminated all corporate loopholes. That proved to be the last straw, and Jack saw it coming. There was no way the shadowy powers behind the scene would take this, and the states were already seething. To make matters worse, President Manley tried to bring the U.S. in line with what many saw as a New World Order: a committee of countries that would have the final say in global decision making, with the authority to override anything passed by the constituent national populations.

It was even rumored that every citizen was to be assigned a number or bar code that would register them in a worldwide database. The religious extremists started denouncing the bar code as the mark of the beast. That set the flame, and in such troubled times, as is always the case, people flocked to religion. Word spread that all private firearm ownership was to be banned, and vehicles were to be strictly regulated. They would be taxed on size, horsepower, and usage. It was hinted that private property could no longer be passed on. After the owner's death, it would revert to the state. A lot of it was hyperbole and speculation, with sides screaming at each other and politicians getting in fist fights on the floors of Congress.

Everything deteriorated so quickly that it came as a surprise to no one when Texas announced it was leaving the Union. Plenty of Southern states followed suit. Unlike the Civil War, in which the Northern states united, mass homogenization splintered the population, and some of the nation's founding cities devolved into chaos. Looting, rioting, and arson broke out en masse, engulfing much of Manhattan and Philadelphia. News feeds were rife with it, as reporters tried to assume an objective stance while the world crumbled around them. One by one the media sources started to wink out. There was jamming by warring parties, sabotage, and arson. Things were getting very bad.

Jack had been ready for this ever since he saw the first rioting. He predicted the splintering of mass political systems, and as the central government broke down first it spread all the quicker. No one paid any mind to the civil authorities anymore, and Jack wasn't going to sit around idly. He listened to Alex Jones' radio show. He knew where this was headed.

It didn't take long to reach the state park. The asphalt quickly degraded in quality, cracks and potholes peppering the road as sandy swaths of soil edged in on both sides. Much of the sand was a prelude to a swarm of straggly foliage, the yellowing clumps growing into a swarm as they spread out, infiltrating the shadows of scattered manzanita and juniper trees. Jack ventured off the main road and onto a barely serviceable trail of sunbaked sand. Stretching out before him were rolling hills, their tan soil besieged by bushes and clumps of yellow flowers. He ventured into the park until the distant hills enveloped him and the road degraded into a rutted path. After some slipping of the tires, he ground to a stop and pulled the e-brake.

Hopping out, he dropped down to a squat next to the front tire and rotated the Warn hubs. The metal was hot, singeing his fingers and forcing a knee-jerk retraction. He was feeling the heat of the sun on his back as well. His shoulder blades were growing uncomfortably hot, his armpits moistening, and the back of his neck was on fire. Standing up with a groan, he circled around, rotated the other hub, and climbed back into the FJ. Shuffling over into the driver's seat, he shifted into 4 High, backed up to engage the hubs, and launched forward. The truck bounded over a bump, losing traction for a minute, and then powered forward into the wild, plumes of dust and loose gravel spewing up in its wake. Following a brief dip through a sheltered grove, rolling fields surrounded him on all sides. Wiry green sage bushes dominated, yellow brittle bush and red chuparosa dotting the wild grass in between. The savannah was punctuated by tridents of thick-trunked saguaro cacti, their grooved limbs towering over everything beneath. Mountains of limestone and basalt rose out of the plains ahead, escalating in size as they ascended toward the northern reaches. The climate was cooler up there, and forests of pine dominated the terrain. That was where Jack was headed.

He peered upward past the canvas rooftop and into a sky of purest blue. Fleecy white cumulonimbus clouds rolled across the heavens, their cottony wisps unraveling in slow motion. It was easy to forget everything you ever knew about civilized society out here. You could survive off the land, as Native Americans had done for thousands of years. Jack even felt a special affinity with them. Not that he liked them personally, of course. He was too racist for that. All he really liked was the idea of being free, of living without the constraints of government.

The arid sandy smell commingled with the aroma wafting off the foliage. A gentle breeze brought it to him and he peered up at the sky. Everything looked so tiny in the firmament of the heavens. Out here mankind didn't matter. He was boorish and obscene. An oily, contemptible intrusion. Jack even felt a little of that. He viewed himself more or less as a sweaty sack of meat. Yet the will to survive was strong, and he'd have to look past it.

Upon reflection, he realized that he would need a woman at some point. He despised himself for the weakness. It was a chemical addiction, like nicotine or heroin. He realized this, while at the same time surmising that in the apocalypse he was strong, and when push came to shove, he could have his pick. He'd scoop up some weak-willed mountain biker or outdoorsy type who was flustered by the collapse of everything she knew. No more iPhones, no more MacBooks, no more lattes—this would be the real deal. A slap in the face by reality. A world where his type was finally on top once again. She'd learn how lucky she was. Or the next one would. In the end, it didn't matter.

He had been mentally chastising himself, afraid that life would pass him by and he would amount to little more than a blip in the grand scheme of things. He'd shown a little promise early on, but this was followed by a series of unrealized expectations. Old age, with its one-way trip, had crept up as the years rolled by. Life had worn him down, and he had come close to succumbing.

This time, however, he would shine.

THE MONGOLIAN RIM

The clouds had started to coalesce, their shifting masses darkening into deep purples and cobalts. An array of tree-swathed hills spread out in corrugated rows, the peaks touching the sky. As they descended, the thick forest opened into a cadence of woodsy groves and grassy meadows. Across the valley, distant hilltops were laid out in pale blue queues, the silhouettes of the farthest ones barely distinguishable in the haze. On the hillsides, spurts of flowers were starting to bloom, their pink and yellow petals wafting in the meager wind. The clean scent of foliage and warm soil permeated the air.

Jack pitched his tent near the road yet under the cover of trees, and he made sure it was uphill so he could keep an eye on the spread below. A mountain bike trail cut a level swath through the upper echelons of the scarp, and he had set up in one of the few areas where the sloping hill leveled out into an overhanging embankment. There was a majestic view of everything below, clear to the horizon. This was a perfectly strategic spot. He could hunt, fish, and retreat to high ground when needed. He inflated his air mattress, an olive-green Litespeed, and nestled it snugly inside the dome of his tent. He dug a fire pit in front. Behind the encampment and several feet away, though still in sight of the tent, he dug another hole to eliminate in.

He swaddled and hid a Bowie knife and a .45 ACP Springfield in a brown blanket next to his mattress, and then stretched out his sleeping bag over top. He hoisted one of the five-gallon drums of water out of his FJ and positioned it next to his bugout bag in the corner. Everything was looking ready. He unzipped his case, took out his Remington Sendero, and flicked the bolt to make sure the action was good. Gripping it upright in his right hand, he stooped, exited the tent, and once again beheld the magnificent spread. He breathed in the air. Crisp and clean. No fumes, no chemical smells. A bird chirped somewhere in the distance.

He realized then he had no job to report to anymore. No boss. Not that he really considered anyone the boss of him, that had been a temporary inconvenience. Glancing around at the tall oak trees glimmering in the midday light, he took in another deep breath and headed left, up the winding trail. He'd get the lay of the land, and maybe luck out and find some dinner while he was at it.

Hours passed with no animal in sight. The bluer suffused light and cooler scent of dawn had burned away in the midday sun, replaced by the doldrums of midday. Cool, refreshing air had been usurped by an unrelenting heat and the smell of stale, dry earth. Jack sat down on a rock, momentarily impressed with how dull this might actually prove. He hated humans, in theory, only he was beside himself with boredom at the idea of being completely and permanently deprived of their company. That bothered him, more than he wanted to admit. While he had no insight into this paradox, it existed nonetheless. There was a time, long ago, when he loved all of this. The isolation and sense of oneness with nature. Even though he told himself he neither needed nor even liked any of it, he had grown dependent on social media. While decrying it, he also made sure to check it every day. He had built up so much of the image he wanted to portray in his little virtual world that it might have very little to do with him, although that wasn't a comfortable thought, and certainly nothing he wanted to admit, even to himself. His mind had wandered and he had peered deep into his inner consciousness for a few minutes. It was terrifying, he felt lost, and he wanted nothing to do with it.

He rose from the boulder he was sitting on, hoisted the Remington, slung it over his shoulder, and headed back to the camp.

He descended the steep incline of the hill. It was mostly

hard soil intermixed with boulders, all of it under the minimal shelter of pine trees. Although it kept the burning sun off him, it did nothing for the heat, and he was already sweating. When the trees ended, he lifted his path higher to tread through the tall yellowish grass that had sprung into prominence. A few feet of that, and he was back onto the cream-colored sand of the trail. It was a mile to camp. He hadn't meant to go so far, but an early spurt of enthusiasm had overtaken his better judgment. A little ways down the trail the trees closed back in on the right, cloistering together into a forest that scaled back up the mountain. The other side had fallen into a sheer drop of segmented granite, a wide savannah spreading out at the foot and tapering away into distant hills that paraded across the landscape in ever-fainter lines. The sun was almost directly overhead now, blazing down on everything in relentless fury, and his skin felt gritty. Oily grime mixed with perspiration and sheathed him in a coat of filth that disgusted him.

Nearing the encampment, he heard voices and curbed his steps. They sounded distinct, one male and one female. From the tone Jack guessed they were young, and they sounded naive. Soft even. The curve of trees at the bend blocked his vision, and he hunched over as he drew closer to the edge of the roadway. He hoisted the rifle, pulling its sling over his shoulder and settling it into his outstretched hands. Sweat mixed with the salt and grime on his forehead, and trickled down in irritating rivulets. He shrugged his shoulder into the corner of the eye, catching a stream that was about to drop from his eyebrow and blind him.

As the trail rounded the bend, two kids came into view. The girl was tall and slim, with slightly darker skin. Jack guessed she was Mexican or Native American, only with the sharper facial features more common to a European. She immediately reminded Jack of the Italian girl he had dated, only this one was even better looking. She had long black hair, and was wearing a white T-shirt with some yellow and red logo stretched tight over small, perfectly shaped breasts. Her slim, dark blue jeans flowed down into brown sandals.

Even the little you could see of her feet looked smooth and

perfect. Jack reasoned their attire meant they must have arrived by vehicle. There was nowhere close by, those sandals and jeans were not meant for a mountain bike or hiking, and only a four-wheel-drive vehicle could make it this far out.

The guy had sandy-brown hair, shaved down into maybe a half-inch swathe that encircled his head, and stubble that thickened into a well-trimmed goatee near the chin. His face was square, and he was on the stocky side. Jack found it amusing that he was plainly shorter than the girl. They made an odd couple. The tall, thin girl and a short, stocky guy who had on black BDU shorts and a red T-shirt that proclaimed "Red Hot Chili Peppers" in bold white letters.

Thick tree trunks for legs flashed a partial image of calf tattoos. He had the look of one of those alternative types, the kind who went to the last Woodstock and worked at Starbucks.

Jack immediately disliked him. The kids were having a casual conversation, standing in a relaxed slouch next to the pile of gray rocks that circled an as-yet-unused fire pit.

The guy saw him and turned, raising both hands palms out and drawling, "Woah, man...just stopping to see who's here. We didn't take nothin'."

The girl looked on with a mix of mild interest and indifference. The guy kept one hand raised, reaching out with the other toward Jack.

"My name's Curtis. My girl is Penelope."

Without lowering his gun or easing his gaze, Jack barked, "What are you doing here?"

"We were listening to the news, man. It's all gone crazy. We figured we'd be better off if we hopped in my truck and headed out of town."

"And what? You saw my shit and you figured you'd take it?"

"Naw, man, it's not like that. We were just looking for other people."

Curtis starting walking backward, lowering his left hand and bringing it down to encircle Penelope's waist.

"We'll just leave, man. No harm no foul."

The girl was a real piece. She would need a man like him in the days to come. Even though this guy she was with looked a little tough on the outside, Jack could see him folding when the chips were down. This was a new world.

Time to cull the herd. The trick would be to separate them without putting negative vibes in the girl's head. Society hadn't degraded to the point where he could get away with just shooting Curtis, even if it was headed in that direction. Of that Jack was certain. Given enough time, she'd see that this was for the best. The dilemma was how to take Curtis out of the picture. Jack tossed it around in his head and decided that, if he kept them around, he'd have plenty of opportunities to dispose of Curtis. But that might not even be necessary. The girl might come over to his side in the natural course of events once she realized the way things were now. Then again, Curtis would be a drain on resources, and if Jack stole his girl, it wasn't likely that he could be trusted. He decided his best move was to lighten the mood.

"Hey, man, things being the way they are, I'm just a little suspicious. You seem like decent people. Let's join up. Wait this shit out."

Jack risked a slight smile, hoping it would increase his semblance of good intentions. It only added to his creepiness, and Curtis wasn't buying it.

"Naw, man, we're cool. Thanks for the offer. We're goin' to keep truckin', see what else is out there."

Nervous energy hit Jack like a truck, and he grew unsure of what to do. He glanced over at the girl, trying not to make it too obvious. She struck him as even more of a standout than he had first thought. A fragrance that reminded him of lilacs drifted over to him from her direction. The sun drew a line of illumination along the far side of her face, highlighting her delicate features. The soft glow rolled down her forehead, circled her eyelid, and glinted off her thick lashes. Her lips were sharp and full of expression, her gently cleft chin smooth and straight. She had a deep, natural tan, her dark brown hair dancing gently in the breeze. Jack couldn't help noticing that she wasn't wearing a bra. Her nipples were dark bulges on a slightly small T-shirt and her head was slightly downturned as her right foot lazily drew circles in the sand.

Jack's throat tightened. His head was full of cotton and his palms grew damp. He swallowed hard and tried to come up with some clever words. Only his mind was a blank, and all he could think about was not letting this girl get away.

"I didn't mean to drive you out..."

He mumbled it, and Curtis shot him a wary glance. Jack's heart sank. He was going to lose her, he knew it. This was his best bet and he had to do whatever it took. It was all for the best anyways. The world was headed toward the end of days and he needed this girl by his side. Once they were out of sight, she would be lost to him. He might never have an opportunity like this again, and he knew he would regret it forever if he didn't do something. The scent of pine and soil wafted up to him, strangely digging in with an edge of loneliness and sadness. All he could think about now was the isolation yet to come, and how he might miss this chance like he did everything else.

"You... can't go."

Curtis had taken Penelope's hand and turned to walk away. With that remark he whirled around, his face changed so much that it caught Jack completely by surprise. Curtis's features were contorted with rage, and his free hand was brandishing a black knife.

"Fuck you," he spat. "We're out."

Jack raised the rifle to take a shot, still not completely sure he wanted to take things this far. Curtis charged him. Jack managed to get a round off, but it went wild, and then Curtis was on him, plunging the knife into his chest.

Then it all dawned on Jack, and he realized for the first time how real the situation was. The knife dove impossibly deep, like it wasn't real, and he was feeling some strange pressure. It didn't even hurt that much, it just felt all wrong. His mind was racing, his body wired with adrenaline. He looked down and couldn't believe the image his eyes were sending to his brain— that of the knife buried up to the hilt in his left pec. He lurched back, stumbling awkwardly. His body felt flushed and his ears filled with a rushing sound. It was drowning out everything around him, and he started to get lightheaded.

Penelope was yelling. He thought this so strange. She hadn't made sound until now. Curtis pulled out the knife and turned back around. Jack was collapsing backward. He saw Curtis take Penelope's hand and start walking away in slow motion, as if they were underwater. Then he realized that he couldn't catch a breath. His thoughts were getting cloudy. Like a mantra, a sentiment ran through his head: *No... don't remember me like this... I'm not this guy. If only... I need... I...* Consciousness faded as he collapsed, the last spark of it winking out before he could even hit the ground.

Walking at a brisk pace, Curtis and Penelope reached their truck, a silver Toyota Tacoma. She was dazed, in shock, her mouth agape. Curtis opened the passenger door and hoisted her inside. It had a lift and oversized tires, so even with the black side steps it was still a high reach. Penelope was limp, forcing Curtis to do all the work. He grunted as he stuffed her into the passenger seat. Sweat poured from his armpits, but he barely registered it. Adrenaline raced throughout his body, every hair pricked up in high alert, and he kept glancing around nervously. He slammed the door, circled around back, and snatching open the door, jumped in the driver's seat. With a flick of the ignition keys and a desperate pull of the stick into reverse, he backed out onto the road in a flurry of flying sand and squealing rubber. He chanced a quick look in the rear-view mirror at Jack's body, which seemed to appear miles away to him, punched the shifter into first, and roared out onto the road.

Jack's eyes had glazed over, and for the most part his nerve endings had stopped transmitting impulses. Except that he felt cold. So strange to be cold in this heat. And he was thirsty. Terribly thirsty. He wanted to move. If only he could get his body to respond. His thoughts were clouded, and he forgot about moving for the moment. A collage of mental images flickered in front of him. Scenes from his teen years. He was at his friend's house, and there was a girl there he had a crush on. He tried to make moves on her, but she pretended not to notice him. Then he was somewhere else. A pudgy, long-haired metal-head was yelling in his face, shoving him. He stumbled backward and tried not to look like a coward. Then he was at his job at the warehouse. Again he was being yelled at, this time from his boss. His thoughts grew murky. It was so hard to concentrate.

Then consciousness passed. His still body lay outspread, the upper torso edging out onto the road. His eyes stared at the pale blue sky, his mouth agape in the aftermath of the shock. As the leaves rustled in the wind, nothing else moved. The sun scaled the horizon and languidly fell. The temperature dropped, the mountains darkened, and Jack's body grew cooler.

BLACKSBURG, VIRGINIA

A aron had always felt like an outsider. In North Carolina, as a metal deviant, he was part of a group. His only real buddy was a guy named Kevin, who lived in a trailer with his mom. Sometimes at school he managed to hang out with this girl Dannielle. She was cute, blonde, and had huge tits for a fourteen-year-old. She would sneak out with him and Kevin to smoke cigarettes and look at horror magazines. Aaron had managed to befriend a couple of older types who had fallen through the cracks of mainstream society. A guy in his thirties who worked at the local comic book store and a college kid who worked weekends at the used record store. When he moved to Northern Virginia, however, everything had changed. He was in high school, and for the first time he found himself on the downside of the outsider social cliques. In North Carolina, he was the young kid who'd smoke a joint with the older guys. In Northern Virginia, he was the misfit from down South who wasn't hip to the intricacies of their scene. Nothing stings like the rejection of the circles you want to identify with, especially at that age.

In the beginning, he was pretty much left alone. Ignored. He made a few friends, people he didn't feel much of a connection with. They were kids he would see at a concert or hang out with locally. But he always felt different than them. They were too run-of-the-mill, too plain. He could tell they set their sights low and were going nowhere. They were ordinary, drones who would grow old, get 9-to-5 jobs, and accept their place in the social structure, no questions asked. Although he didn't know why, he knew that had nothing to do with him. He was weird.

Different. He had bounced around the country with his military family, so he had a broader outlook, only that wasn't all of it. He could stare out at the night sky in whichever country his dad happened to be stationed, and it would trigger a feeling inside him that there was more out there, more to this life than resigning oneself to the fate of being a worker ant. He believed he experienced existence in a more significant way than the worker drones who surrounded him. He'd walk between the military houses at night, and the lights of the local ball court or the reflections on the asphalt pathway were a little brighter. The shadows in the woods a little deeper. He couldn't explain it, but he felt their pull more intensely. At first he thought that was how everyone experienced the world, but Kevin made him rethink that.

Kevin was the same age, fourteen, but he was taller and already had the trace of a mustache. His dark brown hair was slicked back, and he always wore a lightblue coat he'd picked up from the Salvation Army. He and Kevin would steal beer from the fridge and lay on the rooftop of Kevin's mom's trailer. It was a rural white trash scene stuck in a time loop that made it feel nostalgic. The problem was, although Aaron realized this, he knew Kevin had no clue. Then there was the time he ran away to New York. Everything was all the halfhearted softness of youth up until that incident. In NYC, he had seen someone die right before his eyes. Not the movie or Internet version, the real winking out of existence of someone who had been there a split second earlier. And if that wasn't bad enough, then the dead guy started to talk to him.

With the move to Northern Virginia, he had mentally buried the past. After a struggle, he discovered punk rock, and it was the first subculture that truly spoke to him. He wasn't a fan of the more abrasive stuff like the Crass or the Subhumans. But the Sex Pistols and the Dead Kennedys? Or especially early Black Flagg? Those groups spoke his language. It was like they were reading his mind, pointing out all the things that everyone else was trying to pretend didn't exist. He was excited and dove in head first. Only social circles can be cruel. Aaron was a newbie, and the fact he took a year to get into punk rock was one more thing that was held against him. At least this was the case with some of the taste makers, which is all it takes in high school. This wasn't the beginning of the scene, when all comers, the more different the better, were accepted. By this point the scene had codified into an identifiable clique, and he didn't fit the mold. It wasn't quite Hot Topic yet, but 1977 was long gone. He felt that was unfortunate, and it went completely against punk as he knew it to stand for. Fortunately he had a strong sense of self and he knew what he was. Fuck everyone else.

He ended up spending a lot of time alone, walking the byways of Fairfax, Virginia. He would listen to music, lost in thought as he wandered the deserted streets and parking lots of suburban hell. He would consider this world and how it wasn't quite the place everyone appeared to think it was. He knew most adolescent kids thought like that to some degree. Then again, most adolescent kids probably didn't talk to dead people.

After a year, he finally began to be accepted into some of the social circles. Mainly by people in grades other than his, or misfits from other school systems. The farther they lived from his local high school, the more he felt he could be himself. Then it happened again. He saw someone die right before his eyes. And then the dead person started talking.

That led to a crazy, week-long journey. Some shadowy segment of the government had come after him, and even though he didn't what they wanted, he knew it wasn't anything good. The police were never on the right side of anything. A string of false charges, mugshots, and community service gigs had proved that to him. In his flight from them he had ended up walking between worlds. Even though the multiverse proposal was still a theory, it was the best argument he could think of. It was the only thing that made sense to him, and the places he went certainly weren't the real world in the present. In these environs, mankind was the prey to strange creatures, or under siege, or riddled with weird diseases. He had met a girl who spoke no English in a community under assault by something from out of this world, had slept with her, and had lost her immediately, stepping out into a Washington D.C. that had gone to hell. People were shooting at him, others were dying right before his eyes, and the darkest corners of his worst nightmares had come to life. He would open a door, or round a corner, and be greeted by a scene utterly different than the one he just left. If this was him going insane, the rest of the world was playing along. The last surreal trip had landed him in a cemetery near his friend Tommy's house. When he stumbled onto the house, he found Tommy's grandfather bound and gagged. A government agent had shown up, and Tommy wound up blowing him away with a revolver that Aaron had never seen before. It was like something out of a Quentin Tarantino movie. Bound and pleading people, violence, screaming, and finally a bloodbath. They left in a hurry, fleeing in Tommy's Monte Carlo to Blacksburg, Virginia.

The world was falling apart, and Blacksburg was the most isolated place they could come up with on short notice. Aaron didn't know the people down there that well, and Tommy was as shifty as always. He claimed to have many good friends in Blacksburg, but Aaron doubted that Tommy knew anyone outside of a girl or two he had macked on. In its favor, Blacksburg was in the boonies, at least compared to D.C., and the house down there was populated by punks. So they must be cool. Or so he hoped.

HUMANS ARE A DYING BREED

Day shifts into night, and back into day. Clouds trundle overhead in a leisurely dance, the cottony threads falling away and merging back together as they spiral through a pale blue sky. The initial onslaught of dry sand and desert shrubbery have grown up in the distance into a forest of pine trees.

Beyond the woods, limestone cliffs rise grandiosely from the leafy escarpment. All about me thin grass has edged in on the endless tracts of sand, popping up in straggly yellowed tufts amid the caked, sun-scorched soil. Pausing and craning my head, I see that the elevation gives me a glimpse of the long path I've tread. Varying queues of hills spread out below, their details growing more chimera-like as they fade toward the horizon. Perhaps it's only memories and traces of old associations that make the vast spread seem more beautiful that any of the off-world trips I've been on recently, but it does nothing to diminish the impression.

It's been said that humans favor something because they associate it with other positive events. They prefer a song because it reminds them of a time in their life they view pleasantly, so perhaps I find this view so scenic because I appreciated it when I inhabited an Earthly form. In time, that might change.

Some of the sentiments based on human sensations, like fond childhood memories, are elements that will wane in priority over the years. At the thought I feel a pang of regret, and I speculate on what I will eventually become. If all sentience is merely a complex butterfly effect, and I have both a larger and more accessible data bank than any human, I certainly won't be human anymore. Everything is constantly evolving, so no one is ever the same person they were a year ago; however, without the chemical-based input of Homo sapiens, will I lose all emotions? And even if I do, is that a bad thing? Plenty of those inputs represent flawed pathways put in place through natural selection and evolution. When those are gone, what will be left? I train my view forward and continue ascending.

The forest swallows me as I forge ahead. The sun falls in the sky to my back, lengthening the shadows. The tree trunks throw dark lines across an uneven carpet of pine needles and brush. Only my shadow is alive with movement, the edges of it swooping over the forest floor as a silent harbinger of my approach. I hear the rustle of a small animal in the distance, probably a fox. Mammals apparently do not view my presence as a threat. I give off no scent, and I'm not warm-blooded, so they must not consider me an immediate danger. I've also noticed that they give me a wide berth, too, as if they sense something there that is best avoided.

The ascent levels off into a dirt road, the tree line opening into a thin shoulder of yellow grass and loose soil. In less than a foot, the forest levels out into a concave path of packed dirt. A thin shoulder picks up beyond, and immediately scales up into another tree-covered hill. This is the first road I've encountered in this park, and it looks empty. I'm about to cross and continue my ascent when I see a wavering form off to the left. I magnify my vision and see a human hand jutting onto the road. Zooming in still closer, I can see a bare arm just beyond the concealing trunks. I head toward it, steadily concentrating my vision on the hand. As I draw closer I perceive that the skin looks saggy and wrinkled, the flesh blotchy and loose. As I round a slight bend, more of the body comes into view and I can see the back of a head.

As I draw even closer, the trees open up to reveal the full picture. A withered corpse stares up at the sky. The eyes are black holes, the skin dried and drawn to reveal a row of glimmering teeth. The nose has collapsed, not completely, but the skin has sunken in and the nostrils have nearly caved. The chest is torn open, and ragged skin droops in thick coats over a framework of ribs.

Inside is a hollow vacuum, the organs long since cleaned out. I can see the torn remnants of a black T-shirt, rags encircling the tops of the shoulders and running along the lower edges of the ribcage. Although the clothing is hanging loose over shrunken skin, the fabric looks fairly unmolested. I doubt humanity has yet fallen to the point of tribalism, much less a black market for stolen organs. My guess would be some wild animal opened the chest to access the tender vittles within. The body looks like it has been lifeless for several months. It would be hard at this point to tell whether or not it was as a result of natural causes.

There is a clearing a few feet beyond him harboring a military-issue tent. Olive drab, and propped up like a dome, it looks perfectly intact, the anchoring ropes still taut. A blackened fire pit lies a few feet in front, the dark timbers scored with sand and the dried rivulets of several rainfalls.

Beyond it, nestled among the overhanging pine trees, is a silver FJ40 that looks like a redneck's wet dream. Sporting a four-inch lift, 35-inch Thornberg tires, and a winch in front, I absently wonder if it still runs.

Stepping over the corpse, I amble through the clearing and up to the FJ. Opening the door, I see that the floor is diamond plate, the seats black velvet racing buckets, and there are no keys dangling from the ignition. Taking a quick look in back, I see that it's crammed with supplies. Jugs of water, rifle cases, and military duffel bags stuffed to the brim. Maybe this guy was ex-military, although from the looks of it, it's more likely he was a redneck playing soldier. I duck my head out of the vehicle and stroll over to the tent. Unzipping the front, I peer inside. A green sleeping bag is spread over the deflated rumples of an air mattress. There is a plastic box of Wise emergency food, another five-gallon jug of water, and a brown blanket. A stuffed backpack sits in the corner, the leather handle of a large knife sticking out of it.

I step in to take a closer look. Flipping the blanket, a semi-auto .45 and sheathed Kabar roll out. I dig through the backpack, tossing aside a gas mask, an aluminum coffee press, a "Woodsman's Pal", binoculars still in the leather case, and a ton of other survivalist crap. The backpack swarms with pockets.

Out of them I pull clear tubes of waterproof matches, a black Lensatic compass, nylon parachute line, a tiny folding shovel in a black case, and a few microfiber towels, but still no keys. He was definitely a survivalist. No military guy would carry this much. This must have been his "bugout" bag. Ducking out of the tent and walking to the corpse, I kick him at the waist.

Sand has crusted up on the sides, and he makes a squelching noise as the cloth and soil break apart. Now rolled over on his side, I rifle through his pockets. The folds are stuck together and the worn fabric tears as I probe. Scaly fragments of skin puff out in gaseous bursts as I dig. This is probably one of those times when not having a sense of smell is a good thing. I register a few gas emissions, their density increasing as I twist and rotate the corpse in an attempt to get through the pocket. Butyric acid predominates among them, and I sense traces of putrescine and cadaverine. The probing of my fingers fights the glued-together strips of cotton, the pressure of my hand pushing the pocket down into a slippery coat of still-damp flesh. The tissue shreds off the bone, sinking the corners of the pocket down into an oily morass. My fingers fight through a frustrating entanglement of stuck together cloth and damp fabric until finally alighting on a sharp edge that feels metallic. I clamp my fingers on it, and pull. Whatever it is, it catches in the folds and the rest of the corpse comes up with it. Grabbing the edge of the pocket with my left hand I tear out a ring of keys. The cloth shreds with it, trails of string following the emerging metal.

I shake the keys to remove the remnants of cloth. There are two rings. One holds a set of generic looking silver keys, and the other holds a slightly smaller brass key. Heading back to the FJ, I climb in, shift into neutral, and try the first silver key. No dice. I try the second. The lock spins, but there is no crank of the starter. I see a lit button on the dash and try to push it, but the hard plastic cover doesn't move. There is a black rubber button below, and I try that. This time the starter cranks a few times. I climb in, pull up the lever under the seat to roll it back, step lightly on the gas, and try again. The engine catches and dies. I examine the dashboard but don't see a choke lever. Giving it a little more gas, I try again. It roars to life, and then almost dies immediately. I hit the pedal to bring the RPMs up again and keep it slightly depressed. As well taken care of as this rig looks, I'll bet it has a good battery in it, probably an Optima or the like. I let it warm up. The engine is now emitting a hearty rumble and the rear exhaust pipes are belching smoke. I zip down the window and wait for the temperature gauge to rise. When it has reached 120, I spin the wheel, hit the gas, and head out onto the trail.

I know where I am headed even if I have no idea where this path leads. Left leads northwest, and that's good enough for now. There were two five-gallon gas cans strapped to the back, nestled next to the spare and high-lift jack. If this guy was a survivalist, the cans are full, the tank is probably full or close to it, and this vehicle will most likely make it to a gas station. Or whatever is left of one.

Things have picked up for a change. I have a vehicle again, and I'll bet I lost any pursuit months ago. The engine throbs with a deep rumble, the tires kick up dust whenever I bounce through sandy areas, and the dark is settling in, transforming the wooded sides into thick walls of black. Branches rustle with my passing, a slight breeze kicking in, and I look up past the treetops. Dark purplish-blue clouds are tumbling overhead, their thick upper layers winking with a few bright stars. The lower atmosphere pales into cottony strings of deep red, brilliant hues of orange underlining crimson clouds that trail off into a shining yellow horizon below. Barely cresting the tops of the hills is the shiny orb of a setting sun.

In my youth I would have thought this view spectacular. The knowledge of age has tainted me, and now I see it as a momentary glimpse of how fragile the Earth really is. It's simply a tiny planet in a miniscule corner of an incredibly vast universe. A universe that is trying its best to destroy us. If it weren't for Jupiter, a meteor would probably have taken the Earth out already. Not to mention climate change, the melting of the icecaps, the precession of the Earth, and so many other variables. Even without a quick means of destruction, this world will eventually die. In billions of years the sun will balloon out into a red giant and scorch the atmosphere off this world. If

I'm still around and tied to this planet, humankind may have ventured out into space and even colonized other worlds. What part, if any, will I play in all that?

The Dark Corners of Rural Virginia

A aron entered Blacksburg at nightfall. The one other time he'd ventured down there he was tripping on acid, and the whole thing was a cool, rebellious adventure. Cars were flying past in glowing streams of red, glimmers of orange and yellow blinking in their wake. Blinding white lights burst into view whenever the car closed in on another traveler. Air gushed through the window in a noisy torrent, carrying on it a cool and slightly metallic smell.

Aaron had finished his cigarette and he wanted another, but he didn't feel like enduring the verbal abuse associated with bumming one from Tommy. The acid kept kicking in and sending his mind off on a tangent. He'd forget all about smoking, zoning out with the cool breeze pouring in through the window.

The world seemed more real to him without the glass barrier.

In the passenger seat, Tommy looked his usual bored self, the dash lights bleaching out his already pale face. His appearance was older than his nineteen years, a shadow of dark stubble shading a weak jawline. A leather baseball cap graced a head of greasy black hair that was shoulder length; he just usually had it slicked back under his cap. He wore the thin leather jacket of some trendy scenester, and Aaron was always confused by that. It wasn't befitting a punk rock look at all.

Aaron, on the other hand, looked the part. He was more like a crust punk, despite having the fresh face of someone like Edward Norton—well, Edward Norton on his most punk rock day, in a painted-up, spiky leather jacket, a belt of M16 bullets, and black jeans tucked into combat boots.

They were headed down to a house owned by local punks, most of whom had been attendees of Virginia Tech. This time he had a clearer head, if only marginally so. The events of the last couple of weeks had been so overwhelming that they seemed like something out of a dream, only that wouldn't be his luck. His dreams were usually simpler, grounded things. In them, he was with childhood friends, doing kid stuff like riding BMX bikes. Sometimes he dreamed he had found a lost item and he would be gripping it tightly, hoping that somehow he could bring it from the dream world into the waking one, though he knew this was impossible. Most of them had the same common elements: one crazy ingredient, a few things that didn't make sense, and a slightly fantastical edge. Even while in the midst of them he knew that they were not real. A few times he had even recognized the dream while still in it, and tried to force his eyes open. The last few days had been nothing like that.

He had witnessed horrible violence. Seen worlds populated by monsters, fled through apocalyptic landscapes, and met an awesome girl. One who didn't look down on him or cast judgment. She had saved his life, seduced him, and then disappeared. It was crazier than any dream, yet it somehow felt solid and real. He had no idea what was going on and was coming to the realization of a dark underbelly to the exterior shell of reality. Pulling out of his thoughts, he straightened up and rubbed his hands.

"How much farther, Tommy?"

Tommy didn't reply.

"Tommy?"

"Would you shut the fuck up?"

Tommy was always a dick and grumpy like that. Aaron had no idea why anyone tolerated him.

After a good two hours, the car rolled into a sedate little town. The darkened forms of one-story brick houses popped up along the roadsides, their driveways a varied lot of trampled dirt and the rusty traces of chain-link fences. Behind it all ran the omnipresent shadows of tree lines. Aaron remembered it being fairly dark and inert last time, although this looked bleaker than normal. He leaned over to the window and peered up. The sky was dark. Starless. Only the contorted edges of thick clouds. Although they had passed a few cars on the interstate, the roads here were empty, making it all the creepier. Most of the houses weren't even lit. The few that were emitted only the faintest of glows.

"Where do you think all the people are?"

Tommy grunted in annoyance. Aaron was curious as to what exactly had gone on while he was away. Tommy had to see that this was strange. He always liked to play the silent type until things got serious, and then he usually opened up.

"I don't know..." he mumbled.

Tommy slowed and rolled left onto a driveway of packed dirt. Aaron figured they must have arrived. It looked familiar, even if he had been way too fucked up last time to recall. All was dark, and they were plowing through a field of tall grass. They bounced along the unpaved trail, the path arcing up a wooded hill. After a few feet trees took over and it was hard to see anything. There were the twin tire grooves of the trail in front of them, visible in the beams of the headlights, and a fluster of leafy branches popping in on the sides whenever they broke the circle of headlight illumination. Then the dark cover overtop broke a little, and they were rounding the silhouette of a two-story house. Everything had lightened up a little now that they were out of the woods, and Aaron could see again the waving tops of tall grass on either side.

From the view between the trees, the house looked like a concrete base that scaled up into a flurry of cheap wooden planks. The trail dropped abruptly, the last of the trees fell away, and a gloomy depression in the wall loomed on the left. Aaron narrowed his eyes, making out what looked like the tail end of a garage, a cheap wooden staircase scaling up on the left. The car pulled to a halt, Tommy shifted into park, and they got out. Aaron shuffled his feet in nervous anticipation. Staring straight ahead, Tommy buried his hands in his pockets and headed for the staircase. Aaron followed.

At the top, the stairs spread out into a wooden porch. Tommy strode forward and tapped lightly on the door. There was no response. A few tense moments passed, and right when

Tommy was about to knock again, the door cracked open. It was only a sliver, and a rough voice, obviously a kid trying to sound tough, called out, "Who's there?"

"Tommy."

"Tommy... Oh, hey, man. What are you doing here?"

"Just let me in."

"Uh, yeah. Who's this with you?"

"My friend Aaron. He came last time."

"Yeah, okay. One sec."

The kid closed the door and there was the sound of a chain sliding back. When the door swung open, a shadowed figure blocked the way. It took Aaron's vision a moment to adjust to the dark. When it did, he was faced with a kid sporting a rat's nest of nappy, long brown hair that was on the verge of knotting into dreadlocks. He was trying to come off as some sort of crusty punk, only more of the college, wannabe rebellious type than the real McCoy. His arms were lily white, and with the exception of a wide black leather wristband and few metal rings decorated with skulls and occult symbols, nothing about him was authentic. Definitely nothing so definitive as a tattoo. He was wearing an old "The Mind is a Terrible Thing to Taste" Ministry shirt, black jeans, black boots, and dog tags, and his face had the thinnest trace of a beard going on. Aaron didn't think much of him, but figured he'd better be nice until he figured out what was going on. "World's gone to shit out there," he commented.

He was trying to present a stoic front, leaning forward with his hand resting against the doorframe. All this was in vain, though, as Aaron noticed an edge of nervousness that betrayed him. The guy didn't even look at Aaron, keeping his eyes trained intently on Tommy as if he were the only one that mattered.

Tommy sighed. "I know, man. Crazy. I just shot a guy."

The kid's eyes widened, and his jaw slackened. "You what? What happened? He attack you? Society's breaking down, man!"

"I don't want to talk about it."

That was Tommy for you, always the dick. He shuffled sideways and let himself in, the guy at the door raising an arm to let him pass. As an afterthought, he turned to Aaron.

"Hey, I'm Mike."

It was uttered without energy or enthusiasm. "Aaron."

With that, Mike headed in. Aaron followed, closing the door behind him.

The hallway was narrow and dimly lit, and consisted mostly of white drywall and stained wooden floors. Even though it was dark, Aaron could make out graffiti on the walls. The sloppy scribbling was accompanied by a sticker or two. A hazy orange-ish light filtered in from the kitchen, and Tommy strode confidently toward it. Following Tommy into the room, Aaron observed that it was a particle board affair of light wooden cupboards, fake marble countertops, and a dented stainless steel fridge. He didn't remember it being so shabby, but then again, he was pretty fucked up last time. The table was a huge oval slab of pale wood, choked with liquor bottles, empty Pabst Blue Ribbon cans, and a few red plastic cups. Some were half-full of beer, some held an unidentified murky liquid populated with cigarette butts, and still others were in various crumpled states.

A large girl named Dana—cute despite being built like an Amazonian— leaned forward and hugged Tommy. She tossed back her curly mop of purplish-red hair, revealing a smooth, lily-white face. Her nose was sharp, her chin cleft, and pale bluish-gray eyes stared out from under stark brown eyebrows. Definitely attractive, if a bit oversized, she was wearing black stretch pants, jean cutoffs, and a Sisters of Mercy shirt. Tommy mumbled to her as he passed and headed straight for the plastic cups on the counter.

"There's a keg on the side of the fridge if you don't mind Bud."

Mike was holding a cup to his mouth, the other hand pointing at a keg in a cheap aluminum can filled with ice. It was tucked into the corner between the wall and the fridge and some stocky guy was bent over it, filling a plastic cup. With his shaved head and a cutoff Pantera Fucking Hostile T-shirt, he gave the impression of being a local tough guy. One of those people who liked fighting for fighting's sake. Aaron waited for him to finish up before shuffling over and scooping up the tap. He didn't know these people and didn't want to commit any social blunders. Still gripping the tap in one hand, Aaron quickly downed two cups and poured a third. The last thing he wanted was for the keg to be kicked before he had a buzz.

Everyone—and that meant about ten people in the kitchen—was clustered together and talking in lower than normal tones. A chunky guy, with a black leather cowboy hat and a matching black leather trench coat, was going on about something. He kept making random gestures with his hands, sweat running down in streams from the tufts of black hair jutting out from under his hat. It glistened in the incandescent kitchen light, making its way down chubby cheeks before it dribbled off of a weak chin. Seated next to him was a skinny guy with a Mohawk of brown braids who kept pointing at the floor intently as he talked. His hair sheltered a slender face covered with patchy stubble and a childlike mustache. Thick silver rings jingled as his fingers moved, a myriad of leather and silver bands clanking together as his skinny wrists jerked to and fro.

Sitting next to the comically fat standing guy and the rail-thin jerky punk was a nonchalant-looking girl. It was hard for Aaron to discern her body, hidden as it was under a loose Skinny Puppy T-shirt, but her face was nice. She had sharp, goth features and raven-black hair. Her eyes were looking at the floor, her head nodding with every word from the skinny guy. Aaron stared at her for a minute. She was beautiful, even if she didn't look that bright. Although it may have been that the beer was romanticizing his vision. All this made Aaron feel weird and out of place, and he pulled away and looked around.

The keg bordered a doorless frame and beyond it a dark corridor ventured into the depths of the house. Everyone was busy talking, their conversation confined to whichever little social clique they belonged to. Aaron wandered over to the doorway and looked in. After a few feet of drywall the shadows took over and he couldn't see anything. He stepped over the keg and headed in.

As the darkness enveloped him, he let his mind wander across the events of the past few days. He had seen people's heads explode right in front of him; a tank rolling down the streets of D.C.; and the girl, that sexy girl who didn't speak any English. She had saved his life, fed him, fucked him, and then disappeared. All of it had transpired in a surreal landscape populated by monsters, or aliens, or whatever they were. It was then he realized that he could barely recall the details of their appearance, which was unusual. He had a virtually photographic memory. They had large black eyes, glistening teeth, and a preternatural aura. Something not of this word, and the more dangerous for it, but he still couldn't recollect a clear image.

Snapping back to reality, he sensed his steps encountering more resistance than usual, like the ground was thick and tangling his feet. The beer was kicking in, so it might be his buzz, but he felt a very strange vibe. He was cold and clammy, shivering under his leather jacket, and the air smelled strange and sort of briny. But the ocean was miles away. He also caught a whiff of something rotten and ground to a stop. It suddenly felt like the air around him was throbbing. He heard a scuttling noise in the distance, the kind of sound you might expect an enormous crab to make. Aaron tensed and wished he were sober. His skin grew taut, his arm hair erect. There was a wet, hissing sound, along with a rank fishy smell. Lightheadedness struck and he leaned into the wall. It was too dark to see anything, and he desperately groped for a surface. His fingers touched on wet, slimy stone, and he immediately pulled them away. Unzipping the front of his leather jacket, his shaking hand dug through the inside pocket for a lighter. His cigarettes were there, and he debated pulling them out before his fingertips brushed against the zippo. Flicking the wheel, a flame spurted to life, and Aaron's eyes grew wide with terror. The wall on his left was made of rough, curving stone, resembling some subterranean cave. Off-white streaks of lavender rippled through the white rock. Symbols, vaguely cuneiform, only more spidery and delicate, glistened under a sheen thicker than water. He had seen pictograms like these recently in his travels.

Stepping back, he held the lighter aloft. He was in what resembled a cave, the walls pale stretches of contorted rock. The floor was more of the same, only flattened out and coated with a thin layer of chunky sand. Damp sand at that, with water gathering into rivulets that navigated through the gullies. From the corner of his eye he caught movement, and instinctively he scuffled backward into the wall.

He bent over and swept the lighter across the floor. Its flame flickered toward his thumb and he instinctively let go of the button with a gasp of pain. His finger throbbed, and he swapped the lighter between hands. Sucking on the burnt finger in an attempt to alleviate the pain, he held the lighter aloft with his other hand and reignited it.

There was definite movement in the sand. Everything was a little blurry, and his head felt thick and strange. He lowered himself into a squat as he tried to clear his head and get a better view.

Rising furrows in the sand announced the presence of something he could not yet see. He leaned closer, but the lighter was growing hot and the flame was close to his thumb. He tried to push the pain aside so he could get a better look. Staring intently at the rising queues of dirt, he noticed that one hit an intersecting stream, and a form emerged under the current. It looked like a tiny armadillo, sporting pinchers like a stag beetle. He felt a wave of revulsion, and wondered if these were what was making the noise or if there was still some further horror. The heat from the lighter was unbearable now, and he took his finger off the button. Listening in the dark, he could hear a distant, muffled, crashing sound, like a wave striking the seashore.

Whatever the clicking and scuttling sound was, it had now vanished. He flicked the wheel again and the tunnel came back to life. The furrows in the sand had changed direction, and it dawned on Aaron that they were headed straight for him now. Terror washed over him and he backed up until he was against the wall. He hit the slime and instantly recoiled, dropping the lighter. Total darkness swarmed in. Terrified, he turned in the direction from which he had come and broke into a run. He was instantly stone sober, fits of hot and cold washing over him in sickening waves. His lungs felt raw, and his thighs started burning, only it didn't matter. Adrenaline kicked in, and he was running for his life in wide-eyed, open-mouthed shock.

The Decline of
Western Civilization

Hindsight is 20/20. There is plenty I could have done differently, although planning ahead is the first thing to go when the apocalypse comes. My trip across a decimated U.S., in a body new to me, was one entangling incident after another. My trip back has been less eventful. So far. I don't know if it's a factor of the new wiring of my brain, the weight of experience, the passage of time, or a combination thereof. Initially I felt personally invested in the downfall of the U.S. But that all changed. Now I gauge the situation on a completely different level. Why the U.S. fell is an overarching issue. The questions that follow, however, are of more immediate concern. Namely, what is the outlook of the general population, and how will they respond?

Specifically, how will they respond to me? Whereas before I might have been afforded more leniency by certain segments, people tend to fall prey to dogma when the going gets tough. They also tend to become more contentious and less open to new ideas, which sets me against the current.

There are fewer local governments, but those that remain appear to have tightened security and ramped up hostility toward outsiders. I don't know if they will try to utilize me, or be more defensive and withdraw from any confrontation. So far it appears the current climate fosters a shoot-first-and-ask-questions-later mentality, although I arrived at that conclusion while in the thick of the crisis. I can't be sure how long I've been away or if anything has changed.

When I worked for the central government, it was in a

closed, high-security environment. Ironically, that meant we heard more than outsiders. Not about the general population, which might have prepared me for this twist of fate, but about the inner workings of our political and military system. Everyone in the system suspected there was a bureau that handled the paranormal side. Although it wasn't as high profile and dubious as Project Blue Book, this division was rumored to have clearance for almost anything, and they operated with impunity. I don't think the various branches were unified, even if they all shared some of the same intelligence, but the indication was that everything was connected. Because this is the central government we're talking about, I doubt the bureau dispersed completely in the face of all this chaos. They may even have caused it, although that's a stretch, as it would only complicate their job. But they may have inadvertently pushed everything over the edge. The U.S. public has this idea of individual liberty, even if they tend to be slow-witted and susceptible to instigation. Too many secrets held too closely could be the root cause of all this, although considering all the false flags and intrusive government agencies they put up with, maybe I'm giving them too much credit. The real issue is how active said bureau still is, and what precisely do they know? I'm not even sure that their overlooking the potential of the body I now inhabit was an oversight. It's possible that the compartmentalization of incoming intel kept the right people from looking in a certain direction until it was too late, if there wasn't another plan afoot. The path to obtaining this body had its obstacles, but it also had plenty of lucky strokes. If the theft was engineered from on high, how much do they really know about the suit's potential, and what is their real agenda? More importantly, is their game plan still in play?

The engine rumbles smoothly as I pass through the wilderness of Arizona down a trail of red sand. A series of short rock walls blossoms on the right, following the road for a mile before breaking down into squarish chunks of rubble. Behind it all, fields of yellowish grass spread out toward a distant tree line, their verdant expanse dotted with bushes and stubby oak trees. I pass two large conical tanks squatting in the midst of the field on my right. Darkly tinted rust coats them, white letters spray painted on the sides declare: "Please Do Not Shoot. Wildlife Water". Society might fall to the point where water is a rare commodity. If that happens, I wonder how long the lifespan of these tanks will be.

The road progresses into a paved trail. A short wall of tree-topped granite ascends on the right, the left falling down in a grass-covered slope. As I round several bends in the road, the wall of rock on the right drops dramatically, a rising forest of oak trees taking its place. Cottony white clouds lethargically pull apart through a pale blue sky.

Hours pass, and now hills spread out on all sides, their undulating terrain fading as they stretch toward a distant horizon. A forest overtakes the rolling slopes, the trees taking on a blue hue as they pale into the distance. A slight wind blows steadily, tossing about the leaves and grass. In the past I would have found this scene relaxing. Now all I really notice is the absence of that impression. I have only a distant sense of how my human body would have reacted a lifetime ago.

My arms are little more than stiff levers. The left one grips the steering wheel, the right one the shift lever. A year ago I would have relaxed the muscles so that the weight of my left was resting on the windowsill, the palm of my right on the shift knob. Now the positions are strictly mechanical. I no longer feel the buildup of lactic acid, and my arms remain rigid. The scene around me presents no evident challenge, it's just land that must be crossed.

As with the majestic sunset earlier, I feel nothing. I recognize the difference, and that inspires a faint twinge of regret. Am I losing my humanity? If so, am I okay with it? Not that I have any choice, but I wonder if my humanity is part of what makes me... me.

As I survey the surroundings, I start to compartmentalize. I analyze the rock, try to deconstruct its type. How it got there, and how it interacts with its surroundings. Then I look at the trees, and I start to do the same thing. I examine the bark, the thickness of the trunk, the neighboring elements and how they interact with it, the root system, where the underground tendrils extend, and where they draw water from. I'm consumed for a moment before realizing that I have to cut off this train of thought. I have a sense that this is taking me down a mental road I do not want to travel. Even worse, my appreciation for nature's beauty is fading. That insight first came to my attention in the Amazon, and remorse would wash over me as I cursed at what I'd done. A few times it gripped me so intently I could barely function. I would end analyzing all conceivable angles of my new outlook, questioning whether the comprehensive analysis was a new adaptation or a re-emergent aspect of my old self that was now heightened. Claustrophobia would follow, and I would start to feel trapped in this body, convinced my human emotions were being tampered with and I was becoming a new thing altogether that was not at all what I intended or wanted. Then cold reason would snap me out of my reverie and I would start backpedaling. I think this mental drama accounts for why the Al'lak couldn't remain in this body.

I focus on the road. The hills are now far off in the distance, the shoulders short, sandy stretches of wild grass that run into a nestle of low-lying trees. A ranch-style wooden fence starts up on the right, its stretches of timber graying and cracking with age. It stirs a distant memory, and the vague sensation causes me to let up on the gas as I try to discern the source.

The fence falls away before long, a wide open lot of red sand taking its place. On the outskirts of the lot, a few hundred feet from the road, a strange-looking cabin is nestled among a dense stand of oak trees. Long blocks of red sandstone bolster the foundation. The walls are a queue of heavily weathered brown logs, piling up until they reach a terminus of rusty, corrugated tin that serves as a roof. As I draw closer, the premonition grows. I have a presentiment of danger and yet an undercurrent of necessity. Or obligation, I can't tell, but I feel somehow drawn to it.

The FJ40's tires crunch over the gravel as I pull into the wide lot. I shift into neutral and leave the vehicle idling. Upon closer inspection, I find the cabin to be even older and more decrepit than I initially thought. The rustic logs that make up the walls have gaps between them, as if the place were constructed as an afterthought. The red foundation blocks are haphazardly mismatched, with the remnants spilling out into crude piles. Bordering the foundation, wiry brush contends with patches of wild grass for space.

I dismount the FJ and approach. I get an external temperature reading of 110 degrees Fahrenheit. Everything, even the trees, looks beaten down under such sweltering heat. The sky is now a static blue. No clouds, no movement—nothing disrupts the utter stillness. Some trace of human emotion tells me this is too much. I'm not sure what it is, but nothing feels normal.

A central walkway bores through the dwelling, splitting it into two equal halves covered by a common roof. The right wall sports a single, boarded-up window that seems to exude a dim light. I focus my vision on the gaps and zoom in. I can't get a clear view of the inside, and even the source of the brightness remains elusive. I should be able to focus clearly, although it might be merely an aberration of my newfound sight that I haven't learned to control. The walkway between rooms has an opening on either side. Neither portal has a door, but my glimpses of the interiors tell me they are darker than they should be.

My thought patterns have grown oddly discordant. Nothing too extreme, but I am so used to the clarity and sharpness that come with this body any degradation hearkens back to my old human self. My vision has become less precise as well, and a faint humming began resonating in my head. I drift toward the left, feeling out of sorts, and then I realize I've lost control of my motor function.

I close my eyes and try to clear my head, and when I look up I've already stepped into the cabin. It's much bigger on the inside than I suspected. More modern as well. Chestnut-brown trunks are nestled against tall, scratched-up gray file cabinets. Papers flow from mounds atop the trunks as they make a disorderly sweep across the floorboards. A crooked painting hangs on a far wall papered with a sepia damask pattern. Wait… outside this appeared as a ramshackle log cabin. This makes no sense. The mental thumping intensifies as I lean forward and grip my head. I see a row of three doors on the far right, all folding wooden slabs of venetian blinds. Light pours in through the slits, and I stumble in that direction. The thumping grows louder—to the point of pain, in fact. I didn't even know I could feel pain anymore.

"You can't see them, you know."

I crane my head to the left. Nestled in the corner, a shadowy form sits atop a folding chair, an antique-looking wooden desk positioned in front of him.

What with the fog in my head, I hadn't even noticed him. He looks human, only a human from seventy years ago. With sharp features, a gray suit, and matching fedora, he resembles a square-jawed movie star of yesteryear, a la Clark Gable. I try to zoom in, but my vision control is shot. Still, something about him resonates as particularly odd. He has a barely perceptible glow, like that from a distorted projection, and his form is semi-transparent.

"You're not Al'lak. What are you? Human?"

His words are garbled and hard to understand. He's talking out loud, and I am unable to respond verbally. I'm not sure if he registers this.

"I know you can't talk. Think your response."

That was definitely in my head, which makes me think this is a projection. That would explain the out of place look. Someone is trying to put up a pretense that they think I'll respond to, and that level of technology means that whoever this is, it isn't human.

"Who are you? What is this?"

"Ah, the ten-million-dollar question. Isn't that how you humans say it?"

"You assume I'm human?"

"You think like a human. An eastern United States human at that. It took a moment. Your species can be a confusing breed."

The throbbing in my head hasn't budged. If anything, it's gotten worse. "What do you want?"

I'm trying hard not to show how bad I feel. It's like I'm in a mental haze, and it takes a minute to refine my thoughts.

"Definitely not you. You're a curiosity. A primitive inhabiting a structure built by a boring genus from elsewhere."

The pounding has escalated to jackhammer intensity. I fall to my knees and grip the back of my head as the world roars around me. The periphery grows hazy, and unidentifiable streaks of gauzy mist whip past. Everything trembles beneath the impact of a huge, percussive wallop. More thunderclaps follow, the blows interspersed with a deluge of smaller thumps. My thinking is disoriented. I put forth thoughts but they never last long enough for analysis. They are only sounds crashing into the maelstrom of chaos. Indistinguishable voices punch through my mental fog, angry demands that promptly morph into screams. Wet, gushing noises follow, and there's the liquid slap of soft tissue against something unyielding. The pain in my head is now a living thing, and I curl into a fetal position.

Abruptly, everything is normal again and my mind is clear. No swirling vortex, no headache. Confused, I rise from my huddled position and view an empty room, only it's not the empty room I entered. Everything looks long abandoned. The floor is a primitive spread of red dirt. The dried remnants of weeds and twigs litter the ground, building up in little piles of detritus that sidle against the coarse sandstone blocks of the foundation. Sunlight pours through the gaps in the wall's loose arrangement of timbers, the beams commingling with the long rays descending from slits in the roof, their brilliant shafts piercing the darkness in a complex array of sharp angles. I turn to my left and see the weather-worn frame of a doorway. The vertical beams are merely crooked timbers that sport breaches rivaling those in the wall. Beyond the doorless portal can be seen the sun-bathed trunks of oak trees. Saplings crowd in around them, their wiry boughs drooping along the ground as they struggle for life. I walk forward and step out into the blazing sunlight.

Rounding the corner of the house I freeze. The front lot is the scene of a bloodbath. Spread throughout are the remains of perhaps twenty soldiers, their bodies pulped into oblivion. Judging from the scraps, they appear to have been Army National Guard, although most are utterly unrecognizable, the gory remnants looking like they've been wrenched inside out. Pink intestines weave in and out among a soupy morass of darker glistening organs. A slick sheen of crimson coats the entire scene. It flows over the bodies, stains the sand, and enswaths the mangled equipment. A dark-skinned man is sprawled before me. Eyes closed, his cheeks and forehead are abraded, pinkish gristle bubbling out of the gashes. The torn shreds of a military shirt encircle his outstretched right arm, a limb that is shredded near the wrist, the flayed skin peeled back there to expose a nub of bone. Not far away lies another body torn in half and missing a head. The pale skin of the lower belly is split open and a writhing mass of intestines pours out over a pool of dark blood. Next to the torso, a severed right arm lies next to a similarly cleft left arm. Both might belong to the remnants of that soldier, although it's hard to tell for sure. A few feet to one side is a blond-haired soldier who must have been all of nineteen. His blood-speckled face stares through pale blue eyes at an indifferent sky. His left leg is mashed to a pulp below the knee, strings of gristle splaying out beneath a protruding thigh bone. A few feet behind him is the burning frame of an HWWMV.

Beyond that, parallel with the road, is an M1117. It's an Army security vehicle that as far as I knew was only used overseas. There are the shredded remnants of troops between the burning HWWMV and the M1117, but that last vehicle looks like it might be untouched. Spread out across the lot are whitish lumps of brain matter, severed appendages, and countless organs, most of them mired in drying pools and trailing veins like strings. Most of the bodies are far from intact, just solitary chunks of gristle and blood. So much blood. More than even seems possible. Pooling in sinkholes, soaking the earth and clothing, and slung across everything like some crazy abstract painting. What the fuck happened here? It had to be while I was in that house. I'm getting the impression that this was the epicenter of the storm I caught the tail end of, and that there was a lot going on before I arrived. It was pure chance that I stumbled on this. That thing inside hinted that I wasn't the focal point. Is the military trying to hide something, or did they happen upon something that was way out of their depth? This carnage looks a lot more gratuitous than anything I've seen from the Al'lak or the race they are at war with, which makes me think they might be small fishes in a very big pond.

My FJ is off to the right, on the edge of the lot. I should have known that instantly, but that incident in the cabin fucked with my recall. It's something I haven't experienced since I was human. When I rolled into this spot I was lamenting my loss of humanity, which may now prove to be my weakness. If whatever was in that cabin could so easily fuck with my system, where does that leave me? Everyone so far has been on edge when I showed up.

Whatever it was in that cabin, it viewed me as chattel. What *was* it, and who was it really after? There's something going on here, and it's much bigger than I suspected.

My FJ is not unscathed. The sidewalls in front of the rear left tire boast a few bullet holes. The passenger side, which once sported a metal rod supporting a round mirror, now holds aloft an empty metal dish. The glass it once held is gone, a few remaining fragments pooled along the bottom lip in jagged shards. Light streams through a bullet hole. The vehicle is also no longer running. A glance through the passenger window reveals that the keys are gone. Probably taken by a soldier, the remnants of whom are to be found in that gore spread across the lot. I can always hotwire the FJ if I need to. I back up and take a look. There are a few bullet holes above the right fender, suggesting the engine took a few. So even if it runs now, it might not do so for very long. I turn around and scan the area, searching for an alternative.

There are two HWWMVs on fire, and the only intact vehicle I can see is the M1117. Most military vehicles don't have keys. I'll bet that truck isn't fast… and guzzles gas—but it's better than nothing. I saw one like it when I was stationed at a military base, but only at a distance. It strikes me at this point how funny they look, like giant metal boxes that have been partially flattened. The middle folds out above the wheel well, and I think the idea was that the curved sidewalls would deflect rockets launched by hand. It is olive drab and has oversized knobby tires and tiny rectangular windows. Stranger still, on top is a swiveling turret that looks like it belongs on a tank, only it's half the size and has two barrels, one for a Browning .50 caliber and one for a rocket launcher. The entry door is smack in the middle of the body, and it just happens to be open. Leaving the door open in a war zone goes against military procedure, which leads me to think that things happened so quickly it caught everyone unprepared. Not to mention these are probably National Guard troops, not trained soldiers.

As I close in on the M1117, I see the walls on the inside are streaked with blood. This is an ominous sigh. I step inside and it only gets worse. Clumps of gristle are pooled in the corners, a sheen of crimson spreading across the diamond-plate floorboards. The central metal stand, essentially a chair ringed by a circular cage of wire mesh, is empty. Albeit bloody, but empty. The dual rectangular windshields in the far front are coated in blood. The angled windows beside them contain more of the same. The sunlight filtering through it all reaches the interior as a smoky red haze. A few thick knots of gore cling to the windshields, casting eerie shadows across the upholstered surfaces. The dashboard, a complex maze of gauges and buttons, is sheathed in a sticky coat of coagulating blood. Pinkish bits float atop the larger pools, their pulped contours frozen in place like so much shredded human meat.

Round nuggets resembling egg whites decorate the lip of the windowsill. Chunks of brain would be my guess. The barely recognizable remnants of two humans spill over the seats. Like most of the soldiers outside, they look as if they have been twisted inside out. Pools of gelatinous gore cover the seats, with intestines navigating around glistening organs and spilling out onto the floor. A few ropy strings of flesh stretch out from the central pools and wrap around the shift levers. Most of what were once bones have been splintered and partially pulverized, the ashy bone dust commingling with the blood and oozing down from the seats in a chunky red paste.

I hear a dripping sound coming from overhead, and look up to see that a syrupy red fluid coats the roof. It dribbles down in long, viscous tendrils that coalesce in gelatinous pools on the floor. There is no wind, no noise, save the patter of falling gore. It's like a lost scene out of time from the *Twilight Zone*, and in a grotesque appeal to some trace of my humanity, it's slightly repellent.

On second thought, this vehicle might be far too conspicuous, what with its military bearing and the gory interior. Although if I'm really honest with myself, the truth of the matter is that I really don't have the time or inclination to clean the thing.

Ducking back out, I scan the lot. Parked on the far edge, next to a fence that borders the road, is a black Toyota Tacoma pickup. Nestled under the shade of an overhanging tree, it looks fairly new, rear bed cap and all. That thing should be easy to hotwire, and far less conspicuous than this filthy military affair. There's a gas can in the FJ along with a few water jugs. I'll empty the jugs, throw them and the gas can in the back of that Toyota, and see how far I get.

THINGS GET COMPLICATED

A aron's front foot caught on an invisible protrusion under-foot and he stumbled. A quick shuffle enabled him to avert a full-on face plant. Tears of frustration welled up as he resumed his jog. He had slowed down, and wasn't quite sure what he should do. He couldn't see anything, and the only noise that came to him was the sound of rushing water somewhere in the distance. It had been twenty minutes, and he should be back in the kitchen by now. He cursed himself, spitting out strings of "*Fuck! Fuck! Fuck!*" in a barely audible hiss, his flesh vacillating between hot and cold sweats.

The briny smell had transitioned into that of a moldering old basement. The concave floor felt like it had flattened out, and he could swear he was treading on a path that was dry and solid. The air had grown warmer, and Aaron was now soaked in sweat. Rivulets had formed on his forehead and trickled down his face. He plodded almost to a halt, fumbling around in his pocket for cigarettes, never mind the fact they wouldn't do him much good without a lighter. The pocket was ripped, and he wiggled his hand through, contorting his arm and feeling along the bottom seam. His fingers hit matches and he twisted around, trying to establish a grip on them. Eventually he managed to maneuver them to the edge of the pocket. Running his other fingers outside of the jacket, he located the lump and secured it. A little more struggling and he had managed to free them. Opening the cigarette pack and extracting a Winchester, he nestled it in his lips and struck a match.

It was only then that he realized he had been standing still for several minutes, and he glanced at the floor in a panic. He could see no signs of movement. He lowered the penumbra of light to the ground for a closer examination. He had been right after all—the trail had flattened out and now consisted of trampled dirt. The walls had transformed, too, into an assemblage of tightly clustered logs, the uneven gaps packed with dark soil.

The match quickly burned down, and Aaron flung it aside. He lit another and held it up. The path in front extended before him, tunnel-like. It reminded him of an old mineshaft, like something he once saw in a movie. *Indiana Jones and the Temple of Doom* maybe. The flame burned his fingers again, and Aaron released it with a curse. Although the blackness swarmed in again, he could make out a faint glow in the distance. Taking a drag from his cigarette, he exhaled a roiling stream of smoke. Strangely, the smoke appeared to hang in the air like a suffocating cloud. It dawned on him that smoking inside such a tightly enclosed space was probably not the best of ideas. Not wanting to waste the cigarette, he moved forward, hoping to put the cloud behind him.

His surroundings remained stuffy, and if anything, it got even harder to breathe. He dropped the cigarette and crushed it with a twist of his boot. He was sweltering in the heat, inhalations were difficult, and claustrophobia was kicking in. He picked up his pace and squinted toward the light in the distance. Panic started to set in, making him wonder whether the air were truly getting scarce or if it were merely his imagination. The glow he had seen had turned out to be the glowing frame of a doorway. His heart skipped a beat and he quickened his pace.

A few more steps and it was in front of him. He gasped for breath, hands on his knees, and pulled out another match. Sparking it to life, he could perceive an old oak door in front of him. Two dark, ancient-looking partitions met in a seam running down the middle. A large rustic ring hung from a triangular slab mounted on the left-hand door. Aaron took hold of the ring and pulled, but the door didn't budge. He set the heel of his boot against the right-hand door and used both hands. With a grating sound that called to mind sandpaper, it moved slightly and light poured in through the newly formed slit. Aaron tried again, bracing his legs and pulling with all his might. The door budged a fraction more. His muscles were throbbing, the skin on his palms raw, and he released his grip in frustration. He sucked in air, shook out his hands, and readied himself for another attempt. The light grew more intense with every ounce of effort he expended, and after several more laborious tugs he had managed to create just enough of an opening for him to slide through.

The dramatic increase in lighting on the other side of the door momentarily blinded him. Clamping his eyes shut, he squeezed through. And with an instantaneous pop, he found himself awkwardly flailing his way toward a hardwood floor. Dust kicked up and swirled about him in a choking miasma. He coughed and lifted his head, struggling to view his surrounds. Everything was still a blur with the intensity of the light, but he could make out the dark form of a man looming over him. He blinked, his eyes moistened, and the figure slowly came into focus. It looked for all the world like the guy he had seen in D.C. right before the world went to shit. This one was wearing dark trousers, polished black shoes, and a charcoal jacket. His shirt and tie were black, and he was wearing a fedora that looked straight out of some 1940s hardboiled-detective movie, even if Aaron couldn't quite distinguish the facial features. As the world came into view, there was a tremendous flash. Aaron raised an arm to shield his eyes but was too late, and he was once again blinded. He squeezed shut his eyes and rubbed them, shaking his head. Dots swam before his eyes, and he waited for the flashes to pass. When he opened his eyes again, he blinked and then stared in disbelief. He was inside a long-abandoned cabin, surrounded by ramshackle walls formed of loosely fitted timbers. Bright light poured in through the copious gaps. Scraps of wood and chunks of stone spiraled out in loose medleys from the walls. To the left and right were doorless portals. The one on the left appeared to lead through a sheltered overhang and into a similar chamber. The one on the right opened into a vista of trees and sunlight. Scrambling to his feet, Aaron darted toward the sunlight.

The heat was overwhelming. It was much hotter than

the Blacksburg Aaron had been in just moments ago. It was brighter, too, and the vegetation was different, like it belonged in a more arid climate. In fact, everything did. It even smelled like a desert, dusty and sun-baked. He was apparently on one side of a cabin, loose patches of trees spreading out all around him. To the right they clustered together into a vacant woodline. Around the bend of the cabin could be seen the outline of a driveway. He flattened himself against the wall and edged backward toward what he assumed to be the rear of the building. A musky, slaughtered animal scent washed over him, and he gagged. It had an iron-like and sickly sweet aroma, all commingled with a trace of bile. He felt an onrush of nausea and bent over, trying to shield his nose under his shirt collar. The noxious odor was coming from the front of the cabin. He drew in closer to the wall and crept toward the back. Then he heard a faint crunching of gravel, and it sounded like something was advancing in his direction. He flattened himself against the wall and moved in the opposite direction. When he passed by the doorway, he glanced in. The room was still dark and empty. Shafts of light cut across it, motes of disturbed detritus wafting through the beams.

He kept edging along in this way, jumping with fright when his back lost touch with the wall. He whirled around, but it was only the rear corner of the cabin. He cast desperate glances into the woods. The trees were spindly black things, twisting out of the ground in a maze of trunks, their boughs warping into a plethora of long branches bearing flourishes of green leaves as they rose. Half-dead grass scratched its way through sandy soil all about the skinny trunks. The scene was one of barrenness, and was more than a little sinister.

Aaron dislodged himself from the wall and scampered along the back of the cabin until he reached the recess in the middle. It was unusually long, and this break in the middle resembled an open tunnel. He glanced up and realized he had entered a breezeway formed by two cabins spanned by a common tin roof. Edging up next to the wall again, he craned his head and peered through the gap. What he saw made him stumble backward in shock.

Spreading in front of the cabin was the scene of a massacre. Blood covered everything, and there were so many gory chunks of what once were humans that Aaron couldn't even tell them apart. A few feet from the front entrance was a severed head. It was lying sideways, the eyes staring listlessly to the left. The tip of the nose was partially crushed, the short black hair matted with some dark, sticky liquid. Thick eyebrows arched over blood-swelled eyelids. The neck had been pulverized into strings of gristle, two stiff white segments jutting out. The first was entwined with dark, bloody chunks, the second split in two and was swathed in pinkish clumps. Blood pooled in semi-coagulated lumps at the base of the neck and spread out in a wide fan of diminishing thickness. The skin on the head peeled away near the jugular to reveal a chunk of pinkish muscle, the gash continuing up the neck until it split the side of the head open. A fresh, gamy stench permeated the air. It reminded Aaron of the deer his dad had strung up in his garage years ago, only this time with the sickening smell of sweating human flesh added to the mix.

Spreading before the cabin was the scene of a massacre

Aaron looked farther out and realized that this was only the outskirts of the carnage. There were bodies without limbs, limbs without bodies, inside-out clusters of organs splayed out in pools of blood and gore, and crushed heads. The flattened human remains were a perversion of reality.

The frames of two burning Humvees staked out the edges. Propped against the one on the left were the bloody remnants of a soldier. The fires had withered into licks of flame fluttering over a chaotic skeleton of dark ash. Whatever had torn through these vehicles was monstrous, and Aaron surmised that the fires were merely the aftermath.

At the end of the lot sat another vehicle, this one of a type Aaron had never seen before. It resembled a tank, only with a bigger body and a smaller turret. A scraping noise caught his attention and he froze. It mimicked the sound he had heard on the other side of the cabin, only farther away this time. He edged into the tunnel, keeping flat against the wall. He shot a glance into the room he had just exited, then quickly darted past the portal and into the safety of the far wall. Inching forward, his skin tingled and sweat built up on his temples. Closer to the front meant closer to the carnage, and although he tried not to look, the stench was growing more intense. He could feel the last beer he'd had coming up. Fighting back sickness, he peered around the corner.

Far to one side of the lot was an old silver Toyota truck. Sort of jeep-like, he figured it must be rare, because he had never seen one like it. Standing near the front with its back to him was the strangest sight he had ever seen. It was humanoid, tall, and vaguely muscular. It was more athletic than bulky, although it still looked somehow... off. Aaron was no expert on anatomy, but the muscles didn't appear to flow quite right, and the... thing was naked. It was matte black, hairless, and even though the buttocks rose and fell like an ass there was no crack. Even the skin had a strange, satiny quality, and he was unable to focus directly on it. Try as he might, the only impression he was able to perceive was that of a blur.

It stood there, observing something. Aaron ducked his head in and inched backward. That strange, silent being was far more terrifying than all the gory carcasses in front. The carnage of the lot popped back into his head, and he experienced a fresh wave of nausea. A whiff of metallic bile hit and he fell to his knees, the regurgitated beer back in his throat. His cheeks swelled and he felt like a puffer fish, fighting the urge to puke. If he spewed, that thing might hear him, and whatever happened to all those people out front might happen to him. He kept crawling backward, eyes fixed on the dirt, his mouth full of vomit as he tried not to retch. A tingling sensation passed over him when he crossed over the threshold, but he didn't dare look.

Finally, at the rear edge of the tunnel, he reached his limit and spewed it all out. Frothy liquid cascaded out like a firehose, splattering the ground and stinging his throat with stomach acid. Strings of white foam trailed from his lips as he dry-heaved. His head light and his stomach queasy, he rubbed his mouth on the sleeve of his leather jacket. Paranoia swept over him and he quickly raised his head, swiveled around, and stared back. There was still the spread of genocide on the lot beyond, but that creature wasn't coming after him. At least not yet. He scrambled to his feet and ran.

Aaron rounded the back side of the cabin and crossed into the woods. He didn't even care about the noise now, he only needed to put as much distance between him and that thing as possible. He darted between trees, trying to hide behind their trunks as he scanned for any signs of pursuit, only the trees were too thin and far apart to offer much cover. Spindly black things, they pitifully bristled out of wide-open patches of sand and scraggly yellowed grass. Glancing over, he caught sight of one of the burning Humvees. That weird figure was nowhere in sight, although much of the lot was obscured by drifting smoke. The scent of smoldering plastic and metal mixed nauseatingly with that of the arid woodland. Aaron listened intently and could only hear the crackle and pop of dying fires, the gentle tumult of the smoke. It was all disconcerting, and it provided him with no hint of where that *thing* was. It could be on top of him for all he knew. Nervously, he glanced around. Off to his left, nestled against the trees shouldering the road, was a black pickup. It had a cap sheltering the back, and it was the closest place he could see to hide. Aaron took one last look around and darted toward it.

THE NATION'S CAPITAL

Job was in his twenties. Almost thirty actually and pretty unassuming. He was a bachelor and had once had a reputation as a ladies' man. Neither aggressive nor passive, he safely tread the middle ground. His politics tended to lean left. He maintained a decent level of fitness, mostly biking and running, hitting the gym a couple times a week. Nothing too extreme, only what was needed to stay in shape. He was tall, about six feet, and muscular, built more like a swimmer than a football player. He kept his dark hair short, his chin shaved, and his everyman face was a little more handsome than normal. While it was definitely not the chiseled face of a movie star, he wasn't exactly the ugly guy at the party either. Even his clothes were indistinct—not quite the dress clothes of the financial crowd, just the casual slacks and sweaters that projected a cool, middle-of-the-road personality. Not 9 to 5, locked in a career bubble, and not so lowbrow he would be mistaken for a blue-collar drone.

His apartment on downtown P Street a few blocks from DuPont Circle in Washington, D.C., was genial, if unremarkable. Tan-colored carpet, a bookshelf with some interesting, left-field-but-not-overly-so books; a couple of framed prints on the walls, all of them of the mild scenery type one sees in upscale hotels. They were marginally more artistic, but pushed no boundaries. Everything about him displayed every sign of playing it safe, which made his choice of profession all the more surprising.

Job worked at a nonprofit that monitored the government, all of which seemed harmless enough. He even told his friends just that, and the subject was typically dropped without further probing. The LLC *did* watch the government, although it was mainly concerned with the cases that had been shuffled off to the sidelines. Weird stuff that was barely acknowledged, if at all. When Job was hired, the LLC had started out by looking for false flags and pork barrel politics—more down-to-earth material that had taken a weird turn. Although there was plenty of health- and wealth-style rigging and the *de rigueur* political favors, there was also a whole political game taking place below the surface. A racket that Job's clever boss had been the first to discover traces of. Money—a lot of it—was being siphoned off and disappearing down some very shadowy channels. Initially it brought to mind the Iran-Contra scandal. Then the incident and the people concerned quickly disappeared, which made it more efficient and professional than was normally the case with the usual political shenanigans. A cover story surfaced, one that could not possibly be true, and all the parties involved vanished.

The government had a long history of lying to the public. The Gulf of Tonkin incident that was used as a justification for the Vietnam War was entirely made up. The CIA was trying to create an incident in Chicago and blame it on Cuban terrorists. They called it Operation Northwoods, and the idea was to give Kennedy an excuse to invade. Communist paranoia was used to justify anything: eugenics; dosing academics with drugs; exposing soldiers, prisoners, and minorities to diseases or high levels of radiation. The list went on, and rather than diminishing with the end of the Cold War, it continued to grow in scope and daringness. The forces in power had grown smarter after the debacle of the Vietnam War. They kept the heavy stuff out of the mainstream news, which wasn't that hard since most media outlets had consolidated into a few global interests, with the politicians in their pockets. The newscasters flamed minor issues into major crises, and doggedly followed the lives of celebrities. It became a known fact that you couldn't trust the major outlets on anything. In a way, that only made it worse, as it empowered conspiracy theorists and special interest groups to pitch their heavily skewed views all over the web. It was a nightmare of conflicting information, and one that bored the average citizen to tears.

The NSA and Federal Reserve grew stronger. Glaring

violations of the Constitution such as the Patriot Act were passed. The push and pull of local parties only heightened stress levels and increased violence.

The government had proven it could compartmentalize and keep unsavory secrets, the Manhattan Project being a prime example, and it had only gotten worse in the ensuing decades. With the demise of most real reporting, and the ability with which anyone even remotely close to a real secret could be tarred and feathered, no one knew what to believe. There was a persistent rumor that the president, on the day he was inaugurated, would be given access to a "book of secrets." Naturally such a claim had proved impossible to verify, and there were obviously things even he wasn't privy to. While dark and sinister forces swirled all about whoever sat in the office, no one viewed the president as anything more than a puppet. That big interests controlled everything was a known fact, and the figureheads voted into office were at best the lesser of two evils. Most of the population didn't even bother to vote.

This was the scenario into which Job was eased. Coming from a liberal arts college, he honestly believed he could make a difference. As the overwhelming reality of how things truly worked set in, Job grew less and less idealistic. At the same time, intense habits set in. He drank too much coffee, stayed up later, and became exceedingly nihilistic. He stayed in more often than not and socialized less.

He was surfing the Internet one day, part of the long hours of research that had become his daily routine, when his live-in girl approached him.

Shoulder-length brown hair, a curvy Latina body, and a model-gorgeous face, Job figured he had won the lottery with this one. She was smart as a whip, and they would sit with friends at local cafés and discuss relevant events until late in the evening. At least they used to. That lifestyle had gradually dwindled in the five years they had been together, and now such late-night socializing was the exception rather than the rule.

She leaned against the far wall and called to him. He didn't respond at first, as he was in the thick of an Internet diatribe by Graham Hancock and slightly resented the intrusion. She called his name again, and this time there was both an urgency in her voice and an undercurrent of sadness. It snapped him out of his reverie, and he craned his neck toward her.

"Yeah, what's up?"

He noticed immediately that she was visibly shaken. Her eyes were puffy and tears were streaming down her face. He immediately abandoned the debate online and sat up.

"Baby, I think I have to leave you..."

Job was stunned. Bathed in the bright glow of the computer monitor, he could barely make her out. Her voice was shaky and tinged with sadness. Glints of light reflected off her tears.

"Are you... are you... but why? I don't... I don't understand..."

He had left girls before, but this was new. He had never been dumped, although that wasn't even the point. He'd thought they were soul mates, and this was completely out of left field. He sat in wide-eyed, mouth-agape shock while she sobbed.

"Is it... what is it? You don't love me anymore? Is it someone else?"

His mind was reeling at a hundred miles an hour, and he tried to think what, if anything, could be the cause.

"No. It's just... it's just you..."

That was a blow to the head, and it left him searching for how to respond to such a shockingly unprecedented turn of events. He staggered out of the chair, approached her, and fell to his knees. For the first time in ages he sobbed like a little boy. She reached over and rested her hand on his head, tears streaming down her cheeks.

Days passed, and the hopelessness of the situation settled in. He felt like dying, like his whole world had come crashing down around him. Nothing mattered now. Not his job, not the government and all the shady shit they pulled. He didn't care about any of it. All he wanted was his girl back, but the outlook wasn't good. Still, he had to try.

He distanced himself from work. A pall of doom and gloom settled over everything. In time he convinced her to attend therapy with him, and that was a disaster. They both sat in miserable silence while an older woman told them how to work together as a couple. She had short blonde hair, a professional-looking suit, and spouted out words that resonated with no one. Every time she directly addressed Job's girl, she received an increasingly resolute shake of the head. The misery continued for a couple of weeks. Job even tried to have sex with her, in some lame attempt that he told himself was a stab at reigniting the old flame. She didn't stop him, lying like a dead fish and telling him afterward that she felt nothing all the while. Job felt perverse and weird and swore he would never do it again. A couple of weeks later she moved out.

On the surface, Job didn't know whether it was a relief or not. He no longer had to face that accusatory look of late that had been constantly whittling him down. Only now she was gone, really gone, and in a sense it was all worse.

He couldn't sleep, and became OCD, cleaning every inch of his flat and throwing out anything he could possibly rationalize parting with. Days passed. Months. He hit the social scene again, trying to re-awaken single-guy impulses that now were such a part of the distant past.

He started dating again, but now the floodgates were open, and he didn't give any of the others a real chance. He dived hardcore back into his work, and the paranoia had become such a part of his daily life that he couldn't help feeling like he was on some upper level looking down. He even rationalized that as being the reason for his new social awkwardness. He compared each new girl to his ex, even if not intentionally, and that never led to a good outcome. He was clever and witty, still good-looking, and working the game with renewed vigor, so he had managed to net a few real beauties. A few even lasted for a while, although it was never quite the same and they all left in the end, typically amid curses and barely veiled threats.

D.C. wasn't a huge town, and a cute girl's opinion on an ex-boyfriend tended to exert a ripple effect with regard to public opinion. Not that Job had too much going for him. His take on how events had unfolded might have swayed some in his favor, but overall everything was different now, and he found he was continually missing social events. Many of his old buddies just happened to be too busy, and invitations were increasingly few and far between. He didn't have the kind of personality that would take the bull by the horns and change the course. Anxious to do anything to keep himself distracted, he delved deeper into his work. He would spend long hours on the web, watching YouTube documentaries, reading articles, carefully mulling over everything, from the theories of respected intellectuals like Michio Kaku and Stephen Hawking to the more questionable ideas of people like Alex Jones and David Icke.

Then about that time, the world fell apart.

ROAD TRIP

The road stretches out in front of me as a strip of sun-bleached asphalt, the pale gray tract burrowing a trail through the desert hills. Sandy ground, its undulating terrain dotted by wiry underbrush, sprawls out on all sides, with a decent-sized median of low-lying shrubbery splitting four opposing lanes.

The highway is mostly abandoned. It's a surreal trek through wide-open savannahs, the blistering sun beating everything down into a desiccated homogeneity. After a few miles, the desert hills start up again. Rocks and trees scale up into a warren of convoluted hills and peaks on both sides, the roadway ascending an ever-steeper incline. Sunlight pours down from a spotless blue sky, glistening off the metallic hood of the truck. Time passes and the gas needle steadily plummets. This thing gets about twenty miles to the gallon, and it started with half a tank, so I should refill soon. I'll save the reserves stored in the back for the more urban areas. With all the disarray, it's not likely that the local gas stations have much contact with the outside world, which should make them easier to deal with.

The road has leveled out into flatlands, and the landscape has followed suit. Green vegetation becomes scarce, the blistering solar rays having bludgeoned the shrubbery into dwarfish clusters of faded green. Their brood swarms over a spotty grassland, the gaps exposing a red soil beneath.

The occasional truck rumbles by on the other side, scant indications that society hasn't completely collapsed. Even with a dysfunctional central government, most Americans have become too accustomed to the pros and cons of "civilization" to fully recede. Is that still operating, and if so, under what conditions? There are some sizable Indian reservations in this area from what I recall, and this new turn of events has probably been a mixed bag for the natives. Even though many resent the unwanted European invaders, a good chunk of Native American income is based on donations from a government that is now defunct.

The landscape gradually rises, the grass becoming greener, the bushes more lush. Most of the sand is now covered, with weeds jutting up in defiant tufts amid a blanket of ocher. A string of telephone poles follows the right side of the road, their wooden columns a queue of ashen spears. The plain on the left side trails off into mounds of red stone in the far distance, with some of the rock scaling up into veritable mountains. The heavens above have grown darker under an overcast sky, most of it a grim pale gray of churning brume. At the horizon, meager trails of tumbling white clouds pirouette in subdued ranks around a setting sun.

Finally, the solitary shack of a lone gas station materializes on the right. The walls and roof are composed of weather-stained slabs of corrugated metal, the peeling pale gray paint there barely holding its ground against an encroaching onslaught of rust. A red and white Phillips 66 shield dangles from an L-shaped pole. Parked at an angle out front is an ancient Ford pickup that I place as a relic from the 1940s. The forest-green paint is almost completely obliterated from the fenders and hood, exposing a reddish-brown gleam of primer and rusty metal. The bed is outfitted with a lattice of wooden planks, an inch-wide gap between each board. A strange metal crane juts up from the bed, its circular core bearing five spoked wheels, all of it a conglomeration of rust. The vehicle looks like it's been parked there for decades, the sandy lot surrounding it strewn with rocks and bits of wood but devoid of tire tracks.

I pull parallel to the truck, cut the engine, and climb out. I look around; nothing stirs. Behind the Ford I see a chain-link fence sectioning off a jungle of scrap, but I don't see any pumps. I glance over at the shack and spot a closed garage door of rusty gray corrugated metal. Beside it, embedded in the intervening wall, is a wire-reinforced window, which in turn is adjacent to a pale blue door. I walk over and am on the verge of the door when it creaks open.

An old Native American man stands inside, the sun glinting off his deeply creased face. A faded red bandana obscures most of his forehead, tufts of rough gray hair descending down the sides in bound clumps. His hands are heavily veined, his forearms a veil of withered skin stretched over protruding bone. His burgundy work shirt is rolled up at the sleeves, the tails hanging loosely over stiff black jeans.

"We've been expecting you."

I pause, taken aback by such an unexpected utterance.

"The dark man from another world. The warrior of the little creatures. You are welcome here."

Little creatures? Does he mean the Al'lak?

"You come in time of chaos, never remember us, and always need something. What can I help you with, my friend?"

I glance at the truck, and then back at the old man.

"Ah, gasoline," he says. "For your journey. I will fill your tank." He disappears inside, and I see his silhouette flit by the window.

After a few minutes, the garage door rolls up with an audible groan. Half-hidden in the shadows is the hulk of a second old truck. The hood is still attached, even if the grill and radiator are not, thus exposing two belt wheels and the forward section of an engine block. The old man emerges from the shadows carrying an antiquated red metal gas canister. Most of the enamel on its rounded body is worn off, a faded yellow label barely visible under streaks of rust and grime. He saunters over to the left wheel well, pops the gas cap, and fills the tank.

I scan him in spectrums. He appears normal, but to my surprise there is another living object in the bed of the truck. As I start to walk toward the vehicle the old man looks back at me, holding aloft his free hand.

"It is a boy. You will need him. Dark days are coming."

I stop, not sure what to do. This man seems to know more than I do about my predicament. I have no idea how he knows, or who he thinks I am. If only I could communicate with him.

"You probably have many questions. These questions I

cannot answer. But these things from another world, they are real. Humanity is weak, but you will help us. You always have."

The old man shakes out the last of the fuel and screws the gas cap back on. He returns to the garage without ever making eye contact again. He looks so frail, and his whole aura strikes me as uncanny. The pale grass, the dusty old station, the earthen driveway… they all combine to form a nostalgic snapshot, as if of a place and time I once knew. It makes me wonder if this is real. Or if this person is who he appears to be. I have nothing to go on and no idea how to even get a handle on my situation.

I wait for a few minutes, and then climb back into the cab. Whoever had this truck was nice enough to leave the key in it. I'm flipping the ignition when the old man emerges from the garage. He's carrying a green canteen that reminds me of the plastic ones I would see as a kid at Army/Navy stores. He stops at the truck and hands it to me through the open window.

"Water, for the child in the back. Keep him alive."

With that he heads back toward the garage. I watch him for a moment and then peel out onto the road.

ALL IS NOT AS IT SEEMS

Aaron was hot and thirsty, and he would need to piss soon. He was also trapped in an exceedingly uncomfortable situation. The very creature that had probably slaughtered all those people back at the cabin was now driving the truck he was hiding in. What would happen if it got its hands on him? With absolutely no combat training, he wouldn't stand a chance.

Sprawled on his side, he could feel the ridges of the floorboard through his jacket, and as their bite grew sharper, he kept shifting around. Within minutes, the new position was as bad as the old one, the intervening stretch in which it was tolerable lessening with each new shift of position. Next to him were some pale blue water jugs with about an inch of fluid left in each one.

They rolled around at every bend, trailing thin streams and making way too much noise. There were two plastic gas cans back there as well. They looked military and stunk of fuel. Aaron tried to hold them in place with his feet, hoping that would mitigate the fumes, only it was no use, and they grew stronger by the minute. The nauseating odor was prompting a headache, and with every harsh bump they leaked a little more gasoline. When he had first climbed in the truck, the smell of dry plastic had commingled with the scent of the gas and it had all been tolerable. Now, all he smelled was the petrol.

Hugging the floor helped a little, and it also kept him out of sight of the cabin window. He coiled in his head and wondered how long he could take this. He felt sick, lightheaded, and slightly claustrophobic.

They stopped, and he heard that thing in the front open the

door. After a few moments, he decided to risk glancing through the tinted side window. He raised his eyes to the bottom of the window and strained his vision to get a better view. In the blinding sunlight he thought he saw an old Native American man headed for the truck. Aaron was certain he was looking straight at him as well. He didn't say anything or change his gait, but he *had* to see him. A minute later, the man had his hand up and was addressing the creature. Aaron's head pounded, and he decided to risk crawling over to the rear window and opening it to catch a breath of fresh air.

The handle was on the outside, but if he could move the two rods on the inside, he could get it to unlatch. They stuck at first, but it wasn't locked, and by leaning on a rod with all his might, Aaron was able to move them. He debated popping the rear tailgate and making a run for it, but one look at the ambient landscape dulled his enthusiasm. Aside from the ramshackle old gas station, there was nothing else in sight except for desert savannahs and an endless road that stretched toward a distant horizon. At the far reaches, where the earth touched the sky, the vague forms of cliffs were materializing out of a pale blue mist. That must be miles away, and there was nowhere to run in the interceding flatlands, no place to hide, and even if that thing didn't catch him, where would he go? He put aside the notion of escape for the moment and tried to suck in as much fresh air as he could. The air was hot and dry. It burned his throat and smelled of a desert wasteland, all soil and scorched earth. He risked a few more deep inhalations and slouched back, now thirstier than ever.

That thing returned to the driver's seat and fired up the vehicle. With a grinding of asphalt, they were back on the road. Aaron sunk down and cradled his head. He rested his arm across his face and closed his eyes. The fumes were worse than ever. He gritted his teeth, clenched his eyes, and tried to ignore the thirst. Try as he might, he couldn't sleep. His eyes were tired and wanted to stay shut, but his thoughts were racing.

He remembered the friends he left behind in Virginia. Even if some were hardly friends, he was still curious what had happened to them. Had they escaped? Did they even need to?

Was that tunnel in the basement of the last house real or had he done that weird thing again? The one where he ended up somewhere else. Even worse, was the violent slaughter he seem to have stumbled upon recently taking place everywhere? Had it reached Blacksburg yet? Actually, fuck all that, what he really wanted to know was about that girl. It felt so surreal he could easily imagine it was all a dream. He had forgotten many of the details, even if that didn't matter as much as the impressions they had left. For the first time ever, he felt alive and nothing else mattered. Not his parents, not his mediocre friends at school, not his police state town. It was a completely separate experience, one not tied to any aspects of his past. It was as if his past were irrelevant, and he could start fresh. Be the person he always wanted to be. There was no one to drag him down. Only everything had a weird edge to it. He didn't know how he got there, how real any of it was, and then in a flash he was back in this reality. A reality that had something to do with a full-on domestic invasion. That was exactly the way dreams unfolded. The kind where you wake up from some fantastic world, only you don't actually wake up. You are still in the dream, and everything gets strange within moments. Nothing made sense lately. He couldn't even tell what was real and what wasn't. With his luck, he would wake up to his miserable normal life. No, he had to treat it like it was all real. If it was and he pretended it wasn't, he was a goner.

Someone had told him he was special, that he could walk between worlds. What did that even mean? Were these worlds real? Were they in his head? In some other reality? And if so, which reality?

The truck ground to a halt, and Aaron's eyes popped open. He shivered a little, wondering what was going on. The front door opened with a creak, and he heard the heavy footsteps of that thing rounding the vehicle. It sounded like it was made out of solid iron, its footfalls like a sledgehammer hitting the asphalt. He scrambled into a sitting position and backed into the recesses of the truck bed, positioning some of the empty gallon jugs in front of him.

The tailgate rods moved, the rear window unlatched, and

it all opened up. There, in the middle of everything, stood the creature. Aaron's eyes bulged, his jaw slackened, and he scampered back, trying to hide behind the water bottles. His hairs stood on end and he held his breath.

Bright sunlight shown behind the creature, casting its edges aglow and throwing the center of its body into a blurry silhouette. Nothing about it looked human. Its black exterior was more like an absorbent material than skin. Though humanoid in form, its skin flowed in weird convolutions over the muscles. It was smooth and contoured like a swimmer or marathon runner, but at the same time nothing about it was quite right. The limbs were a little too long, the central body too featureless. It had a chest, although there were no ripples for a ribcage, no striations for stomach muscles, and no belly button. It appeared to be wearing no clothing, but absent sex organs it was impossible to say whether it was naked. Aaron had his hand cupped over his eyes. The blast of light that accompanied the tailgate opening had blurred his vision and he was afraid to look directly at that thing. His eyes adjusted, and when he raised his gaze he immediately wished he hadn't. The head was oval, and roughly humanoid, only its eyes… its eyes were recessed, like the lens of some cyborg out of an '80s sci-fi movie, imparting a calculating and inhuman edge to the creature. Aaron realized there was no face. No nose. No mouth. Tiny holes on the sides might be ears, although with a creature this strange, who could say? This first clear impression only amplified the strangeness of the last few days and made him suddenly lightheaded. The last thing he smelled was gasoline. There was the salty taste of blood on his tongue, and he collapsed.

Aaron stirred awake, clueless as to how much time had passed. He was still caught up in a dreamland, and he thrashed about at imaginary covers. Then, in a flash, it came back to him and he bolted upright, crashing into the truck cap and recoiling in pain. He cradled his head, peering up through squinted eyes. That thing was still there. His heart was racing a mile a minute, and he swallowed hard, desperately trying to come up with a game plan. It raised its left arm, and Aaron tried to back even farther into the wall. Only there was nowhere to go. Eyes peeled wide, he stared at the creature. In its outstretched hand the thing held a canteen. Was this a trick? Did it think he was some simple-minded creature that could be lured out? Aaron remained frozen, and the creature's arm stayed stiffly outstretched. Nothing on that thing moved, giving it the appearance of a statue, but Aaron knew better. The wind howled slightly, and Aaron glanced at the desolation beyond. With the scent of warm sand and grass wafting in, the stench of fumes had lessened. His head was a little clearer, though it might not remain that way. It all depended on what was in that bottle. His throat was so dry this was torture, and that canteen was possibly the most appetizing thing he had ever seen. He rationalized that if that thing wanted to kill him, it's not like he had any choice in the matter. His body tense, he reached up.

As soon as his grip on the canteen was firm, the creature released it. Aaron tore open the cap and chugged the contents. He drank so fast he choked and bent over coughing. The thing watched with indifference. Aaron finished the bottle and stared up at the strange creature. It was unlike anything he had ever seen. Its surface was so *dark* that, not only didn't it reflect the light, it seemed to actually absorb it. Suddenly, a horrible thought invaded Aaron's mind.

That thing might be keeping him alive like a farmer does with a pig before he slaughters it. Then, like clockwork, his bladder picked the worst time to act up, and he suddenly had to pee so bad he felt about to burst. He knew that water must have been the last straw. In fact, he could even feel a little release right now. He didn't want to be back here, stuck in the midst of gas fumes, reeking of urine and wearing soiled pants. He decided that if that creature intended to harm him, it would do so no matter what. The upshot was that he had nothing to lose.

He edged forward to the lip of the tailgate, angling to the left of that thing. The creature's eyes rotated to follow him, but it gave no signs of pursuit. He scooted forward, dropped his legs, and slowly slid down until his feet touched the ground. His eyes trained on the creature, he traipsed carefully around it and into the knee-high grass. Unzipping his pants, he let go with a cascade that started before he had fully pulled out. A clear stream pelted the yellowed grass, bending its stiff blades and splattering the reddish soil beyond. Aaron felt so weak and fragile. Here he was, this soft bag of water and skin, with that inhuman thing mechanically observing his vulnerable human state. The release made him feel slightly better, but he didn't want to go back in the truck. He was trying to come up with some plan, even as the piss ended and he was shaking out the last remnants. He scanned the horizon hoping that being outside of the truck might expose an angle he had missed.

Unfortunately, it looked even more depressing out here. Grassy flatlands covered the surrounding terrain, the misty presence of hills materializing in the distance. If he ran for it, and that thing chased him, it would certainly catch him before he reached anything remotely resembling safety. A faint wind blew, bringing more hot air and the dry, earthen smell of the desert. He finished up, tucked back in, and cautiously turned around. Although that thing had rotated to face him, it hadn't moved. A chill ran down his spine, and the ensuing flash of panic almost made him bolt before he snapped to and caught himself. With trepidation, he lowered his gaze and headed back toward the truck. Otherwise remaining stock still, the creature craned its head to follow him. Scuttling back in, he scooted into the far corner. As his back hit the cab, that thing closed the tailgate. Aaron followed its shadow as it rounded the side window. The front door creaked open, and the truck sagged as the thing boarded, straddling the driver's seat. The ignition clicked, the engine roared to life, and the truck lurched forward, gravel pelting the sides as the truck ventured back onto the road.

Aaron's head raced, and he chewed his lip in nervous tension. He had no idea what that creature was. Was it even sentient? Was it under the control of someone or something else? Was this a government thing? Or an agent of that weird man he had met in D.C.? On second thought, they might be one and the same. They all seemed to know more about what was happening to him than he did. And that old Indian man, why wasn't he surprised? Who all was in on this?

The truck rumbled on, time passed, and Aaron grew sleepy. The sun made a languid trek across the sky, the road endlessly coursing under the wheels.

Cliffs rose and fell, cities were skirted, and Aaron slept. A few sparse vehicles dotted the highways, the drivers lost in their own little worlds.

THE FORMER NATION'S CAPITAL

Joe was sitting on the white steps of the marble fountain in DuPont Circle. Wearing a gray newsboy cap, a thin black leather jacket, and freshly creased brown slacks, he was lost in thought as he sipped his daily dosage courtesy of Starbucks. The marble carving behind him featured three nude figures, two female and one male, all nestled against a central column that held aloft a large, water-filled bowl. It had never made much sense to him. And he had hated Starbucks ever since they started to burn the beans in an attempt to fool people into thinking their coffee was stronger. The only saving grace was that they were close, and they sold a red-eye.

He hadn't been sleeping well, so that might have played into his foul mood, and last night had proved to be a real low point. He hadn't gotten laid in a while, and that chemical need for contact with the opposite sex had kicked in. He told himself it was more than that, that he missed a conversation partner and social interaction, yet he knew deep down the motivating factor was purely carnal.

He was at a local bar, and this Latina chick who was always flirting with him on Facebook had agreed to meet up with him. She was attractive. Not stunning, but pretty enough. Although he did find the large mole on her neck borderline repulsive, he made up his mind to look past that. She had olive-toned skin, youthful if mildly sunken features, raven-black hair, and large brown eyes. They talked for a while, during which time Job confirmed what he had already surmised from their online conversations: that she wasn't the brightest crayon in the box. Still, the Sam Adams had lessened the need for wit and heightened his affinity for her. He knew he could get her in bed, it was simply a matter of avoiding saying something that would seriously derail this hormone-fueled train. They both had enough alcohol in their systems to let it happen, and it helped that it was a dive bar. It lowered the expectation level and made everything more relaxed.

The bar was furnished with reconstituted wooden tables whose appearance gave the impression they had been deliberately crafted to give off that vintage vibe. Crowded around them were fake leather-topped barstools. The occasional corner hosted a plush black loveseat, and Job and the girl had snagged one of them, in a darkened nook with a cheaply framed bill for an old Blondie gig hanging on the rear wall. A lit candle flickered on the table, and although Joe's mouth was running, all he could think of was getting her out of that magenta satin top, peeling down those black leggings, and feasting his eyes on the goodies underneath. He was curious if she had large nipples or small ones, and if they were dark or tan. Although he could see some cleavage, he couldn't be sure how big those breasts really were. Anywhere from full As to medium Bs, he decided. Unless she was wearing a pushup bra—and too many girls these days were.

She appeared to be digging the scene. Her lips were spread into a smile, showcasing a glistening row of slightly oversized teeth. Her eyes twinkled, and she talked nonsense as she gently twirled the longneck in her hand. It wasn't too long before he had slid over to her side. It was a tight squeeze, but they were now both enjoying a serious buzz, and in no time they were making out.

The next day his alarm woke him, and he groaned while struggling upright. Hands on his head, he knew he would be nursing a headache. He'd awoken to find the girl's hand lying limply across his chest, and he slid it down in one disgusted jolt. He felt more angry with himself than with her. He had been a douchebag, leading her on when he knew full well it stood no chance of going anywhere. He examined her prone form. She snored softly, her face buried sideways in the crimson pillow with her lips slightly parted. He saw a white fleck on her eyelash, and that her smooth black hair was actually dark brown. It now looked slightly nappy and worse for the wear in the morning light. Her skin was a smooth tan, and the sunlight gleamed off her pale body hair. Everything below the waist was covered by the crimson cloth except for one foot, which stuck out at the rumpled end of the sheet. He barely could recall the sex, yet his memory of the hours of insipid conversation that preceded it made him grimace. He glanced around at the shadowed walls, the heavy drapes obscuring the sunlight. Climbing out of bed, he swatted at the black dial on his plastic alarm clock. The LCD digits flashed green, and the buzzing let up.

First measure of business was his total lack of clothing. His flaccid penis had shrunk to embarrassingly compact dimensions, and he shuffled through his darkly wooded Japanese set of drawers in search of underwear. They were usually on the left, only his mind was elsewhere and he opened a few wrong drawers before hitting the correct one. He pondered how best to get rid of the girl without coming across as too much of a dick. He got what he needed and shut the drawers a little more vigorously than usual. There was a loud thump, and she stirred, emitting a weird, unintelligible sound.

"Wha… omm…"

She rolled toward the wall and went right back to sleep. He repeated his action, opening and closing the drawer. That did the trick. She sat up in bed, the back of her palm against her forehead. She *had* been wearing a pushup bra, although her breasts weren't all that small. Bs was his best guess, with areolas that took up most of the breast and nipples that stuck out like eraser heads. While it had all been a turn-on the previous night, here in the light of day it simply reminded him that he didn't want her to see it getting his attention. Anything sexual would complicate the task of getting rid of her.

"You want some coffee?" he asked.

"Uh… what?"

"I'm getting some coffee. Do you want some?"

"Uh, yeah, sure—light and sweet."

He came back a few minutes later with the coffee, and his

demeanor announced the bad news. The warm brew gave off a strong aroma that seemed designed to mask the whole sordid affair. He could smell the stale sex of last night in the room. They exchanged a few sentences, hugged, and his goodbye kiss was more of a peck. He wasn't getting stuck, and he already had a low enough opinion of himself without her exacerbating it. Any conversation about future meetups would merely be promises he didn't intend to keep. Fortunately, she shot him a smile, one that held a silent reprove in it that made him cringe, and then walked out with a modicum of dignity.

He tried not to beat himself up about it, deciding finally that all of this bothered him more than it deserved to. It was a stupid distraction and a waste of time. He needed to focus on things that didn't involve the carnal trappings of hormones that made him act like some stupid animal. What he really needed to concern himself with was the weird turn the world had taken lately. There was massive deception, only that was nothing new—organizations within organizations that made getting at the truth a sticky proposition. While Fox News and the mainstream press were trying their best to obscure the identity of who was pulling the strings, they couldn't hide all the trails in this digital era.

The most recent mass terrorist act had been 9/11, and that was probably at least in part an inside job. All those YouTube videos said as much, not to mention the string of documentaries that followed. Even Jesse Ventura had tackled it, and not long afterward his TV show had been abruptly canceled. But that was only the tip of the iceberg, as it would be far from the first false flag that the government had engaged in. The Gulf of Tonkin was a blatant lie. The Mexican War was an excuse for a land grab. The Kuwaitis provoked Desert Storm, and we gave Saddam the go-ahead to respond, then invaded and ruined his country. And those were only some of the more obvious modern events. Who knew how real anything truly was? It might all be as it was presented to the media, or it might be a carefully calculated plant. The people in power were way more corrupt than anyone realized, and that assertion merely skimmed the surface. There appeared to be some sort of government within the public government, and if that were the case then it opened the door for all sorts of far-flung conspiracy theories to be holding a grain of truth after all. It made Job wonder if something had been found at Roswell. If the government had a hand in murdering the Kennedys, Malcolm X, and Martin Luther King. The whole thing might even go back to Lincoln's day. It had been suggested John Wilkes Booth was a plant, and although there were no smoking guns, there was plenty of circumstantial evidence. Not to mention the abundance of underhanded politicking that had occurred. It all sounded like tinfoil hat stuff, only half that shit proved to be the real deal. Everything had only gotten more convoluted and frustrating as time marched on. The Cold War paranoia and its associated knee-jerk reaction was elementary compared to what they were getting away with these days. The Patriot Act, Guantanamo Bay, FEMA death camps, HAARP, Plum Island, and a million other crazy things that were probably in some measure true. At the very least, they led to a different version of the truth than the one that had been fed to the public.

Job ruminated that these were the things he should be spending his time on, rather than frittering it away on social consorts that were a dead end.

A big source of impetus for his nonprofit was the centuries-old warning by Benjamin Franklin, who cautioned about the danger entailed in big financial interests. They had steadily applied their wiles in crisis after crisis, resulting in mass depressions and government-abetted monopolies. Centuries later the same monied elite had grown so bold as to try and depose FDR. Only half a century later, they had given themselves raises and golden parachutes in yet another financial crisis they caused with money they had tricked the common man into believing was needed for a failing economy. As an idealistic young adult, all this had made him furious, and he had dived into the whole complicated web head first. Much of it ended up being so obscure it was difficult to ascertain the truth of anything, but Job was certain there was a hidden agenda going down. Accusations were thrown at the Bilderberg Group and the Federal Reserve, as had long been the case. The Bilderbergs and their ilk fit right into the military-industrial complex, and the Federal Reserve wasn't even a government institution, only he could sense that there was more to the story. If he could figure it out, maybe Job would get somewhere for a change.

The political scene had hyped up when the newly elected President Manley mentioned there might be a one-world government some day. Whatever he meant by that, it had caused a serious uproar, and many states began talking about secession. But again, that was nothing new. Every few decades something emerged that drove everyone into histrionics, and this appeared to be no different.

Lost in thought, Job was completely caught off guard when a concussive force slammed into his body and flung him through the air. He was saved only by his high school Judo classes, which instinctively kicked in, reminding him to fold into a roll as he crashed down onto the lawn. Sharp branches tore at him as he smashed through the bushes and tumbled awkwardly onto the grass beyond. The scent of freshly rent foliage assaulted him with its thick, sappy odor. He raised his skinned-up palms, trying to wipe the gravel off them. He rubbed the back of his bruised neck, noticing the sandpaper feel of his shredded palms as a headache started to kick in. He felt filthy, his ears were ringing, and a wet stream trickled out of his nose. A quick swipe confirmed his suspicion. Blood. A couple of drops had made it onto his pink dress shirt, and he cursed silently. He looked down at his slacks, which sported fresh streaks of chlorophyll around the knees. Even worse, his shiny Kenneth Coles were scuffed beyond repair.

Then he heard the screams.

The central sculpture in the fountain was gone, in its place a stubby base of rock. Jagged chunks of white marble littered the courtyard. The moat that had surrounded the statue still had its low-lying walls intact, but most of the water had splattered out. Pieces of marble rose like islands in the shallows that remained. A young girl with bobbing blonde hair flitted by, her track suit a white and blue streak. Job's vision had been knocked askew by the freefall, and most everything registered as a blur. A black kid came into view.

Running across the courtyard, he was relatively distinct in his red alligator shirt, skinny frame, and closely cropped hair. Job absently marveled at the alligator shirt, assuming such styles were things of the past. His head cleared little by little, and he realized the danger of his situation with a start.

Scrambling to his feet, he took off running toward his place on P Street. The sky had darkened, gray clouds choking out the daylight as thunderclaps crashed. He ran down neatly laid-out streets filled with townhouses, the buildings a blur as he fumbled in his pocket for his keys. He rounded a curb and nearly ran into a middle-aged black woman. Plump, with short, curly hair that touched the collar of a crimson silk shirt that struggled to contain her enormous breasts, she stared wide-eyed at the sky, her mouth agape. She barely registered Job as he darted around her. With a stinging pain, his once-rapid gait had deteriorated into a fast limp. The fall had wrenched his left knee, and that sudden veer around the woman had been the final straw. The lady's cheap perfume commingled with the dry smell of pulverized asphalt, and it was all making it hard to breathe.

He arrived at his block, in one of the more yuppified neighborhoods that featured a colorful procession of row houses, their tiny, neatly manicured lawns cordoned off by Victorian-looking black guard rails. In consideration of the way things had just shifted, it struck him as fake and fragile. He hurtled across the street, pawed open the gate, and bounded up his steps. Gasping for breath as he collapsed against the gray door, he turned around to look back.

The street was empty. Hastily digging through his pockets, he grabbed his keys and started flipping through them. They all looked the same and he could never remember the right one. Panicked, he tried to jam one in the lock. He cursed when it didn't fit, and started palming for another. It was only on the third pass that he made it in.

He cracked the door and peered inside. The entrance hall looked empty. It was all a dark recess of floor-to-ceiling pale brown tiles, a wide staircase dominating a central space that led up to his second-floor apartment. He dashed up, stumbling in his haste. A twist around the guardrail, a painful stab in his knee, and he was at his door and jerking out his keys even before he'd arrived. He thumbed through until he found the right one, jammed it in, and slipped inside. Slamming the door, he flipped the bolt and collapsed against the door. Letting his body go limp, he sank as he exhaled in shallow bursts.

He felt winded and dangerously out of shape, and his knee throbbed, making his mood all the more miserable. He cursed himself for not having a gun, or even a car, and kept repeating, *"I knew it! I knew it!"* under his breath. Only he didn't know anything, he just had a sense that things had gone to shit and he wasn't prepared.

OKLAHOMA

Aaron tried to sleep, but it was an uncomfortable ride. The ridges in the truck bed bit into his side, and he continually shifted in an effort to get some relief. Fortunately, the open window had managed to excise most of the fumes. He wasn't hungry or thirsty; in fact, he could go all day with barely eating, and he even had a little water left. More water would make him have to piss sooner, and it was hard enough to nod off as it was. Although he had dozed for a few hours, now he was too awake to fall back into oblivion. He kept his eyes closed and remained as still as possible, but his mind wouldn't stop racing. He wondered where his situation with that thing stood. Was he a captive? It must have acquired him by accident. Now that it had him, what did it plan to do with him? It was possible the creature knew he was there all along. So much weird stuff had happened recently, he wouldn't be surprised if it was in some way connected. There were people that pretended they knew far more about this than he did. That might only be a ruse, but he had no idea where that left him in the scheme of things.

Long progressions of endless flatland passed by in a boundless array. There were no hills, no forests, only the solitary trunks of telephone poles lining the roadsides, their gray regularity adding to the bleakness of it all. Cloudless overhead, it was all a dreary, slate-blue expanse. This might have been the most boring place on Earth, and Aaron wanted nothing more than to sleep through it. Only his mind was on fire. Every time he felt ready to doze off, some new thought popped up and shocked him wide awake. He just wanted something to come to a resolution, and this waiting was the worst. He was trapped, and that creature was in control. He felt like some lab animal. Some very bored lab animal.

He finally managed to doze off, and when he awoke there was one less gas can. The creature must have stopped and used it while he slept. He raised himself on one arm and rubbed his eyes. The wind was blasting in through the tailgate window, rustling his hair and throwing the strands of his Mohawk across his face. He could detect the slight odor of gas, although fortunately for him the smell of fresh air was stronger. His headache had dramatically lessened, and he felt a little refreshed. Almost normal, in fact, and his mood was a little more positive.

He heard what sounded like human voices. Gruff human voices, barely audible above the sound of the wind. They were growing louder, and although he could feel the vehicle slowing, meaning the voices might have been there for a while and the roar of the wind had drowned them out, he sensed something else as well. It was the reek of grease and gear oil, and it reminded him of the military trucks on the bases his dad had been stationed at. The truck rolled to a stop, and without the cooling breeze the interior started heating up. Sweat pooled in his armpits and beaded on his back, and his feet felt warm and swollen inside their leather boot and sock cocoons. He scrambled into a crawl and headed for the rear window. As he was about to rotate the latch, a voice broke the silence.

"What the fuck is that! Back up! Back up!"

Then a torrent of gunfire. Bullets tore into the sides of the truck in a piercing screech, and pinged off the dirt roadsides at a speed that seemed way too fast to be real. Aaron instinctively let go of the rear door and curled up, his arm over his head. Plumes of dirt from the bullet impacts escalated into a wafting cloud, and he heard projectiles ricocheting all around him. The side window collapsed. Something punched through the back pane near his head and the glass cracked into a million spider webs.

"Fuck! Fuck!"

A bullet tore through the sidewall, flew past, and tore out through the tailgate, missing him by maybe an inch. Aaron blanched, reached his hand over to the tailgate, and fumbled for the lever. Shards of glass tore at his cuff, streaking the black leather in ragged gashes of gray.

Popping open the tailgate, he tumbled out onto the metal door, catching himself just before he rolled over the edge and onto the pavement. Another round ripped through the sidewall and barely missed his head. In a panic, he dropped down, rolling onto the bleached highway below with a thud that knocked the wind out of him. Dirt and the smell of gunpowder assaulted him, and he belly-crawled under the truck. He heard shouts that sounded close and popped up, nailing the rear drive shaft with the top of his head. Seeing stars for a moment, he let out a groan and then immediately regretted it.

"I'm out of bullets, let—"

A wet, gurgling sound resounded, and Aaron peered forward just in time to see a pair of black combat boots descending below the front bumper. An M16 clattered to the ground, followed by a bloody torso cloaked in desert camo BDUs and the pulpy remnants of what could only have been the head. There was a shirt collar, and beyond it was a twisted mass of gore. Bulbous bits of white poked through the morass, accompanied by bloody strands of what must have been sandy-blond hair. Aaron felt sick, the scant contents of his stomach resurfacing. The raw smell of warm slaughter and putrid bile washed toward him and Aaron lost it, the last bitter liquid in his stomach coming up in yellow, foaming spurts.

Still gagging, his chest convulsing in dry heaves, Aaron crawled toward the back. As he ducked under the spare tire, more gunshots rang out. Despite the now-constant ringing in his ears, the fire sounded a little farther away, so he dared to peep around the rear tire.

Concrete barriers were blocking the lanes. The closest one, just off to the right, remained unscathed. The one immediately behind it was crudely hollowed out in the middle. Iron support beams jutted out from the ragged hole, the ends twisted as if they were cheap wire. Chunks of rubble trailed from the torn gap, vanishing into the smog beyond. Partially visible through the haze were two HMMWVs, the one on the right in rough shape. The windshield was a splintery mass of shards, the sidewalls were pocked with bullet holes and large dents. The body of a black soldier hung out of the doorway. Only his torso from the waist up remained. His camo shirt was stained with a large patch of blood, the whitish stub of a spinal column jutting out underneath, dark gristle commingling with torn cloth as it wrapped around a stub of bone. Thick crimson rivulets streaked the soldier's right side, trailing down the arm and into a thicker pool coagulating around his hand. From the angled doorway perch, they sluggishly dribbled in shiny ropes into the smoke below. His features were chiseled and looked young. Thick black eyebrows arched over rust-colored eyes that stared lifelessly at the sky. His mouth hung open, a whitish saliva commingling with blood and pooling in the right corner, a stream of it meandering down his chin.

Aaron heard another shout and jerked his head to the left. His eyes popped open even wider and his cheeks sunk in, his lips puckering together as he held his breath. That thing was tearing into a soldier right before his eyes. Its head was bent forward, the back hunched up like a pit bull's. An inhumanly long arm slashed out like an uncoiled spring, the back of its open hand tearing into the head of a soldier like it was papier-mâché. The chinstrap snapped, the helmet flew off, and the fragile flesh beneath erupted in a burst of blood and brain matter. An eyeball popped out, and Aaron only realized what it was when it rebounded like a rubbery ball a few feet in front of the truck.

Aaron was nauseated, terrified, and unable to move. The roar of heavy projectiles exploded off that thing, not even fazing it. Concrete dust wafted in thick gusts across the carnage. Scattered screams commingled with hoarse yells. Muzzle flashes pierced through the haze, the spurts of bullets followed by the screeches of rent metal and the crunch of collapsing flesh.

Aaron felt dizzy. He nodded forward, the scene before him blurring to dark as consciousness faded. When he snapped to, the chaos had quieted, the dusty maelstrom was thinning, and aside from the rattle of a soft wind, all was silent. His eyes were watering, his vision still a little blurry, and his nose was running. Despite being congested and lightheaded, his sense told him that underlying the gritty cloak of pulverized concrete was the smell of raw meat. Of iron and fresh blood, intermingled with the fetid odor of intestines. It reminded him of the time his dad hung a skinned deer carcass in the garage. A silhouette emerged from the smoke in smooth, confident strides. It was that monstrous, alien-looking thing and the smoke was toying with it, curling about its legs and dancing in its wake as it approached. Then it was upon him, and he didn't have the energy to run. It was coated in blood and bits of gore, gelatinous remnants trailing down its arms and dripping off in dark strands of syrupy liquid. It knelt and extended its right hand toward him, and then everything grew dark.

The next thing Aaron knew, he was aloft in the creature's arms, the thing carrying him as if he were a pet. Through blurry eyes, Aaron saw the torn shell of a HMMWV on the left. Its front door was gone, the top of the frame bent upward. The smoke cleared for a moment, and he saw the remnants of a soldier in the driver's seat. It was just the torso and the legs, the waist an open gash clustered with the bulbous crests of organs. The ridges of pelvic bones jutted out of the bloody mire, the ropy strings of intestines emerging from the mire, trailing across the doorframe, and drooping into the smog below.

Aaron's head rolled back, his world a half-conscious dream, and he passed out again.

When he came to, he found himself sitting in a black cloth seat. It was really stiff, and the firmness of it was forcing him upright. He raised his head and saw that in front of him was a flat, olive-green military dash. There was a panel door on the dash that he assumed was for a glove box. Beneath it was a black data plate. He kept his head down, trying not to make it obvious as he slowly rotated his eyeballs and saw that the creature was seated next to him. It had its extended arm on the wheel, the top aglow in the sunlight. He leaned against the door on his right, trying to act like it was an unconscious, natural act, attempting to get a good look at the scene. A large lever jutted up between the seats, and that creature had its hand wrapped around it. It was similar to a human hand, only one that was modeled to be comparable, the angles all off. The lever jolted forward, the whine of heavy machinery doubled up with the bottom-heavy rumble of the engine, and the truck pitched backward. Spinning around 90 degrees, the vehicle ground to a stop, the creature yanked the lever backward, and they jerked forward.

Emerged from the smog in a M35 Deuce, a six-wheeled diesel truck manufactured for the military by AM General, a large exhaust pipe on the passenger side bellowed a thick stream of black smoke as they bowled forward. The fumes trailed back from the boxy truck, skirting over the canvas top in a grayish smog. The vehicle slowly picked up speed, forging ahead into a deserted highway.

The brume behind died out, its gritty residue settling in thin layers on the tattered frames of military vehicles and the gory remnants of soldiers.

SPEED BUMPS

I'm not real familiar with these trucks. I came across them when I was looking to build up a vehicle to raid Fort Bragg, and they always struck me as too conspicuous. I do recall some of them accepted multiple types of fuel—gasoline, diesel, kerosene, heating oil, even vegetable oil. The survivalists loved them, what with their PTO winch, 46-inch tires, and assuming secrecy isn't a concern, they are big enough to plow through almost anything. From what I read, these were highly valued as workhorses long after their intended military use, explaining what the National Guard, or whoever that was at the roadblock, was doing with one. Given the current climate, it might not even be odd to see one on the street. It all depends on how it is taken—since everything seems to be about survival of the fittest right now. States appear to have clustered into small nations, all of them shooting first and asking questions later. That doesn't affect me, although my vehicles so far tend to be less fortunate. None were planned, they were spur-of-the-moment acquisitions. This truck, on the other hand, was more like a vehicle I would pick, although national disintegration might not have been anything I would foresee. Regardless, it's a real combat vehicle, making it more resistant to small arms fire, a resource the local forces apparently have in spades. They appear to have more powerful weapons, RPGs and the like, although I doubt they'd waste it on a single truck, especially if I keep moving and present it as more of a nuisance than a threat. The ammo for those higher-caliber firearms will soon be in questionable supply anyway. The most difficult part will be keeping the kid alive, making this vehicle all the more valuable.

Coming across the old man had changed everything. I learned in the Mexican jungle that the Al'lak visited the natives long before the Europeans arrived, although no one knows how frequent the visits were, how far they were spread out, or even if the Al'lak were the only race involved. And civilization might have existed much earlier than what was initially thought. Historians established a timeline, and then archaeologists uncovered Göbekli Tepe. Not to mention that some of the more established ancient civilizations like Machu Picchu and the Great Pyramid of Giza had complex base elements that were in place long before the structures were constructed on top of them. All those ancient societies had sophisticated mathematical models of the planet as well, and even more telling, detailed information on what lies beyond. Trajectories of stars and planets, orbits that would take hundreds of years to calculate, and topographical maps of the Earth that would only be possible from a high altitude. Their foundation architecture revealed feats of construction not even possible using today's machinery, and even more confusing, they exhibited a structure that was more advanced than any of the civilizations that followed. It's all a mystery, hidden in the dustbin of history, and unfortunately any evidence that wasn't destroyed by religious fanatics had eroded with time.

Anything that challenges a confirmation bias is often misinterpreted or buried, so later finds by archaeologists were often overlooked or misinterpreted. Treaties and agreements could have risen, fallen, and faded in the turmoil of the millennia. All I know is that the current U.S. government is lying about some of it, and if they lie about one thing, who knows what else they may be trying to hide.

That old man was not surprised by my presence, implying a history of previous visitations. He also said a few things that stand out, like how the child would be useful and that the Al'lak come back on a regular basis. At least I think it was the Al'lak. *Somebody* came back on a regular basis.

It does strike me as not entirely out of the question that keeping the kid alive could be part of an attempt on my part to retain the last vestiges of my human self. Regardless, his presence doesn't appear to endanger me, and I would prefer to see him survive this current maelstrom. Although I might need him after all. I have no idea what awaits me in Maine.

TENNESSEE

L ight beamed in through the windshield, warming the otherwise chill metal cab. Aaron's dizziness had mostly abated,
at least provided he didn't move. No seatbelts were present to
restrain him, and he sprawled half off the seat cushion, leaning
across the gap and slumped against the cold metal of the passenger door. Although the rigid metal frame dug into his back,
Aaron didn't dare straighten up. He wasn't getting any closer to
that thing.

The air was thick with the fetid odor of gore. A bloody iron
smell dominated, the fatty, sickening aroma of gristle slinking
in behind. A faint hint of military canvas and gun oil bolstered
the mix, heightening Aaron's nausea.

He kept his eyes closed. The last thing he wanted was for
that creature to see him staring. That thing was so... strange.
It sat bolt upright, its posture more machine-like than organic.
One arm stretched toward the wheel, the other toward the
shift lever, the hands not so much resting on them as hovering
above while fingers spanned the gap and wrapped around
like delicate probes. Muscles bundled up and down the arms,
their shapes verging on human. Yet the arms were too long,
and some of the muscles surfaced where Aaron could swear
no humans had muscles. They were made up of an odd black
material that seemed to absorb the light, giving the whole
thing eerie, indefinable edges. The only element that looked
solid were the thick streaks of dried blood, and even those
edges were diffused into the strange material composing the
creature. Aaron wanted to blink, thinking that might help clear
his swimming vision, but he was afraid that thing might notice.

He was concentrating on the creature when he realized they were slowing down. He dared to swivel his head in the direction of the windshield and observed that the scenery had changed as well. The four-lane highway now had a long, curving concrete median. Steep pine-covered hills scaled up on both sides, with the narrow corridor of the road ahead opening into a distant horizon of undulating highlands. Gauzy mist rose from the valleys between the faraway embankments, their vapor curling into the bases of the distant hills, giving the summits the appearance of floating. The sky was more of the same thick, off-white mist, and it cast the surroundings into a gloomy half-light. The right side rose into jagged cliffs of rock, their serried masses of granite rising a good thirty feet before softening into more level slopes. The spindly branches of a few pine trees poked out from a far-removed peak. A section of the cliff had broken free, the resulting landslide blocking much of the road ahead. Enormous boulders had slid down, and the avalanche crossed the lanes in a gently sloping ramp, the larger chunks petering out into ever-smaller bits as they sidled up against the dividing sidewall.

The truck ground to a halt and the creature rose. Dismounting with perfect fluidity, it left the door open and headed toward the blockage in steps too synchronized for anything human. Aaron watched until that thing stood at the foot of the rocky barricade, and then he finally dared to breathe deeply, feeling like a giant weight had been momentarily lifted. The very presence of that thing scared him.

The creature was making quick work of the rock slide, shoveling aside the boulders as if they were Styrofoam. Its arms were a blur as they tossed aside rocks in a cascade of rubble, resembling darkened streaks that were shooting tan-colored torrents of debris. Rubble pounded the roadsides, the resonating thunderclap booming like dueling jackhammers. The mechanical preciseness made Aaron think about how that thing must have handled the soldiers at the blockade. And probably the cabin, too. He felt his internal temperature rising, his body hair stood on end, and he decided he had to get away from that monster as soon as possible. He uncoiled his legs and stretched them over the edge of the seat. Inching forward until they were just shy of reaching the floor, he dropped, trying to make as little noise as possible. The pounding of the rocks drowned out everything, but it would be just his luck that the monster would pause at the wrong instant.

The creature was still shoveling as he crept up to the open door. Still buried in the interior shade of the vehicle, the harsh light of the opening was an inch to his left. Surmounting the driver's seat, he ducked his head out and could see that the road behind the vehicle was sandwiched between rocky cliffs.

But in about fifty feet, it angled to the left and disappeared around a rocky bend. Both walled sides ended at the turn in the road, and all he could see at the tail end was a guardrail, distant tree-covered hills that were alive with the colors of fall rising out of the far-off mist.

Aaron glanced back at the creature. It was still at work on the roadblock. He jumped out and took off down the highway.

Every minute that passed felt like ten. His chest felt like it was about to burst, and he could swear his boots were making a horrendous thumping noise. His hands scissored back and forth in a mad rhythm, his Mohawk whipping out behind in a blurry stream of black. Fresh air burst into lungs that felt like they were on fire, the damp, earthen scent of the wilderness all about a far cry from the suburbs he was used to. As he rounded a bend, he caught a glimpse of the road they had traversed. It trailed off to the left, hugging the side of a cliff that made a sharp rightward twist, proceeded a few hundred feet, and then twisted right again. They must have blasted this road out of the side of a mountain. Brightly colored woods rolled through a gully far below. Drifts of soupy mist drowned some of the tree trunks, giving the leafy bundles an isolated, aloft appearance. The highway twisted left again after running along the far side of the mountain and disappeared. The earlier cloud cover was parting, illuminating everything with the clear light of day. There was no way that thing would still be working on the roadblock in the time it would take to get to that twist of the road. Aaron slackened into a jog and started to panic. He desperately looked around for any way out.

As he drew closer to the stubby metal side rail, he could see that it was a precipitous drop into a forest far below. A look at the opposite side and he assumed the drop was the same, a steep cliff that leveled out into woods. Aaron might have been able to disappear in that, only he had no way to reach it. The slope on the other side was too steep to even support trees.

The air had grown cold, and Aaron's breath came out in cloudy bursts. A gentle wind kicked in, tugging at his jacket and throwing the loose strands of his hair across his face. The spicy scent of autumn wafted up from the valley below, clashing with the cold, wet bite of a nose that had just started running. He wiped it on his sleeve and dolefully looked around. Everything was so isolated. The left was all monstrous blocks of granite, their jagged edges cracked into a depression of wedges and nubs far above before erupting again in a clutch of sheer stone. Topping it all were the branches of pine trees. They looked safe and secure, and very high up. Above them, a thin queue of clouds tumbled through a vast field of blue. He was going to die here. Desperation and blind terror set in, and his eyes were peeled so wide they felt like they were popping out. His mouth was slightly agape, and he looked around in disbelief. Then he saw that part of the cliff folded into a slight depression a few feet ahead. He took a chance and darted for it.

Aaron didn't know what he was hoping for. Maybe it was merely a shallow cleft in the rock, but he was desperate and would accept anything. As he drew closer, he could see it might be way better than he thought. The cliff was within a foot of the road and fronted by a ribbon of sand sporting a few yellowed blades of grass. All was open and provided nowhere to hide, but this indentation was a true break in the wall of stone. It even had the appearance of a manmade cave, the cut in the granite around it too precise for it to be natural. The sandy roadside trickled into its maw in a downward slope that grew rockier as it descended. Aaron couldn't see far into it—after a few feet the darkness swallowed everything. He shook his head, glanced over his shoulder nervously, and stepped in. This thing scared him, and he didn't dare enter yet. He remembered how things like this ended in all the horror movies he'd watched, and a chill ran through him. He cleared his running nose with a snort, and caught a scent of rotting vegetation. He was sure it had come from down in the cave, and he kept telling himself that this was a really bad idea.

He glanced back at the distant truck. There was no movement. He stepped a little closer to the entrance, trying to hide himself from sight, and bent to examine the sand leading into the mouth of the cave. Grayish white, it looked dry and ancient, like most sand. Tiny ridge-like patterns marred the track that led in. It was cool and dry out here, and those patterns might have been the result of rainwater. Or they might imply something far more malevolent. Tight, dark spaces in weird environs were pretty high on his list of things that are best avoided. Images of those mangled soldiers kept popping into his head, but as bad as those were, that blood-covered monster was worse. He didn't know why that thing was keeping him alive. With the gory scenes fresh in his mind, did he dare venture into an unknown abyss? Panic washed over him again, and he whipped his head around the rocky outcropping for a look. Still nothing.

What was the worst that cave could offer? Threatening animals? Whatever it was, it had to be better than that thing out here. He cupped his hand over his eyes and ventured in.

THAT FUCKING KID

I managed to clear the path of most of the larger debris. Only a few fist-sized rocks lay scattered across the road. All the over-sized boulders are now piled up on the sides in large mounds. I decide the 45" tires on the M35 can handle the few left and I head back. Scanning the vehicle's windshield, it looks vacant from this distance. The sun has emerged from the clouds, casting a glare across the glass. Still I sense a loss and an associated regret. This is odd enough, as I would think that was linked with human emotions that I should no longer have. Although there might be some sensory apparatus at play here that is influencing my impressions. Or it could be a probability based on my past history, which often involved some of the worst luck possible. Either way, I switch on my infrared.

There's no heat signature. The kid is gone, and I'm not sure what that means. I thought he was a nuisance at first, then he became a possibly important element. His presence triggered some recessed memory of a childhood I wish I had. No, that's not quite it. I don't know anything about this kid other than he's a rebellious teenager who doesn't seem harmful, and also that he strikes me as somehow nostalgic. It's the association that attains the elevated status, not the object itself. I can rationalize and break it down even further, but what it comes down to is that I don't like the idea of losing something. Especially if it's something I might need in the near future. That old man said he was *necessary*. I don't know how literally I should take that, although there is no way that old Indian knew what my agenda was. Not that I even have a clear one. I'm traveling to Maine under the premise that it might provide some answers, even though I'm not even sure I know the right questions. If this is as scattershot as I suspect, it makes me question what possible importance that kid might have. Then again, it's better to have something I don't need than need something I don't have.

I climb in the truck, circle it back around, and head down the road. This highway has been traversing cliff sides and sheer drops for miles. Unless that kid committed suicide, I'll find him on this road somewhere. It's only a matter of time.

DEEP SPACE

Everything was a suffocating, lifeless black, the nearest stars barely pinpricks in the limitless void, only the slight glow of a far-distant nebula visible. The gas cloud's center was a dazzling orb of white, its voluminous expanse dwarfing that of an entire solar system. Tendrils of purplish blue arced in from the vacuity of space. They twisted through its exterior, their gaseous strings growing lighter as toward the center they descended into a web of magentas and pinks. A solitary ship drifted on its outer banks, the harsh edges standing in stark contrast to the swirling vapor all about. Its hulking mass resembled a corrugated tube of chromite, the satin edges barely visible amid the celestial maelstrom. A few pinpricks of light dotted a core encircled by evenly spaced rings.

Minutes dragged by and the K'kl waited. This was where the wormhole had appeared, one that the Al'lak seemed way too interested in. If nothing else, the Al'lak were predictable. They pretended to be the peaceful arbitrators of this quadrant, only they would retaliate ruthlessly whenever challenged. This time, though, they had stepped onto perilous ground by violating K'kl space. It was the K'kl who had discovered this celestial aberration. That made it theirs by right, and the underhandedness of the Al'lak had been revealed.

They had established a hidden base on a moon deep within K'kl territory. Although old and apparently inactive, it should never have been there in the first place. And if they had that, who knew what else they were up to? Their inept meddling had forced the K'kl's hand in destroying an Al'lak armada, and now all bets were off. This was war. The K'kl had beat back the great imperialists, and the cracks were showing. Whatever this thing was, the K'kl were going to have first dibs for a change.

Dwarfish, troll-looking creatures, the K'kl sported lumpy, oversized gray heads with beady yellow eyes atop stout little four-foot-high bodies. They all wore the same textured charcoal suits, the only break from the visual monotony a metallic ring that opened up at the neck and wrists.

A glowing fleck opened in the vacuum, a singularity that the K'kl watched with baited anticipation. The mote expanded, quickly swelling to the size of a small planet. It was now a pulsating mass of light, its edges ever-shifting bands of crimson. The back of the K'kl ship emitted a blue radiance as it started to move forward. The tendrils of the singularity picked up pace, whipping themselves into a frenzy. Pulses of electricity shot out, arcing around the K'kl ship. The intensity of the bursts abruptly increased, and a stream lanced through the K'kl ship.

The surge knocked out most of their systems and they were spooked. The control room was a hive-like cavern of protruding black stumps on a floor that resembled black lava, and ten K'kl were occupying it. Seated on the rough stumps, most were wearing wide paper-thin bands around their heads that gave them control of a ship that was not responding. Light poured in through the latticed windows and the craft was picking up speed. The K'kl nervously looked at one another and called out for any neighboring ship.

They received a garbled, weak response, and the ship was sucked into the singularity.

Instantly a cluster of K'kl ships swooped in. Some forty strong, they formed a mass of black, egg-shaped globes outfitted with parallel fins. Following behind was an enormous craft, its hulking mass a tangle of oblong spheres. A few large rods protruded from the central cluster like long, spindly poles. The ships swarmed toward the singularity. A good twenty of them had closed in when the thing imploded, sucking in the foremost ships with it. The last few were far enough away to avoid being sucked in, but the singularity had disappeared, leaving them floating in an empty void.

Dan Henk

Instantly a cluster of K'KI ships swooped in

The smaller ships executed a few looping runs and headed back. Cursing their luck, the K'kl waited for the short-range craft, gathered them all in the belly of the larger ship, and fired up for a return trip. It was to be a trip they would never make.

A swarm of fighters streamed in from out of nowhere. They looked like plated wings, their disc-like exteriors corrugated like armadillo hides, the spine a cone that blossomed in the forefront into a rounded cluster of windows. Slender tubes crested the wing edges, their tips lit up with snarls of blue lightning. The large K'kl ship flared up in a legion of successive explosions. Although they tried to scramble the fighters, it was too late. The massive ship started to look like a pitted asteroid, its bowels losing pressure as it expelled squirming bodies into the vacuum.

Cracks spider-webbed around the craft and it started to tear apart. The central pods on top cracked open, their innards spewing forth a convoluted snarl of wriggling bodies and debris. The central rods broke off and pirouetted violently through the main tube of the ship, their whirling trajectory ripping apart the shredded core before they whipped out into the void. The fleet of attacking ships banked, arced around, and headed back. A vessel resembling an immense black beetle lit by a hundred tiny lights emerged from the darkness. The smaller ships swarmed in like insects entering a hive.

The Al'lak realized how dangerous the wormhole was. Most were narrow and unstable, and anything as large and long-lived as this one had to be artificial. Not to mention, it was acting unlike any wormhole they had seen before. The Al'lak weren't sure where the K'kl had acquired the technology they currently had on display, but it was clearly a step above their presumed capabilities.

They were a primitive race, one that could barely harvest the energy of their own star. The Al'lak were older and much more advanced. But the universe was more ancient still, and there were rumors... Fairy tales really, though if they held even a grain of truth, the consequences could be devastating.

THE WAY BACK TO HELL

It was pitch black, dry, and gritty. The smell of sand and damp rock wafted in, and the air felt smarmy and thick. Aaron was crawling on his hands, trying to stay on the balls of his feet so his jeans didn't scrape along the ground. He was scuttling quickly when he banged his knee into a rock. Reeling in pain, he curled up on the ground and cursed softly. It didn't take long for fear to wash over again, though, and he tried to ignore the pain as he struggled back onto all fours and kept moving. Something crawled over his hand and he bolted instinctively, banging his head on the low ceiling so hard he saw stars. He grabbed his skull in agony, rocking back and forth and gritting his teeth. Shuffling his feet forward, he crouched and dug inside his jacket pocket for matches. There was a pack of smokes buried in there, and his fingertips found them, even if they couldn't locate the matches. The pocket had a hole, and he dug down, gripping the bottom edge of the jacket with his left hand and raising it so his burrowing fingers could probe a little farther. He felt a lump, and angled toward it. His digits brushed against a lighter, and with a little more wrangling he managed to get a grip. Pulling it out, he flipped it around and spun the wheel, and the features of the cave sprung to life.

He was momentarily blinded, but as his eyesight normalized he looked around. The flash of the initial flame was still hovering as a white spot in the center of his vision, and he tried to stare past it. He could make out striations of gray rock arching overhead. They were taller than he imagined. Not quite head height, yet not as suffocatingly close as he had suspected. The tunnel curved to the right in the distance, and then abruptly arced to the left, giving him no clue as to how deep this rabbit hole was. He lowered the lighter, angling the burning flame toward his fingers. Although his thumb was screaming in pain, he needed to see the floor up close. It was the same trail he saw before him, only the grains of sand looked a little rougher, and he could discern the jagged edges of whitish rocks erupting out where the edges curved up into stone walls. His thumb was on fire, and he let the lighter go out. He switched hands while he shook out his right. He hadn't noticed any creatures or insects in the soil, but then again he had not made an effort to look for them. He thought about lighting a cigarette, rationalizing that the glow might help. Then he took another whiff of the stale, thin air and decided that might be a bad move. That creature might be able to track him from the scent. He crawled a few more feet, left hand aloft as he flicked the lighter back to life. Still more of the winding tunnel, and the ceiling appeared to have dropped. He tried to whip the lighter along the ground, only the flame kept bending back and burning his finger. He cursed, pocketed the lighter, and kept moving.

The place was as silent as a tomb, and Aaron's head filled with nightmarish scenarios. Rocks collapsing, underground fumes, carnivorous animals hiding in the depths. He was vividly impressed with how fucked he would be.

Except this cave gave him a chance, whereas that thing outside was probably worse. Something crawled across his hand and he freaked out, picking up his pace and shambling forward recklessly, his hands and knees shuffling through the dirt as he plowed forward in terror. He lost his grip and nearly lost his balance more than once, the curves of the wall bouncing him back into his mad scramble. His knees brushed outlying debris, the powdery remnants flying up and clogging his nostrils. The air was thick, disturbed with floating detritus, and he could barely breathe. Between bouts of hacking up his lungs, he realized that his movements were making a crunching noise, and it was more than just the soft padding of boots against sand. The ground had changed—it felt stiffer and less sandy—but he was still in panic mode and didn't dare slow down.

His hands hit hard, cold tile, and he recoiled, losing his

balance in earnest as he tumbled across a ground that he suddenly realized was completely flat. He rolled up against a perpendicular wall and carefully rose to full height, trying not to bump into anything. Desperately digging for his lighter, he pulled it out and flicked the wheel, which rolled a few times before sparking to life. What he saw in the flickering lighter confirmed that this was no longer a cave. In fact, he could swear he was in the same abandoned Section 8 building he and his friend had broken into ages ago. Although that was in D.C., and they were both smashed, this had the same vibe. The floor sprawling beneath him was composed of heavily stained black and white tiles, scaling up the walls in a flurry of pink. The tiles on the floor were completely flat; those on the wall were shinier and buckled outward. Moldy grime darkened the caulked edges. Greenish-brown smears streaked across, caking up into dried lumps. Above it, ceiling panels sagged down. Some were stained in ocher smears, a few were missing entirely, the ceiling opening into a black void in their absence. Several were cracked, ancient-looking cobwebs cloistered into the dusty corners between the wall and ceiling. Aaron scampered to his feet, disgusted by the filth all around him. His military father had instilled a regimen of cleanliness in him, and germs simply creeped him out. He started to pat the back of his jeans with his hands, then realized he was probably getting it on his skin. Something clicked and scurried by, and Aaron looked around wide-eyed. The smell of mildew and decay was inescapable. He wiped his hands on the front of his jeans and dug in his jacket pocket for a cigarette. The nicotine would help, and it would hide the smell. The bacteria and untold germs were freaking him out. Pulling out a pack of Winston Reds, he grimaced when he saw that there were only three left. He stuffed the pack back in his pocket.

If this was anything like the same place he had been in months earlier, it had a roof hatch somewhere. Most of these industrial downtown buildings did. He and his friend had hopped a fence and climbed a tree to get into that abandoned building. Fire escape scaffolding scaled up the side, and there was always a hatch so the residents could flee to the roof and exit through a series of ladders. A nearby tree had come in handy for accessing the first fire porch, but he didn't need one to get down. He just had to find one of those exit doorways and it should have stairs leading to the roof. Considering their typical placement and signage, he should find one at the end of this hall marked with a big, red EXIT. He rose to his feet and shuffled forward. Every muscle was tensed, the air thick with the smell of decay. He had the lighter in hand, and he flicked it every few feet. He had no idea how much fluid was left, and his finger was still throbbing.

IT ALL GOES TO SHIT

A single window faced the street. The dearth of lighting was the only thing he didn't like about his place. Except for today. Today it was a saving grace.

Decorated with mustard-yellow walls, tan carpeting, and a simple dark wood couch with matching loveseat, Job's apartment was a hipster cliché. The cushions were sheathed in cloth covers imprinted with a cream and crimson floral pattern, the edges fringed with throw pillows. He had outfitted it more for the sake of company than as an expression of personal style, something he had never had in abundance. Basic wooden furniture and a few framed prints displaying milquetoast modern art rounded out an apartment that, stylistically, was one step above a hotel room. Across the room, the couch was nestled in a cubbyhole that played host to the single window. He darted for it, climbed onto the cushions, and nervously groped under the crimson curtains. He was still wrestling with the cord for the blinds when the wall to his right exploded. Chunks of brick whizzed by, cratering the wall behind.

Pulverized dust followed in a swirling, choking cloud. A last hurtling fragment grazed his forehead and he was thrown back onto the couch. Blood trickled down his face, and his left kidney throbbed in pain from a collision with the armrest.

"Fuckin' hell!"

More explosions rocked the building. A colossal gap had opened in the corner of the ceiling and sunlight streamed in, pieces of frame breaking the blazing light into a kaleidoscope of beams. A thick cloud of dust swelled up from the closest corner, its upper reaches breaking apart into thin strings that pirouetted lazily through the rays of sunlight. Job, his vision swimming, was reminded of cigarette smoke. He lay befuddled and stunned for a moment, then he snapped to, sprung off the coach, and bounced across the carpet heading for the door. A minute later he was flying down the marble steps, racing through the tiled entrance hall, and bursting out into the blinding sunlight.

The air was thick with the scent of fire. The brick rowhouse across the road harbored a smoldering crater, its curved façade now missing its dominant window. Most of the frame was gone, only a serried wall of broken stone encircling the coarse hole that remained. The carnage tore a gap below the floorboards, their splintered beams poking out in a row of jagged spikes. The gaping hole revealed an interior that was eerily identical to Job's. It took a moment for him to focus past the glaze of sunlight, but as it cleared, Job could see a soupy crimson design splayed in chunks across the floorboards. The mess looked vaguely human. The head and arms were gone, blood-enswathed intestines snaking around protruding organs, a lumpy splatter of wet chunks scattered across their glistening veneers. Legs flanked by blue jeans jutted toward a gap that had once been a window, the booted feet twisted at impossible angles. Job shivered and glanced up the road. It looked clear. He bounded down the steps, onto the sidewalk, and started running.

The air was heavy with the scent of fire

Iron-fronted rowhouses flitted by on the left, their façades a rippling blur. Despite being in flight mode, his senses still observed that the sky had grown darker. The streets were grungier as well. Townhouses he could have sworn once stood as lush examples of gentrification flashed by in a queue of dilapidated shacks. He passed the remnants of a brick house. Overhanging trees obscured most of its worn façade, but the second-floor window was gone, replaced by a craggy breach in the crumbling brick that looked ancient. Upon reflection he decided that maybe ancient wasn't the word he was looking for. This place looked *abandoned*. The second-story hole opened into a dimly lit display of rotted floorboards and soiled junk. The sleeping bags and blankets of squatters were nestled against filthy walls whose floral green wallpaper was streaked and sullied from years of neglect. Some of it was peeling off in large clumps, revealing a framework of thin broken boards. Job was so wrapped up with the view that he came close to colliding with the remnants of a glass-walled bus stop, a jolt of nervous tension burning through at the near miss. He calmed down enough to take a good look at the thing in front of him, and it was unlike anything he had seen in years. The kind of shelter that might be seen on a street in New York. It might even have been a D.C. thing once upon a time, but if it was, that was long before he arrived. A glass wall at one point, the pane had been knocked out and a dented aluminum frame was all that was left, the inner lining of the frame harboring jagged shards and tattered paper fragments. The broken hovel stretched over a painted bench, its coat of green wearing away into patches of black undercoating and rust. But the shelter wasn't the only thing that looked out of place. The streets were filthy, the sidewalk a collection of cracked and stained blocks that once aspired to a degree of whiteness. Used napkins and fast food wrappers mingled with the detritus of inner-city life, extending in a sprawling swarm of neglect across the rain gutters and out into the street.

Job had been here a week ago, and the area had looked nothing like this. He tried to retrace his steps, thinking maybe he had inadvertently veered down a side street. No, that couldn't be it. Some of the glittering shards lay atop blue scraps of paper that looked to Job like what had once been a movie poster. He tried to guess which one, toeing the glass about inquisitively, only the scraps of paper formed a hopeless jumble. A rustling noise caught his attention and he snapped back into focus. It came from the far side of the street, and he scanned it intensely. While the distance made everything hard to discern, he could see that a kid was scampering down the fire escape of a dilapidated building. The gnarled, leafless limb of an oak tree abutted its black railing, and the kid was trying to clamber up onto it. The monolithic building behind him was constructed of pink bricks and looked like some Section 8 atrocity from the Marion Barry years. Only Job didn't remember there being any such thing left in this vicinity.

A thud broke his reverie. The kid had dropped to the ground. He was curious, in an absentminded way, what the kid's story was. This was an upscale area, and that kid was all decked out like some crusty punk. Then again, nothing made sense right now. With that, it came back to him what he was fleeing from. Panic washed over him, and he started to look back. His head was still rotated when a concussive wave hit, like an approaching train. His ears popped, and everything went blank.

He awoke minutes later, blood streaming from his nose for the second time today. The ringing in his ears had resumed, and the pounding in his head now was much more intense. His vision was fuzzy, waves of nausea flowing over, his balance destroyed, and all he could make out were the scents of scorched asphalt and gunpowder. He tried to move, but it was like he was underwater. He had to will his arms to shift, as if they were no longer under his control. It was surreal, and it reminded him of a poorly dubbed movie he had seen recently. He tried to recall which movie, if only he could focus.

"Hey, mister, you all right?"

It was that kid. Job was sprawled out in the middle of the road, and his pelvis was killing him. Every few seconds another flash of pain would shoot down his leg. The misery radiated through his hands as well. They were shaking, and a stinging sensation hit him. He flipped his palms over and looked down at scraped and mangled flesh, extending his bent fingers for a better view.

Jagged lines scrawled across a canvas of torn pink flesh. He clenched his eyes tight and shook his head, trying to clear his vision. That grassy lawn at the park was nothing compared to the pavement he had slid across this time. He opened his eyes and stared at his mutilated palms. Everything was slowly growing sharp again, and he could see dark bits of rubble amid the bloody groves of peeling skin.

"Hey, you're gonna get killed if you stay out here."

That kid from the apartment was leaning over him. Crimson tips of hair dangled in Job's face in a surreal wave of color. Long strings of black trailed away in a blur from their red edges, leading upward until they morphed into the fuzzy contours of a face. A metallic row glittered next to the face, and he speculated about what that could possibly be.

Job struggled to sit up. He couldn't find his balance and kept collapsing. All he wanted was to rest, only he felt if he succumbed, what would follow would be worse. A heavy thump cut through the ringing, followed by the sound of falling concrete. The heavy artillery was still going off. The fact that he was still alive probably meant that everything so far had been collateral damage. Or perhaps whoever was responsible was shooting wildly. All he knew was that he had to get out of sight. Aaron was running down the street. Job managed to gain his footing and follow suit. He narrowly avoided kneeling over in a flash of vertigo, and with a wobble he managed to stay upright. After a few loping hops he shambled into a weak run. A sonic boom rocked the air, and bits of stone from some nearby building pelted him in a cascade of stinging shards. It came close to knocking him over, but with some stiffening of his body and awkward shuffling, he managed to stay on his feet.

"Hey, kid. Hey, kid…"

Aaron halted and peered over his shoulder. "What do you want?"

"Where are you going?"

"I…don't know. Out…of here." Aaron tried to say the words,

but they came in stuttering gasps. He regretted every cigarette he had ever smoked. His chest was on fire, he couldn't catch his breath, and his nose was running.

Job loped after him and called out again. "Kid, I have an idea."

Aaron didn't know who this guy was and wondered why he was even trying to connect with him. The dude looked to be in his thirties, and anyone over twenty-five was suspect. That, and the way he was dressed, meant he was from a different world. That nine-to-five, downtown-suit-and-tie business crowd.

Aaron hated those guys, and to judge from the abuse he had taken back home, the feeling was mutual. What could this man possibly want? He was wearing a dress shirt, creased slacks, dress shoes, the works. Aaron was a skinny punk kid in a painted-up leather jacket with a bullet belt, dog tags, and black clothing. People like this guy looked at him with either disgust or pity, or both. They lived in their own little bubble, and even the few who tried to make some sort of connection still had no clue. They merely tried to be more "understanding," all their prejudices and clichés still intact. And most of these types had been dangerous recently.

Job was hurt. It felt minor now, but he knew how it worked. The swelling was already kicking in, and it was all getting much worse. He was out of his element and terrified. In theory, he had friends he could call on. In truth, though, he knew they weren't the kind of people who could handle something like this. They were "hang out at the bar and enjoy a good time" together types, not the kind you could rely on when the going got tough. Fair-weather friends, not a close-knit social group, but he bet this kid had the exact opposite. He had never known any of their kind to be overly bright. Their saving grace was that they appeared to unite over anything, and they were too on the fringe not to hang out together. If anyone knew the streets and had friends who lived under the radar, this kid would be his option. His friends were probably essentially a less-dangerous gang. All he needed was to prove his worth to them and he'd win their trust.

"Hey, kid, I know where we can get a car."

Aaron stopped. "You have a car?"

"I know where one is."

"Where?"

"Follow me."

Aaron waited for him to catch up. Job had almost reached him when everything went to hell again. There was a heavy crunch of gravel, and then a concussive force knocked them to their knees. Rocks rained down out of a sky thick with smoke. A dense, suffocating smog rolled in. Though only feet away, they could barely see each other. The dry thickness of pulverized rock clogged their nostrils, a layer of white powder overlaying everything. They looked like old men in clay masks, the only breaks their red-rimmed eye sockets. Doubled over and gasping for air, Job crawled forward and tapped Aaron on the shoulder. Aaron's head was bent, and he could barely make out Job. The ringing in his ears was too loud for him to hear anything. But he could make out a blur that he assumed was Job, and he appeared to be motioning toward the left. Aaron rose to his knees, the white sand trailing off his leather coat in rivulets. He gripped Job's hand, a gritty hold that expelled clouds of powder, and followed. Wisps of pulverized debris drifted by, sometimes entirely obscuring his view, but Aaron held tight to Job's hand and hoped that would be enough.

A moment later they were out, emerging from an opaque veil of roiling fog and into clear daylight. An asphalt roadway lined with distant sidewalks spread out before them. Aaron let go of Job's hand and stayed close. He felt weird and uncomfortable. His nostrils were clogged with dust and he was having trouble drawing air. He pinched off one side with his knuckle and snorted out a hardened wad of snot. He did the other side, and only then could he breathe a little better. His insides felt like they were coated in dust, and his throat was scratchy. His lungs were heavy, his ears rang, and he felt lightheaded. He kept moving, Job leading the way. When he raised his head, a cluster of rowhouses surrounded them on all sides, their desolate red-brick veneers glimmering in the sunlight, carefully manicured trees rising out of neat little plots among the grass. Black metal railings flowed up short staircases and into freshly painted doors. It all looked very suburban and serene. There were no signs of violence here, but there were also no people. Aaron glanced around nervously. He didn't see the cloud of smoke they had emerged from. Job had made it a few feet in front of him before he stopped and turned back.

"C'mon, dude! We're only a block away!"

"From the car or from the thing that was shooting at us?"

"I don't know what that was, but we'll be dead if we try to figure it out now. We're a block from the car. I don't know if that thing is headed this way or not, but I don't think it's after us."

"What is it after?"

"I have no idea. It blew up the park I was at and killed a lot of people. I'm just trying to get as far away from it as possible."

They rounded another corner and were out of the neighborhood and into a commercial sector. There was a Subway, and right next to it a Smoke Shop. This was downtown D.C. They must be somewhere in Northwest. Across the street, the individual storefronts suddenly gave way to a large structure that took up half the block. It was a hipster clothing shop, its plate glass windows papered in white, the blue silhouettes of fashionably clothed people splayed across.

All the businesses were dark, the sidewalks devoid of people, the streets carless. It was like something out of an apocalyptic movie, only it felt way more surreal. Tension-charged air that smelled warm and musky. Aaron could swear it held the bite of electricity. The green sign at the crossroads read 15th Street. The looming structures beyond were a succession of increasingly ephemeral silhouettes as they curved into the horizon. The pall of an overcast sky cast an aura of menace on everything, the sun already sunken. Night was coming.

"Over there!"

Job was motioning with his hand, gesturing toward the darkened maw of a parking garage. Square columns of whitewashed concrete enveloped a descending ramp that sloped down into the black void.

Aaron looked dubious. "It's down there?"

"Yeah."

"How far?"

Job didn't really have a car. He had a friend who worked at a parking garage, and he knew where they stored the keys. It would be in the kiosk, and usually on the wall. His plan was to grab a fairly modern car or SUV, and use the auto-lock to find the vehicle. Aaron had bolted ahead of him and was already crossing the street.

"Hey, kid, we have to get the keys," he called.

Aaron stopped at the nearest pillar, resting his hand against it as he caught his breath. Job looked both ways and darted across the street. He headed for the opposite pillar, the one fronted by a large white sign with the red word "PARK" on it. The sign was fixed to a metal pole, the base a thick block of stone. That thing likely was heavy enough to break the kiosk window. If, by some stroke of luck, the door was unlocked, all the better. It dawned on Job as he was crossing the street that there was a slight flaw in his plan. He didn't have a flashlight, and there was no interior light in that garage. He'd be lost in the dark. Stopping short in front of the sign, he glanced around in desperation.

Aaron looked on with growing skepticism. "What are you doing?"

"I'm just...I—"

"It's buried down there in the dark, isn't it?"

"I...well, yeah."

Aaron shook his head. "How far is the kiosk?"

"Around the corner."

"And what, you have to get your keys?"

"Yeah." Job nodded.

"How are you going to do that? I don't think anyone's here."

"Yeah, I know. I'll have to break the glass."

"With what?"

"I was thinking I'd use this stand."

Aaron grimaced. In for a penny in for a pound. It was probably too late to change course, but none of this was good.

"All right, look. You grab that thing, we'll head down the ramp, and when it gets too dark, I have a lighter. I can't keep it going for long—I have no idea how much fuel is left. If that kiosk is close though, we should be fine."

It felt weird to Aaron to be bossing around this obviously older guy, but this was life or death. He could already tell he had a quicker wit and more street smarts than this chump, but it still felt weird. He wasn't used to any of this, this telling adults what to do, and he wasn't sure how seriously this guy would take him. He pushed those thoughts aside and confidently strode forward. A moment later, he could hear Job following, and after a few steps, darkness had enveloped them. He pulled out the lighter and flicked the wheel. It sparked a few times and jumped to life. The abrupt flash burned a blue dot into the center of Aaron's vision, and he slowed while his eyes adjusted. As his sight acclimated, he could see a small enclosure on the left. His thumb grew raw and he let the flame die. In a glimpse he had judged the garage to be a barren underground lot of open pavement, so traveling a few feet in the dark should pose little risk. Only the shadows had closed in, and recent experience had taught him that usually meant an unseen horror was lurking nearby. Sweat rolled down his face, his skin grew tight, and waves of nervous tension washed over him as he descended. He flicked the wheel again and noticed that the kiosk was still a few feet away. He had drifted to the left, and a raised concrete barrier was partially blocking his path. He held his other arm outstretched before him, let the light go, and proceeded slowly.

When he flicked the wheel again, he was inches away from the kiosk, a white box with large square windows. The thing looked empty. One chair, a desk with a few papers on it, and no room for much else was all he saw.

Job tapped his shoulder. "Light it up."

Aaron barely avoided jumping. He tensed up and grew seriously annoyed. "Dude! Don't do that!"

"Do what?"

"Sneak up on me like that!"

"Sorry! I'm just…hold that lighter up. I need to see if we can get in."

Aaron sparked the lighter. Job put down the sign, walked to the door, and tried the lever. Locked.

Aaron let the light go out. "What now? You want to try breaking in?"

"Yeah, hold on a minute."

Job shuffled behind Aaron. There was a scraping noise, and Job yelled, "All right, go!"

Aaron lit the flame again. With a charging cry that Aaron found ridiculous, Job ran at the box and thrust the parking sign at the window. It bounced off, leaving barely a scratch. Aaron let the light go out, passed the lighter to his other hand, and cursed softly, shaking his stinging thumb.

"Is it going to break?" he hissed.

"I got it. I got it," Job panted. "It must be safety glass or something."

"I can't keep doing this. My thumb is on fire and I doubt I have much fuel left."

"Just give me a little light when I say *now*."

Job had tried the quickest way possible, and now realized that it was going to take more work. He adjusted his grip so both hands were on the metal bars and he was wielding the weighted end like a club. It was black as night and he couldn't see what he was doing, but he was pretty confident this time, even if the block of concrete swayed precariously as he tried to wiggle his hands down to the sign. He could smell his own perspiration, and the awkward wrangling nearly tipped him over. The sharp edges of the sign dug into his hands, but he tried to ignore the pain, shifting it around and positioning it like a mace.

He gave himself a moment to mentally pump up. "*Now!*"

Aaron sparked the light. Job hammered the glass, and a network of spider-web cracks blossomed in response.

"*Fuck!*" Aaron screeched, letting go of the button. He tossed the lighter to his left hand again and stuck his blackened right thumb in his armpit. He squeezed, the pressure alleviating the pain a little, and kept up a soft stream of curses.

"One more time!" Job said.

Grimacing and trying to ignore the agony, Aaron flicked the wheel. In the flickering light, Job pummeled the window. This time there was a husky splintering noise that registered just as Aaron let the flame go out. The burn grew more intense with every attempt. His eyes were watering, and he stuck his thumb in his armpit again.

"I got it," Job said. "Give the lighter a rest. I'll just keep hammering!"

Aaron didn't respond other than to keep muttering "*Fuck*" under his breath. A few more blows resounded, followed by the sound of shattering glass.

"I got it! Give me the lighter, I'll find the key."

Job groped around until he located Aaron's outstretched hand. He nearly lost the lighter in the swap, clenching his fist as it was slipping. Hot metal burnt into a palm already raw from scraping across the pavement. He uttered a curse and quickly traded hands. Shaking out his stinging hand, he extended the other, lighter in the forefront, into what he thought was the gap.

"Ow! Fuck!"

"What?" Aaron asked. "I just cut my hand."

Job's thumb had nicked a jagged edge, and he let go of the button the instant glass dug into his finger. He almost dropped the lighter as well. He was about to try again when it dawned on him he would have to use the hurt thumb to rotate the wheel. He could feel both a stabbing pain, and the cool pooling of blood. He could even smell it. These types of cuts bled a lot, and his unseen finger was probably a wet mess by now. It would be a slippery, painful experience if he applied pressure to the lighter. He retracted his left hand in the darkness, switched hands, held the lighter aloft, and flicked the wheel.

The scene was much clearer this time. A line of glass shards skirted the bottom of the windowpane, a few of them red with blood. The top half of the window was still holding on, the glass so splintered it had degenerated into an opaque sheet of reflections. His thumb was heating up, and moving the lighter forward cast the flame back on his skin, but he needed to see how the kiosk opened. He stepped up next to the booth, moved the lighter inside the breach, and shifted it up and down until its little circle of illumination landed on the door handle. The thing was a simple lever, and the moment the light illuminated it, Job let the fuel button loose. The top of his hand was in agony now, and the lighter felt like a stick of fire, yet he managed to ignore the pain, slide the lighter down his palm, and free his top two fingers. He twisted them around the lever and tried to move the thing, but they slid off with the first few attempts, his fingertips so numb he couldn't even tell if he was making contact.

"C'mon, baby...c'mon..." he muttered, his nerves on edge as his fingers slipped off repeatedly. Finally he managed to flip the lever and cracked the door with his knee. Uttering a sigh of relief, he extracted an arm whose muscles were aching all the way up to his shoulder. "I got it," he said to Aaron. "I'll be right back."

He used his knee to push the door farther open and quickly stuck a foot in the gap. Stepping in and flicking the lighter back to life, he noticed that while the front sides of the kiosk were sheathed in windowpane, the rear wall was a solid sheet of glossy yellow metal. Glued to it was a panel of white plastic that held three rows of metal hooks. The first two rows held a variety of keys. Job held the lighter closer. A Toyota or Honda would be nice, he just needed a newer one with a key fob to locate the vehicle.

Aaron snorted. "You don't have a car here, do you?"

Job debated how to respond. He didn't know the kid well, which made bluffing difficult. If he was caught in anything that was perceived as a lie, he might lose whatever chance he had.

"I never said it was my car. I know someone who runs this garage. I can get us one."

He scanned the key rack in silence. The truth was he *sort of* knew a guy who *used to* work at a garage, but provided he was able to obtain a car, he was sure it would be a moot point.

Aaron, on the other hand, had the impression Job was lying, pure and simple. In his experience, these types of people always lied. He knew nothing about this guy, who had proved questionable concerning the very first thing that had come up. How much worse could he get? People went to some serious lengths to gain the confidence of someone they intended to betray. It had happened to Aaron more than once. People he knew and could read much better had turned on him when the chips were down. Considering how little he knew of this dude, and how shifty some of them had been recently, this did not bode well.

They both heard a hiss. Animalistic and primal, it sounded strange and out of place in an urban D.C. garage. A muffled thud, followed by the sound of shredding cloth, erupted from the depths. A scream followed, followed by a frenzy like the gnashing of teeth. Guttural, high-pitched squeals pierced the silence, followed by the unmistakable splatter of liquid. Then everything was silent. Eyes wide, cheeks drawn, Job and Aaron froze with the same dumbfounded looks on their faces. Job had let the lighter go out. He flicked it back to life and pored over the key rack. His skin was electric, drawn tight in terror as his temples burned and his pulse thumped in his head. Sweat rolled down his face as he flitted back and forth over the keys. There were about ten in all, and his vision darting among them too quickly for a close analysis.

Aaron sprang into the booth. "Dude! The keys! Pick a fuckin' car!"

"Give me a minute!"

"We don't *have* a minute! Did you hear that shit?"

"Just a minute...just a minute...We need to get a good one..."

Volkswagen Golf. That would do. Job snatched up the keys and barely missed Aaron when he spun around. He let the flame go out.

"Is that it?" Aaron whispered desperately. "Help me find the car!"

"You don't even know where the car is?"

"Just look for the headlights!" said Job. "I'll hit the button."

Aaron hated this chump. He had no idea what he was doing, and he was probably going to get them killed. Then a flash winked from across the lot.

"Over there!" Aaron yelled, pointing. He kicked the door open and ran like mad for the pulsing lights.

Job followed, calling after him, "Where is it?"

"To the right! To the right!"

Job stopped and flashed the key again. He caught the shadow of Aaron headed toward a car mere feet from the entrance and took off after him. It was nearly dark outside, only a pale glow streaming in from the entrance ramp. Aaron had disappeared into the blackened maw, and Job kept hitting the button on the keypad as he tried to orient himself.

He was getting close when Aaron yelled out, "Stop it with the button! You keep locking it!"

As far as Aaron could tell, the car was a blue Volkswagen Golf. He had made it to the driver's side and was attempting to open the door, but Job kept locking and unlocking it in rapid succession.

"Click it again. Just one time."

Aaron had his hand on the lever. He let go and then popped it again, and the door swung wide so quickly it almost toppled him over.

"I got it!"

The scent of fresh leather and stale coffee wafted out. He climbed in and slammed the door.

Job could barely see where he was headed. He tried to stay in a straight line, only his footsteps sounded tremendously loud, the noise exacerbated by the reverberating echoes of the empty garage. He debated whether slowing was the smarter move. The car was only a few yards away. He flashed the headlights again and it dawned on him that whatever had produced that sound might be attracted by the flashes. If that was the case, it was too late. The kid was already in the car and the door was closed. He scampered up and rapped on the window.

"Move over! I'll drive."

Aaron looked up at him skeptically.

"I know the quickest way out of here!" Job insisted.

Aaron let it sink in, deciding to go with it. He hadn't driven a car often in D.C., and it was a good bet this guy knew the local streets better, especially with all the one-ways and roundabouts. He crawled over the parking break and into the passenger seat.

A guttural sound rippled through the darkness. It was a throaty sound that rose into a hiss, and eventually a full growl. It was primal and terrifying, and Job froze. His hackles up, Job felt the electricity of tension coursing through. Cold perspiration streamed from his armpits, his breathing reduced to panicked gasps. His newsboy cap had fallen off, leaving him feeling cold and naked, and his bangs were plastered to his forehead with sweat. As he palmed at the door, something razor sharp ripped into his back. His feet went out from under him and he fell against the car. The coolness of air and the wallop of a searing pain together hit the exposed flesh in a blinding rush. The air thick with the musky smell of animal, augmented by the iron scent of freshly spilled blood, he could feel liquid streaming down his spine. He let out a gasp. There was a padded thump, and something set down nearby. Something heavy.

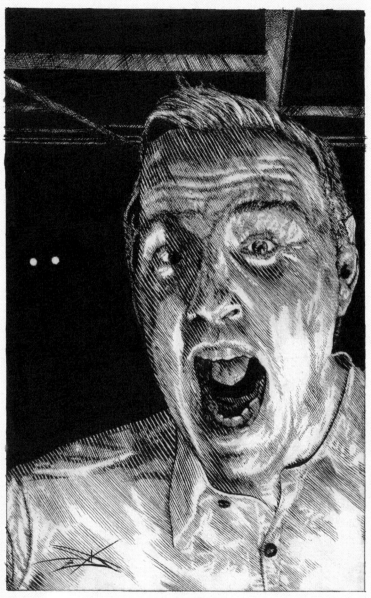

A guttural sound ripped through the darkness

Aaron jumped over and pulled the driver's door shut. It was more instinct than anything. He didn't mean to shut Job outside, but he was dead if whatever was out there got in. The knee-jerk rationalization that he didn't know this guy flashed through his mind. Not that it helped. This was wrong, and a wave of shame washed over him. Then came the realization that he wasn't going to get very far without the keys. That spawned an instant change of plan and another wave of guilt. He told himself that this wasn't merely self-interest. He needed to help that guy. He even tried to bolster the rationalization by imagining himself on the other side, but he still couldn't help feeling like a heel.

Then he remembered that the horn and lights worked without the key. He grabbed the wheel and ran his hand along the column for the lever. Nothing. He slid his hand along the other side. Still nothing. Starting to panic, he cursed under his breath. He ran his left hand along the dash as an afterthought. His fingers hit a circular depression and he groped around the area. A lever felt like it was in the center and he flipped it. The dash sprung to life.

Job had collapsed against the door, his eyes clenched shut. The abrasive squeal of the horn jolted him back to wakefulness. His face was wet with perspiration, his back a field of throbbing misery. Blood-ringed eyes rolled toward the glare of the headlights, and what Job saw sent shivers down his spine.

Large, glowing orbs stared at him. The thing's furry head was down, its lips pulled back enough to reveal a row of glistening teeth. The horn apparently had no effect, as it looked more amused than anything. All Job could think was, *How the fuck did a tiger get down here?*

Its left paw was extended, and it looked supremely confident. The eruption of light and sound had only given it a slight pause. Aaron hit the horn a few times and tried to open the door. The weight of Job worked against him, and Aaron hissed, "Let go of the door and get in the fucking car!"

Job tried to pull his midsection away from the door, his eyes still intent on the tiger. The light seemed to have confused it, and he managed to delicately slide off the door. Aaron edged it open and crawled back into the passenger seat. The tiger was growing restless. It started to sway, its feet pawing the ground as it evaluated the situation.

Astounded at Job's stupidity, Aaron hissed, "Get in!"

Job braced his hands against the door, took a deep breath, and hoisted himself in. His head and upper torso made it inside, but his legs were still hanging out. The tiger pounced, its claws scraping against the outer shell of the door and sounding like nails on a chalkboard.

"Get the fuck in!"

Job grabbed his knees and yanked. His feet rotated onto the floor mat, and in a frenzy he twisted for the door. He was almost within reach of the handle when a flurry of white fur flashed by. The claws barely grazed his skin, although they shredded his shirt. Job recoiled in panic, the new scrapes lines of fire on his arm. In a burst of terror, he lunged forward again. As he gripped the door handle, claws tore into his arm. He threw his right arm over his mauled left and pulled. The tiger's paws retracted at the last minute and the door slammed shut. Job grabbed the wheel with his tattered left arm and fumbled for the keys, finally pulling them out and finessing them into the ignition. The engine came to life with a roar. There were more shrieks as claws raked against the door, followed by a thump as the tiger bounded onto the hood. Now head level, it stared at them through the windshield, and it was the most horrifying sight Job had ever seen. There was no reasoning, no talking. All it wanted was to kill him. The tiger flung out a leg and took a swipe at the window.

Job was too shocked to say anything. Eyes bugged out, his mouth gaped in awe. Desperately, he dropped the e-brake lever, shifted into drive, and hit the gas. The car lurched forward, the tiger dropping off the side as it peeled out. Job spun the wheel like a race car driver, the Golf swerving violently as it headed for the glow of the ramp. The hulking forms of parked cars he hadn't noticed until now jutted out like obstacles in a race course, and Job zigzagged, trying to avoid them. The air in the cab hung thick with the scent of wild animal and blood.

"Where did that tiger come from?" Aaron croaked.

"The zoo," Job gasped. "The D.C. zoo. Someone must have opened the cages."

"Why?"

"I...I don't know, kid. Everything's gone to hell."

Job was scared, yet he also felt a boost of self-importance. He was acting the responsible adult in this scenario, and proving he had some worth after all.

He'd gotten them a car, and hinted that he had some insight into what was going on. More than this kid at least, that much was obvious. Even though he was in agony, if he kept this up, things might work out for him after all. A wave of euphoria washed over, the feeling almost distracting him from the excruciating sting of the claw marks. Almost.

The car burst out onto the main road, everything muted and gloomy under an overcast sky. A misty haze choking streets bare of people and cars gave the block a surreal edge, mammoth walls of glass and stone caging them in on all sides. With a dramatic spin out onto the road, Job managed to get the car oriented into a lane of traffic. He was fighting the wheel, sweating like crazy, and still somehow miraculously avoided sliding over the rain gutter and into the tree beyond as the curb took a chunk out of the rear tire in a jarring skid. He was running on adrenaline and too flustered to slow down. He spun the wheel until he was more or less level, stomped on the pedal, and shot forward.

Trees streamed by in a queue of fall colors, the veneers of industrial buildings forming a somber backdrop of glass and stone. Two blocks down and the street opened into a major intersection. Job figured this must be Connecticut Avenue. Six lanes crossed, the token presence of a city park on the left. If he angled that way, he could take this down to 17th, head over to Independence, and get onto 14th. That would lead to the expressway and out of the city. He decelerated to a crawl and was lost in thought when the piercing shriek of a horn jolted him to attention. He instinctively stomped on the brake seconds before a green Nissan sedan flew by, the force of the impromptu stop throwing him and Aaron forward. His grip on the wheel had bent his arm awkwardly in a spike of pain, but saved him from further impact. Aaron wasn't so lucky, and slammed into the dash.

"What the fuck!"

"Sorry. That car…"

Job felt a flash of panic. He needed to act like he had the situation under control. Fortunately, the dash on Aaron's side was padded, and his collision with it had probably come as more of a shock than anything.

"You all right?" he asked. "Yeah. Just drive."

Aaron was leaning on the dash, his cheek still sore from the impact. He peeled himself off and pushed back into the passenger seat. Ruffling his jacket, he sunk into a grumpy slouch.

Job rolled forward and was about to execute the turn when there was a knock on the glass. He jumped in his seat and spun his head. Someone was standing just on the other side of his fogged-up window. He blinked, leaned back for a better view, and tried to focus. He could make out a black helmet and a Plexiglas visor, the eyes barely visible. The figure wore some sort of uniform.

Black nylon, pockets and cords strewn across it, yet no labels or insignia. A black-gloved hand tapped on the window again.

"Don't open it!" Aaron hissed.

Job wasn't so sure. This might be the nation's response to the violence, and this guy looked official. No terrorist would be showing up this well outfitted, at least not this soon. This had to be some domestic agency already in place. They were in the nation's capital, after all, home of the FBI and at least at one time was the center of government. Job was sure they had Special Forces on standby. Conspiracy theorists loved to speculate about malevolent black ops operations, only when push came to shove, Job felt it was more paranoia than anything. This was serious shit. After all, he was only a bystander, and they probably were here to help.

There was a rattling sound, and Job realized they must be on the passenger side trying to open the door. No doubt that kid had it locked. Job knew these punk rock types were real distrustful of authority, and this was no time for a political stand. He started to angle back to open the door when the window burst. He whipped his head around and something heavy smacked into him. At that point, everything slowed down. He drifted forward, barely aware his head was falling into the steering wheel and not coherent enough to do anything about it.

The glass on Aaron's side broke, and a gloved hand reached in. Aaron grabbed the arm and bit down. There was a muffled "Fuck!" and the arm retracted. Aaron pounced into the gap between the front seats, hit the back, and scrambled toward the door. The latch clicked on Job's side, and Aaron knew the door would be open any second. They had already gotten to Job. His body was slumped onto the steering wheel, and for all Aaron knew, he might be dead. A hand slipped in through the window again, and Aaron pushed the rear door open. It bounced off the soldier, and Aaron kicked it hard on the rebound. It jerked forward and slammed into something. Aaron heard a grunt and a heavy fall. As the door was closing again, he kicked it and jumped out.

He twisted upon landing, almost bouncing off the pavement, but the momentum propelled him forward and he headed for the intersection. Once he cleared the car, he saw on the far right more of those jackbooted men.

Spreading out behind them were some serious looking military vehicles. All he recognized were the Humvees, but there were some other weird-looking ones mixed in. They had angled sides, pinched fronts that resembled a wedge with headlights, and eight wheels. Even more menacing, they had turrets on the roof with .50-caliber guns.

As best he knew, that was some overseas technology. What was it doing in downtown D.C.? If this even *was* D.C. Explosions erupted beside him, and he realized they were firing on him.

"Stop! Take him alive!" someone was shouting, but Aaron was already out of there.

He darted through the lanes of the side road, hopped over the brick median, and ran out into the intersection. Then he was in a park. It was small, only a few trees and a commemorative statue, but maybe he could use it to lose those guys. If nothing else, he would be a moving target. And a moving target was harder to hit. Aaron thought about ditching his heavy jacket, but knew he'd regret it. They had bulky suits, a bunch of gear, and probably far better boots than his skinny combat ones. He hopped the curb, bounded across the sidewalk, and hurdled over a knee-high chain barrier. As his feet hit the grass, electricity resounded through the air. Louder than normal static electricity, twin darts of pain slammed into his back. Jolts arced across his body, his limbs instantly rendered stiff rods. He toppled over, crying out as he fell. Face-planting into the grass, wet vegetation and the smell of soil clogged his lungs. He couldn't move and feared he might suffocate. All his muscles ached, and he couldn't crystallize a clear thought. Desperation ate at him, and the world moved in slow motion. He kept blinking his eyes and trying to move his limbs, but it was like the *Twilight Zone*. Nothing worked.

Feeling took its time in coming back, but when he was nearly strong enough to crawl upright, hands dug into his armpits. The sting of pinched muscle shot through him as he was lifted. He cried out, kicking his feet in desperation, but the grips upon him were oblivious. He swung about, trying to touch the ground so he could relieve the pressure. When his heels finally settled on grass, he was dragged forward. The sharp pain shifted forward an inch and he scrambled into a gait and direction he was being dragged. Despite his efforts, his toes kept catching in the grassy lawn and pulling him back, rewarding him with further stabs of agony.

"I can walk. I can walk. Let me down," Aaron croaked. It did no good. He still could not concentrate. He wasn't sure if it was what they hit him with or the fall or both, but he couldn't break out of his mental fog. He twisted and tried to readjust, to lessen the pain if nothing else, but the restraining hands only gripped him tighter.

He was being dragged toward some heavy-duty military vehicles. They were clustered in the center of the intersection at different angles, looking like they thought they owned the place. Light gleamed off the metal contours, giving their forms a hazy, almost phantasmal appearance. Troops in black clothing milled about. Some held aloft M4s. It all struck Aaron as strange. This was equipment that should be in a foreign country, not here in D.C.

The vehicle he was being taken to was like nothing he was familiar with. He certainly hadn't seen any of them on the bases his dad had been stationed at. It was an overbuilt pickup truck, a vehicle he would associate with the Korean War, when military trucks looked more like beefy cars than oversized bugs. Glossy black, not the military green of the others, it looked like an antiquated troop carrier. The cab was rounded like some older vehicles, and oversized wheels were doubled up in the back. The bed appeared to be a large, removable boxy structure. Four narrow grated windows filed across the top, the rest a clean slate of white wall.

He was dragged toward the tail of the truck. As they closed in, two soldiers stepped forward and opened the doors. Aaron realized with a start it was a prisoner transport. He had only seen them in movies, and this thing fit the stereotype--cold, dark, and with a bare metal interior. Steel walls flowed down into benches that were mere outcroppings, the bases welded into a floor of diamond plate. Job was crumpled against the far retaining wall, absolutely motionless. Still Aaron reasoned that if he were dead, they wouldn't have bothered putting him in here.

The hands relaxed their grip, and Aaron settled down on his heels. He debated pushing off and making a run for it, then he recalled being tasered and thought better of it.

"Get in," one of the soldiers ordered.

Aaron stalled for time. "What?"

"Get in or I'll put you in."

Aaron had a renewed impulse to make a break. He paused and crouched before deciding that now probably wasn't the best time. He rested his palms on the floor of the truck and hoisted himself up. The doors slammed shut behind him, throwing everything into darkness. A pale glow streamed in from the slatted windows on high, yet Aaron's eyes were still adjusting and he had to feel around to place himself. His fingertips alighted on the edge of the bench and he took a seat.

"Hey," he hissed to Job, waiting for a response. After a few moments of silence, he tried again.

"Hey!"

Still nothing. It was high time he found out this guy's name. It hadn't struck him as an issue before, but given the circumstances, it was proving to be an annoyance. Then again, he didn't have any bond with this dude, and wasn't even sure he should. The guy gave the impression that he was just a scared adult trying to play it cool so he could get out of the city. Given how slippery these people were, this might all be an act. And once he hooked up with his peers and was out of danger, Aaron would become chattel. Sure, that might not be the case, but Aaron felt he would be better off not getting too close until he got a better read. Either way, he thought he should at least make sure the guy stayed alive.

Even though it was too dark to see anything, from the quick scan he'd made on entry Aaron could see the slumped form of what he presumed was Job.

His face and hands were mostly hidden from view, and Aaron had seen way too many horror movies to think getting any closer was a good idea. He scooted back on the bench and reclined in silence, hoping he was doing the right thing. He'd feel like a real shitheel if this guy was alive and needed his help.

Time crawled by, and Aaron grew antsy. He could hear the muffled calls of the men outside, but he couldn't make out their words. The prison truck was cold and sterile, and smelled of the bitter tang of metal.

After what may have been an hour, the latch threw back with a loud crash and the doors opened. Aaron was blinded for a moment and threw up his hands reflexively. As his vision adjusted, his heart sank. He could swear the dark shape in the doorframe was a dead ringer for the man who had questioned him at a police station weeks ago. The one that hadn't popped up at Tommy's house and been shot.

Black clad from head to toe, sunglasses hid the guy's eyes. Slicked-back, close-cropped dark hair and the chiseled edges of a face were all he could discern. The guy called to mind that whole "men in black" cliché. Whatever he was, he apparently had a lot of pull, which meant someone much bigger was backing him. He and his partner had used local police to round Aaron up weeks ago. They had showed up at his parents' house, dragged him to the nearest station, and peppered him with strange questions. They knew aspects of his life that no one knew. When he played dumb, they had walked and left the door unlocked. When he wandered out a few minutes later, none of the cops would have anything to do with him. They claimed they didn't know who he was. The very officers who had showed up at his house disavowed any knowledge of him. It was all very strange, only things had gotten so crazy afterward that he hadn't had a chance to give it much thought. Small beans compared to all that followed, only maybe it wasn't so small after all.

Not if they had this kind of reach.

"Hello, Aaron. Good to see you again."

Aaron snapped out of his reverie and debated what to say. What *could* he say? He didn't know who was a good guy, who was a bad guy, or what any of this was leading to. The last thing he trusted was the government. He had dealt with those people all his life, in the capacity of law enforcement at least, and they had proven unethical on just about all accounts. This scenario was even worse, and it was a proven fact that the government would assassinate, torture, and lie to people, all in a shallow effort to get its way. In this chaos, who knew what it was capable of?

"It's a time of great adversity, Aaron. You will have to grow up very quickly. Your nation needs you now."

Aaron hated this man. He wasn't even sure why. The guy seemed to be talking down to him, and Aaron couldn't help feeling he was shady as fuck. He also had the suspicion they didn't know the whole story. Then again, *he* didn't even know the whole story, although he was willing to bet they had some knowledge about all the weird things he had done recently. Still, they probably didn't know that he couldn't control it or that he didn't know when or why it was going to happen. Not that he thought for a minute they would believe him. The government wasn't exactly known for its subtlety.

"For what? I'm just a kid!"

The man smirked. Without another word, he motioned to the guards and was already walking away by the time they closed the doors.

THE FUTILITY OF IT ALL

They called it "the Fort," an admittedly ridiculous moniker. If there was one thing young adults loved, it was to be extravagant. Especially when they think it means they're breaking societal barriers and establishing some sort of identity.

Tommy knew better. He would claim he was here because he had nothing better to do. If pushed, he would shrug and pretend to be indifferent, and while he went along with the group to a point, he made it known he was an iconoclast. The girls loved the "loner on a lost crusade" part of him. The guys were friendly in no small part because the girls liked him so much. It all worked in his favor most of the time.

Nobody pretended to follow the news much, making a big noise about how it was all manipulated by the same evil interests they were rebelling against.

However, this latest development was too much to ignore. There was plenty of debate, as no one knew just what was going on, but one thing seemed clear--the government had fallen. It was a scenario they all yearned for when there was little danger of it actually happening. Now that it was here, everyone was terrified.

Matt had come home early from his job at the mall a few days ago and said that things were getting real weird. The first sign something was wrong was the lack of people. There was practically no one in the stores. Then again it was still early, so no one was too concerned yet. They were all engaged in casual conversations, remarking on how slow business usually made for a long workday. Then things got even more sparse. The few stragglers did not appear to be the typical mall clientele, mostly kids and a few shifty, homeless-looking types. Then even they cleared out. About an hour later the police arrived and ordered everyone to lock up and go home. Most were glad to have a spontaneous day off. The hippie guy at the smoothie store was the only one who raised a ruckus. He started to get in their faces and argue, saying he wanted to speak to someone higher up. Usually, at least in public, the police took a softer approach, but not this time. Without hesitation they pistol-whipped him and barked orders at everyone else. The others were in shock and left without a word. Matt hightailed it to his car, trying to maintain a low profile. He was stocky, tattooed, had a head full of blond dreadlocks, and a rap sheet. If they would beat up an old guy, a local business owner no less, he stood no chance at all.

Matt ducked out to his old Honda Accord. Faded copper paint, the wheel wells barely holding their shape under an infestation of rust, it had a barely legible odometer that read 99,000 miles, which was probably because the odometer simply didn't go any higher. The mileage was most likely much higher and it was a miracle the vehicle still ran. The windshield was cracked, the shocks were shot, the belts squealed, and he'd been driving on an undersized spare for months. Still, it was a running vehicle, which was more than anyone else had at the Fort.

Except Dana. Dana had a newer, silver 4Runner. Her parents' vehicle. She wasn't a permanent resident, though, and she was real capricious about who she let drive it, so it didn't really count. Matt's car was usually so packed with people the back would veer under the weight whenever they went out. He had even been pulled over by a cop who thought he was driving drunk.

The Fort was the cool punk rock hangout. They had a large, multi-car garage, really more of a barn with a dirt floor, and they would host shows there most weekends. Work lights hung from the rafters in yellow strings, the walls cheap slabs of red-painted timber, the entrance more a wooden gate than a true door. That said, this spot was the biggest thing anyone had going in the cozy college town. There were always a few people staying over in the main house, and those were the first to go when all the shit went down. They ducked out amid a flurry of excuses and spacey looks while the group that remained divided into two camps consisting mostly of permanent residents, although a few others stayed on as well. If this was the apocalypse, some people wanted to stick with their social group.

The Fort was a two-level house built on the side of a dramatic slope. Not that the slope amounted to much. The town merely dropped a level and trailed down in a sprawl of houses and small stores. The highway that fronted the Fort marked the start of the seedy side of town. No sidewalk ran alongside it, only a short lawn of dying grass quickly overtaken by the faded red walls of the Fort. There were no front windows, only a slab of rough planks that eventually ended, giving way to a gravel lot that sloped down in an arc toward the barn around back. The whole thing had no doors or windows on the side, and gave the impression of an ugly relic that would be torn down any day.

Tommy's car was parked in the rarely used front lot. Not everyone had a valid inspection sticker or registration on their car, and with a main road passing by, the risk was too great. There were always kids in attendance with illegally obtained parental vehicles, and the local police kept a watchful eye on the place. No one would put it past them to take down license plate numbers.

Two blocks of cracked concrete out front led to the single door facing the street, and this opened into Matt's second-floor room. It was the biggest room, but he was also the only one who paid the rent and bills on a regular basis. The concerts were often a desperate attempt at raising the remaining balance.

The entrance that everyone used was on the back side. A curving strip of worn asphalt led up to the garage, with a side trail of concrete blocks continuing toward the rear door. The door opened into a kitchen stuffed with a reclaimed wooden table and then into a living room decorated with worn furniture and poster-covered walls. Two couches huddled on opposite sides: one sheathed in white, the cushions the bright reds and pinks of some floral pattern; the other a tan leather affair they had found junked in front of a neighborhood house. This place might be a hub of activity during the inebriated night hours, but the daylight did it no favors. A couple of passed-out partiers nestled in the corner and on the tan couch, the wreckage of used pizza boxes and fast food wrappers littering the light brown carpeting all about them. Nestled next to the white couch was a wooden coffee table, an ugly utilitarian thing whose burnt and pockmarked top was cluttered with crushed beer cans and the dust of cigarette ash. Transparent plastic cups half-filled with butts and stale beer covered every horizontal surface.

A tall, slim guy was walking around carrying a black bag. His bowed head spilled brown dreadlocks over a cut-off Lamb of God shirt as he unenthusiastically tossed trash in the bag.

His name was Marc, and he hadn't completely decided what his next move was going to be. He was one of the original roommates, here since day one, and was as responsible for what the Fort had become as anyone. It had elevated him from a community college dropout and a bit of a nerd into a key player in the underground scene, and even gotten him a girlfriend--a hot little chick who was new to the scene and into his status.

He had worked hard building all this, and he had come so far, but he didn't know where it should all fit in the grand scheme of things. He felt he might be lost without it and it was time to make a choice: to go full tilt with this punk rock subculture thing, or give in and crawl into some lame middle-class existence. That was what his parents wanted from him, and it was where he was headed in high school. This whole "breaking into the underground" had been a post-high school move. Hooking up with a hot chick hadn't hurt either. Her naiveté and darkness really attracted him to her, and he feared that he had to maintain some sway in the scene just to keep her around.

If he abandoned all this, there was no going back. He would be ruined as far as this social group went, and he debated how dedicated he should be. He didn't think he was willing to die for it, if it came to that, but the million-dollar question was how far he could push being down with these people without fucking up any more mainstream future he might have.

Some of the more nervous types at the Fort were getting all wired up. They were pulling out their cheap stainless steel knives and throwing stars, getting their taped-up baseball bats out of the closet. It was all bottom-of-the-barrel crap that was laughable in the real world. Most of the weapons had come from some local gun show or Renaissance fair, bought amid drug- and alcohol-induced fantasies inspired by Charles Bronson and Dirty Harry movies. Marc had his doubts about their actual abilities. They might be able to hold off some rowdy kids, but this was gun country, and even though they probably wouldn't buckle under the strain, he doubted they had any ability when it came to real combat. Then again, bluster was part of it. If you faked anything long and hard enough, you might be able to get away with it. What made the difference was how drastically things had changed. If some hard-ass redneck types decided to pull their card, they were fucked.

Matt's group was composed of more athletic, alternative types--the surfers and skateboarders who liked punk and metal yet were more into physical activity than appearance. They were talking about stocking up the car with what they could scrounge and getting as far away from civilization as possible. Large state parks like Claytor Lake and New River Trail were mentioned. Most had camping equipment they could grab, and a few had firearms and bows.

The crusty side was more extreme within their expression of the counterculture. They had less-useful equipment and physical prowess and yet conversely held a higher opinion of their ability to fight authority.

Tommy knew better. He didn't want to side with Matt's crew. They would expect him to carry his weight and do some physical work, but the rest of these losers were walking tall, gathering up their cheap weapons and making grand statements about "fighting the man." He would see if he could get Natasha to leave with him. Italian, with dark hair, descent-sized breasts, and a face that resembled a famous lead from the old days of Hollywood, he had an on-again, off-again thing with her. He would keep her around until some annoying tendency surfaced in her, then he would kick her to the curb. They would be enemies for a while, then pretend like nothing ever happened. That was how most of his relationships went.

Natasha had moved from Tommy's neighborhood down to Blacksburg recently, and although she had a relationship with one of the house members, he was confident he could get her out of it. When push came to shove, he had the edge. Dana was a good backup, but he'd try Natasha first.

Matt's crew packed their shit and departed quickly. They were essentially their own clique, and even though they would exchange pleasantries with the other house members, that was about the extent of it. No one said anything to them, but they often snickered behind their backs, calling them jocks' and the like.

Marc's side of the housemates were more the social pariah type. The dreadlocked, bullet belt-wearing, bar and club crew. About the toughest thing they had going for them were their steel-toed boots and goatees. But they were putting on a serious face, acting like they were well prepared for all of this.

Natasha's boyfriend was Dave. Or Nick—Tommy couldn't remember. He knew the face, and that was enough. She was following the guy around and acting all stressed out and committed to the cause. Tommy managed to corner her and tried to persuade her to leave, but she put on airs of being offended.

He didn't have time for this drama, and it wasn't his style to put too much effort into a convincing act, so he wandered outside to look for Dana.

She was milling about her 4Runner in the back. Shadowed by the overhanging trees, she had two guys with her. With a black leather cowboy hat, dreads, and a goatee, one was a dead ringer for Al Jourgensen from Ministry. The other was just as scruffy, only he didn't have a hat or dreadlocks. His untamed, curly brown Mohawk spilled past his chin, a dusting of dark facial hair shading his pale features. Both were talking to her in hushed tones that ceased abruptly as Tommy drew closer.

Dana twisted her head to look. She usually had a pretty serious presence, but this time there was a slight edge of tension on top of it all.

"Hey, Tommy."

"What's up?"

"Nothing. Just got down here and everything's getting crazy."

"Yeah, I know. We're getting out. You headed back to Virginia?"

"Naw. I can't go back to my grandparents."

"Why not?"

"I just can't. It's crazy there."

Dana shrugged. She knew Tommy was stubborn and she didn't feel like trying to pry any more information out of him. Not when there was so much else to focus on.

"Well, we're leaving," she said. "It's probably not going to be safe here."

There was a moment of tense silence. Dana started to swivel back toward the two guys when, almost casually, Tommy said, "I have a gun."

It wasn't threatening. Tommy was weird like that. It was said off the cuff, but Dana could tell he was putting that info forward as a mark on his side. She liked him, even if no one quite seemed able to get a full picture. It was as if he kept the world at bay with a social wall, and him having a gun was entirely possible.

"What kind of gun?" she asked.

"I don't know. It was my grandad's."

"Yeah?"

"It's a revolver. Looks like something out of *Dirty Harry*."

"You have it with you?"

"It's in my car."

Dana and her party were silent for a minute. Then one of the guys, the Al Jourgenson lookalike, spoke up.

"You're welcome to join us if you want. My dad has some hunting stuff back at his place. We're going to stop by there and get some supplies, then head for a cabin he has up by Jefferson Forest."

Dana whispered something to him that Tommy didn't trust, especially when she looked back at Tommy with a smile. It came off as fake, and Tommy thought twice about joining. He didn't know Dana that well. Then again, who knew anybody that well?

"Let me get something from my car," he mumbled, and shuffled away.

Dana barely nodded, conversing once again with the other

Dan Henk

two. Tommy figured he'd think it over. He didn't like the idea of being out there by himself. Not that any of the other options sounded that appealing.

Matt and his crew were already gone. They were the least shifty of the bunch, which was a plus as far as survival went, but they were way too physically active for Tommy, and would be harder to manipulate. It was a non-issue.

That boat had already sailed.

Marc and his group were dead in the water. They would be the first choice socially, but he was a survivor and he didn't see things going well for them. Their adolescent fantasies would be the easiest to exploit, but the unfortunate reality was that they were soft, and none of their theatrics would hold sway in the real world.

That left Dana and her friends. He'd take his car and follow them. That would also be his way out if things got too sketchy. He hadn't seen Aaron since last night. He looked down on Aaron, but he was jealous of him all the same.

That kid was kind of a newbie in the circle and Tommy had known him less than a year, yet he gave off the vibe that he was sincere, if a bit naïve. He seemed to be intelligent and he was pretty strong-willed, which could prove an asset in this situation.

Tommy rounded the house and ascended the slope running alongside it. Even though there was no sidewalk, Tommy stayed close. The going was way steeper than he remembered. Panting, he crested the hill and was heading for the front door when the ground began to shake. A concussive blast washed over him, and he was thrown a few feet back down the slope and into the side wall. His leather jacket had no padding, and he rubbed his aching shoulder as he struggled upright. He glanced around the corner at the road, then instantly ducked back against the wall. Police cars and a few military Humvees were parked out in front.

And a fucking tank! That's what that noise was!

They had blown up his car, and Tommy panicked. He slinked back down the side of the house and ran to Dana's 4Runner. It was already in reverse and pulling out. Holding his leather cap to keep it from flying off, he swung the other hand fiercely and scrambled for the moving truck.

Dana slammed on the brakes and yelled, "Get in!"

The guy with the Mohawk was in the back and had leaned across the seat to open the door. Tommy dove in, tumbling into the seat with all the grace of a bull in a china shop, and Dana stomped on the gas. The front tires bounced hard as they hit the bump of asphalt between the driveway and the road.

Tommy was still sideways and was thrown forward. Mohawk guy braced his arms, the spur-of-the-moment slam prompting him to screw up his face. Dana spun out onto the road and headed toward the shops below. Loud thundering resonated from the Fort, followed by the splintering of what was probably the front door. There were some cries, followed by the hissing of compressed gas. Tommy slouched back against the rear seat.

Without turning around, Dana called out, "What happened back there, Tommy?"

"I don't know. They blew up my car."

"It sounds like they battered in the front door and gassed the house," the guy in the front seat kicked in. "I'd say we left just in time."

"They let us go," Tommy mumbled.

The guy in the front seat spun around to face him. "Why do you say that?"

Tommy wouldn't even make eye contact. His lids were half-closed, his arms crossed, and he slumped down in the chair as he pretended to be staring out the window.

There was an awkward pause for a few moments as the guy in the front seat stared at him, and then he said, "So I guess you didn't get the gun, huh?"

Tommy grimaced and kept looking out the window.

COOKEVILLE, TENNESSEE

Endless ribbons of highway roll by under a pale blue sky. Even though I'm taking a different route, much of Middle America is all the same. A straight line splitting two lanes of bleached asphalt dwindles as the curving road fades into the hills of the horizon. Slim white plastic cones, their tops painted sky blue, form a symmetrical queue on my left. Their train separates a shallow gravel stretch from a wide grassy median, then the pattern repeats itself in dual oncoming lanes. A deluge of trees wall the sides. Wide open fields and isolated buildings peep through their autumn-thinned clusters. That kid could have easily disappeared here. That he picked an isolated, mountainous region is a mystery. Unless he committed suicide by jumping off a cliff, I have no idea where he could have gone. I don't know anything about him or his story, but that old Native American guy said he was a necessity, although that might have come from the distorted bits and scraps of old tales that he selectively interpreted. Even so, most old legends hold a kernel of truth. All in all, I'm not sure what I'll encounter in Maine, but I have a feeling that his loss is a bad omen.

The M35 is loud and slow, the military cab bare and utilitarian. No radio, no CB, only the whine of the gears as I trundle down miles of numbing roadway through the rural backwoods of the U.S. An occasional truck passes by on the other side, a reassuring sign that society hasn't completely disintegrated.

Perhaps it's even in the process of rebuilding. I'm out of the loop and I don't know how long I've been gone. Most of civilization was still in shock when I left. I wonder what alliances and governments have formed in my absence, and to what degree it is centralized. As best as I can make out, a Northern president's wide-ranging socialist agenda was the straw that broke the camel's back. If that's the case, the North and South might have formed separate nation states. The South being more independent and less populated, the transition to a central governing body could take them a bit longer. There's been no pressure of civil war so far, which would necessitate the consolidation into competing factions. The militarization of borders between them has been far more prominent in the South, bolstering the theory that everything is still in chaos.

There were always plenty of military bases in the South, although not nearly as many research stations. Most of the facilities that did exist were in Texas, and that state appears to have broken away from the central government.

From my limited knowledge of the bureaucratic workings, Texas was used mainly as a warehouse for recovered material. They were so intent on compartmentalization that the locations were essentially nameless storage warehouses. Items were shipped out from their to labs up North that had no idea where the originals were acquired. I stole this alien form from a storage facility in North Carolina. If they had taken it more seriously, it probably would have been transferred for examination. The powers in play appear to have some grand agenda, and this body was just an anomaly. One they didn't understand and that didn't have much to do with their larger plan. I know they were doing things way more complex and far ranging, like experimenting on pregnant women and using disease as a chemical weapon like in the Tuskegee experiments. They've been using the populace as guinea pigs for decades. With a Freedom of Information Act slip-up, the public found out about some of it, and even with the resultant shock and outrage the government wasn't shut down. In fact, the violating agencies' budgets only grew bigger as they became more secretive. The public had become so accustomed to a lying and thieving bureaucracy they merely shrugged their shoulders and hoped they wouldn't be one of the random victims.

Most of it involved shots in the dark, but this time they had stumbled upon something big, some advanced technology they whispered about in back rooms. It was all shrouded in mystery and hearsay, but there was talk about opening a portal. A gateway to some other place, another dimension. I didn't give it much credence until years later, when this body and that wormhole I encountered changed my view on everything. They might be onto something really dangerous this time, and in this current environment, who knows how far they will take it?

The sun had long since set and the sky was growing dark. My new vision was so acute I didn't even think about flipping on the lights until it was too dim to see the gauges. Even then, I only turned on the safety lights. I didn't want to draw more attention to myself, even though the whole area looked pretty vacant and I hadn't seen a vehicle in hours. I held down the release and flipped the three-lever light switch. In the dim red of the dash illumination, I saw the gas was low again. Even though these military gauges were far from precise, the needle claimed I was almost out of fuel. I had emptied the spare cans miles ago, and put off stopping somewhere for more, but now it was inevitable. In the past, that usually meant a spurt of violence followed by the possible loss of my vehicle. And having to interact with humans, something I was increasingly loath to do. This reluctance had put me in the backwoods of rural America, in the dark, and I had no idea how close I was to anything approaching civilization. I would bet this truck called for diesel as well, and I had no way of knowing how common that was around here. Then again, this was Highway 40, a major trucking route, so diesel couldn't be that rare.

At first I grew aggravated with myself for procrastinating, and then it crossed my mind that this was a very human reaction. The good thing was, body chemistry wasn't the extent of it, and I might not be losing my humanity completely. But on the flip side, I was still falling prey to the very frailties I hoped to rise above, which might cost me time I didn't have.

The dimness of the setting sun had overtaken the landscape. The sky had morphed into a cluster of charcoal clouds, the pinpricks of brighter stars glimmering through the haze. The line of the fallen sun faintly lit the horizon, a pale string of illumination tearing across the distant treetops. Sandy stretches shouldered the road, a wood line of leafy trees cloistering behind. The lower edges of the metal windshield frame reflected the red of the gauge clusters below. Breaking the stillness, an object in the distance caught my eye. It was a giant metal cross, the sharp edges cutting a fierce outline in the failing light. Such a strange thing for people to become fixated on. A killing device from the dark ages of man had somehow become the symbol of a worldwide cult, one that had played a large part in justifying mind-numbing inhumanity ever since. Wars, crusades, witch burnings, torture, barbarity. Heads cut off, hearts ripped out, babies buried under the foundations of buildings. Not that other religions had been much better. It's no surprise intelligent life isn't anxious to make its presence known. For most of their history humans have acted like primitives, willing to kill others simply for being different.

The last of the light finally disappeared, the overwhelming darkness of the rural highway swarming in. An overcast sky blotted out all the stars, reducing the road into a worn patch of highway burrowing through the blackened tunnel of a sheltered night. The headlights strobed the weathered asphalt, yellowing wild grass creeping in on the sides. The boxy glare of a white sign with the words FUEL scrawled across it popped up on the right. There were no gas station logos, no exit number, none of the things normally associated with a highway turnoff.

As I closed in, the sign came into starker view but looked no less mysterious. It was a simple square of white painted metal with large black letters stamped across it in a block font. A side road ventured off the highway a few feet beyond, although it was more of a dirt path than anything official, cutting through the overgrown grass of the embankment and descending into the woods below. I slowed the truck, looped into a turn, and rolled in.

The M35 bounced to and fro, its oversize wheels crushing through the rocky terrain. There was a sprinkling of gravel but it was little more than a muddy trail, its clearance kept alive by tire tracks. The stout trunks of a forest emerged, swarming in from a sheet of darkness in a ghostly procession of pillars. Their scraggy branches reached out into the trail and scraped the sides of the truck as I passed with a sound like nails on a chalkboard. I trundled through until the trees thinned out and the beacon of an orange light pierced the distant maze of trunks. A minute later, thick grass was rising on the sides as I exited the tree line, and I obtained a clearer view of the orange light. Its glow mantled a wide set of doors, the semi-dome of an old industrial warehouse stretching out beyond. An assemblage of crisscrossed girders rose behind the tail end of the roof. They appeared to be supporting a water tower. The vehicle sputtered its last and I let it coast down the long, grassy embankment.

With a bump I jolted up onto a clearing of stained concrete. The warehouse was off to the left, the orange glow a single bulb atop a set of double doors that were ten feet high. I had shot a little past the front, noticing as I did that the side walls of this warehouse were merely curved sheets of dull gray metal. I got the impression that it was cheaply constructed and only intended for short-term use. The M35 ground to a halt and I stepped out. I stood in silence for a moment, using thermal imaging and heightened hearing to scan the area. Nothing man-sized was alive inside or close to that warehouse.

Small heat blurs rustled through the grass and nearby woods. Consistent with small mammals, they were probably local wildlife. Mounted on the side of the building right next to the double doors was another white sign painted with the word FUEL in those same block letters. It was a bit strange and austere, although the military weren't known for their verbosity. There was a dwarfish sidewall of plain concrete encircling the building like some half-thought-out fence. Considering how little effort appeared to have been invested in construction of the warehouse, the inclusion of the barrier was a bit confusing.

I debated the best approach. The building looked industrial and probably military, and the military often relied on diesel. It also looked abandoned, although that glowing bulb would have long since died out without someone having been here recently. Unless there was someone in there who had some really expensive thermal suits, and this whole shabby appearance thing was a ruse. That had a slim possibility of being the case, and if this building didn't have any diesel fuel but I was exceptionally lucky, there might be an extra vehicle in there. Even an ATV would be faster than an M35 with an empty tank. I crept across the lot, hopped the sidewall, and made it up the ramp to the doors. They were large slabs of wooden boards, a crack between them revealing an interior chain that probably held the sides together. Since there were no handles on the outside, there was most likely a rear entrance. No point in subtlety now. Punching into the gap in the middle, the doors splintered into a network of cracks that shot up through the fatigued wood. I grasped the links of chain and twisted them free. The restraining handles tore off, and as the chain fell away, I pushed the doors open.

The place looked dark and empty. The large panels of metal comprising the walls curved inward, vaulting toward the ceiling. Steel beams erupted near their apex and spewed forth in a latticework of pipes and girders.

Symmetrical trays of fluorescent lights hung from the rafters, each holding two tubes aloft. Only three were lit, the closest playing host to a single flickering bulb. Torn sheaths of stamped metal were haphazardly piled atop splotches of dark grease, scraps of grimy debris spreading from their periphery across a grubby concrete floor. Light glinted off an oily pool on the far left, the sharp angles of a door visible just beyond.

A flash of light caught my eye and I swiveled to the right, but there was nothing. Then I noticed several barrels stacked in the corner. Oil barrels. Perhaps fuel barrels if I was lucky. This endeavor might not be a waste of time after all. I was pretty sure my M35 could use regular gasoline. You were supposed to supplement it with an additive, but beggars couldn't be choosers, and anything that got me closer to Maine was worth a try.

I looked around carefully as I passed through the warehouse. When I reached the well-lit central space, a stab of pain shot through my head. It was intense, like a burning spike pounded right into my brain, and I dropped to my knees, cradling my head and rocking back and forth in agony. Everything grew hazy and I couldn't think straight. My skull felt like a jackhammer was digging away at the base. I tried to concentrate, to gather my thoughts, to find a focus on something amid the throbbing…

My head was a maze of cotton, and all I could think was that maybe I was wrong, and this was why the Al'lak couldn't stay in this body. Pain wracked me in waves. Old human coping instincts were cropping up. I wanted to grit teeth I didn't have. The torment grew more intense by the minute. I didn't even care any longer what became of me. I just wanted it to end. I had to get out of this body. To escape. I didn't have a form to go back to and I didn't care. I just…

"Hello, David."

My name! My human name!

And like that, the torment melted away. My thoughts started to clear and my vision regained focus.

"David, you're in a unique position to save yourself and everyone else, but you have to listen very closely. Time is of the essence, and they already have the boy."

I relaxed and let my arms drop. At this point, I knew what to expect. I wasn't disappointed. Although the mental onslaught had distracted me, I should have recognized the approach. A form seemed to materialize from out of the shadows. Standing upright this time, it was the same man from the cabin.

"We meet again, David."

I needed to buy some time while I figured out the right course of action. This guy was clearer now, his words sharper and more refined. His thoughts were in English, and my specific variant at that. Even the delivery was soft and familiar.

"David, we have no secrets here."

He was in my head! Not merely my surface thoughts, but everywhere!

"David, you don't have time for this. I've provided you with more than enough fuel for your journey."

"What journey?"

"Your journey to Maine. It's very important you get there, but you must stop and rescue Aaron along the way."

"Who is Aaron? You said you had no use for me! And how do you know where I'm headed?"

"Things change, David. We found a use for you after all."

"Who is this *we*?"

"That...that would take quite a bit of explaining, and you don't have the time. Suffice it to say, this is in your best interest, as well as that of your species."

"I don't give a fuck about my species."

"You say that, only it's a blind reaction. You've been through some rough patches. A brutal family life, the loss of your wife, the betrayal of your government. Those are all minor compared to what needs to be done. You can save the world, David. If you don't, you might not have anything to be bitter toward."

He's playing with me. It's too perfect of an act.

"It's not an act, David. I'm trying to address you in the pattern you feel most comfortable with."

"The pattern? What is that? No, I have an even a better question. What are you and why should I give a fuck what you want?"

"We've been around a long time, since before your world was even formed, and your little out-of-the-way planet has become a crucible for the whole universe."

"What exactly does any of this shit have to do with me?"

"Things were very different in the early days, David. The fabric of reality employed a different set of laws. We live in a multiverse and the walls are thin now, but they were even weaker back then. The story of your race is much more varied than you think, and there are things that should not be allowed back."

"Again, what does this have to do with me?"

"People on your planet are working to open a portal that will have disastrous consequences. You need to prevent this."

"What happens if they open the portal?"

"Millennia ago, something infected this system like a cancer, but the physical laws in this universe have now changed, and they can't get in without help."

"What do you need me for? If you know so much about this, why don't *you* *h*andle it?"

"I'm not even here."

"What are you talking about?"

"This is a projection, over billions of light years. Even this much is...difficult."

"You appear out of nowhere dressed in an outfit that isn't even current or relevant. You slaughtered all those men in New Mexico and you announce your presence by screwing with my brain. I don't trust any of this."

"We had nothing to do with whatever men you are addressing. People can be manipulated, but not when it is something this complex. None of it was meant to cause you distress, only to get your attention. This communication isn't perfect."

"So this thing you want, it's what, in Maine? And why do I need the kid?"

"It's not a thing, David. It's the destruction of a thing. That child is the harbinger of death."

"Kill the kid? Is that what you're asking me to do? You could have killed him at any point. You want something."

"My time is up, David. Go to D.C. Find Aaron. Save your world."

And with that he disappeared. I couldn't even get a clear glimpse of it. One minute he was there, and the next he was gone. I didn't look away. He didn't fade out. There was this feeling that I had skipped a scene, like my memory was a tape reel and something was missing. They were fucking with my head, and I didn't like this at all.

Running with Scissors

Aaron was scared. They had thrown that older guy from the car in with him. The guy's hands were cuffed in back, and he had not yet regained consciousness. His face was battered and bruised, a bloody cut marring the side of his mouth. Dark circles surrounded hollowed eye sockets holding eyes that had yet to open. Aaron figured most of the damage was from the wreck, although he had no doubt this guy had been treated pretty roughly afterward as well.

The room was dark and cold, and stank of metal, blood, and the musty odor of sweat. Light streamed in from high slits atop the walls, specks of dirt fluttering through the beams. It was just enough to make the cabin gloomy and depressing. Although it wasn't that chill out, Aaron felt cold and claustrophobic. He had the feeling that everything was going to shit all around him. No friends left, no family to fall back on, and nowhere to go. He had tried so hard to make his way, to make something work, but it had all been useless and now he didn't see the point anymore. He wasn't sure what was going on in this new world. One thing was certain, though: it had nothing to do with him.

The engine rumbled to life, the back rattling in vibration. The truck jerked forward, the momentum throwing Aaron back along the bench and inches short of the rear doors. He had fallen into a slump as he skidded, but as soon as he managed to stop, he jerked upright. This was all too crazy and over-the-top serious. His parents might have been oppressive, but they had their limits. Basic ethics and morals, if nothing else, only things were very different now. He had been relentlessly pursued, tazed, thrown in the back of a prisoner transport, and was being taken to places unknown. He had no doubt this was the military-industrial complex finally going buck wild. It was obvious before that they had their hands in everything, and this latest crisis was simply the straw that broke the camel's back. There were so few mainstream news sources left that it was just a known thing that what the media fed to the public was little more than an infomercial. All the alternative news outlets talked about it. Maximum Rock and Roll, underground fanzines, YouTube and Facebook bloggers. Even if some of the reports were exaggerated, there was no way some hidden agenda wasn't going down. With every new bout of craziness, things crept closer to martial law. And then came this. The breakdown of normal society. The same society that condemned him, yet held its maliciousness in check. Aaron had seen strange, cutthroat stuff recently. Riots and beheadings in areas that only recently were perfectly normal. It was on the tube, all glazed by a wall of separation that seemed to remove it from reality. Until this. Until it was in his backyard. He had read the history books, he knew how brutal people could be. This was a dangerous downward spiral.

He was lost in thought when the vehicle slammed to a halt. He flew into the front wall, cracked against a sheet of cold steel, and tumbled onto the floor. Shocked out of his woolgathering, he scrambled into a crouch. In full-on panic mode, his brain was running a million miles a minute as he glanced nervously around. That poor guy he was stuck with had thrown him back into one wall, then forward into another, and then back again. Even more disturbing, none of this had woken him. Aaron thought he might already be dead. He hoped that wasn't the case. He didn't know the guy, but he seemed decent. He definitely wasn't a threat. Aaron didn't mean to be so coldly analytical, yet having this guy around probably worked out for him as well.

He felt guilty and tried to shake that rationalization. It struck him as base and mercenary. He decided to concentrate on something else, when he realized he could check this guy's pulse. Done deal, that would solve this dilemma. If he tried to stay busy, he wouldn't be plagued by all this second-guessing.

And he figured if the guy was still alive, he could find out his name.

Aaron inched forward, paused, moved even closer, and paused again. The truck had resumed movement, and Aaron could feel the temperature dropping. A chill swept in. His arm bristling with goosebumps, his fingertips grew numb and started to ache. The cool air brought with it the noxious fumes of the vehicle's exhaust, and it was making Aaron nauseated. The room kept vibrating as well, which screwed with his ability to focus. He felt dizzy and sick, and every time the truck hit a pothole it reverberated in his stomach.

Trying to distract himself, he looked over at the crumpled, lifeless blob that was Job. The guy looked pale and sort of green, although it struck Aaron that it might be the lighting. If he was still alive, he should be breathing. Aaron cursed himself under his breath for being so stupid and scuttled over.

Extending his right hand, he let his fingers drift under the guy's nostrils. Every bump challenged his balance, and Aaron kept shuffling his feet as he swayed to and fro. He was a little creeped out. And if it turned out this guy was dead, he didn't want to touch the body. His fingertips moved directly under the nose and he didn't feel anything. He wasn't sure, but he knew he was only half-hearted in his effort while distracting himself from the possibility that there was a dead body in front of him. No excuses. He had to bite the bullet and get closer. His fingertips felt a draft, and he leaned closer still. The truck bounced, Job's head rolled, and Aaron jerked his hand away. He admonished himself and extended his hand again. Sure enough, there was a slight movement of warm air. So he was alive. Hopefully he wasn't in a coma or brain-dead. Aaron wondered if that was a real possibility and, if so, what these people would do in that case.

Then the truck violently came to a sudden halt, the tail end rising with the abrupt cessation of forward motion. Aaron slammed into the wall, Job's limp form serving as an involuntary pillow. The shriek of shredding metal erupted from the front as Aaron gasped for breath. The wind had been knocked out of him, and he struggled to stay upright. He heard more tearing metal and a scream, followed by a heavy splat. A cascade of bullets erupted, their high-pitched whines skimming by the sidewalls. A few tore into the bottom of the truck with terrifying force, the undercarriage howling as ricochets slashed through. There was a series of momentary pauses, and then violence would erupt again, the bursts coming from all directions. Some sounded like they were right on the other side of the wall, whereas others sounded like little more than distant echoes. A squall of mangled steel broke up the bursts of gunfire. All was quiet for a moment, and the cacophony started again accompanied by a pulpy burble of liquid splatters and tearing flesh.

Nervous tension wracked Aaron, and he trembled as he peered around for a way out. It looked hopeless, and with every near miss he became increasingly desperate. Then everything stopped. He twitched his ears, listening closely, but there was nothing. He debated whether this was better or worse. Maybe he was the last guy. The doors would open and it would be like some Tarantino movie. Or maybe he'd be overlooked, and whoever did this would just leave. Only then he'd be stuck in here to slowly die of starvation. A quick death would be much preferable.

He was crouched and staring at the slits of light atop the walls when the sound of the rear doors tearing apart echoed through the cabin. Backing against the far wall, he debated whether he should play dead. He was still in the midst of deciding when it was suddenly too late. The rear doors swung wide, and standing in the center, haloed by the blinding rush of light, was that creature.

ARMAGEDDON BOUND

Aaron remained with his back against the wall. He was frozen, unsure of what to even think. How had this thing found him? He wasn't sure where he saw it last, but it had to have been in a different state, a Southern state. The trees and rocks there didn't match the terrain he was used to up here. If that was the case, though, wouldn't it have taken the thing days to get here? It had only been a day at most, although time was becoming a hazy construct. He remembered the strange man he kept running into--the one who hinted at knowing what was behind all this craziness. Was that guy in on this? Was all of it somehow linked? Was this creature in the loop? It wasn't military. It had killed enough soldiers to prove that. But the government definitely had some knowledge of what was going on. They were acting violent and confused— nothing new there— but this rogue thing kept throwing a monkey wrench in their schemes.

The creature stared at Aaron for a minute before gesturing for him to follow. Aaron looked on in shock for a moment, then finally crawled to his feet. If this thing wanted him dead, it had already had plenty of chances to kill him. Even if it was doing the bidding of someone else, it was still treating him better than the government. It hadn't tazed him, and its grip was so lax he *had* managed to escape from it before. Maybe the way his encounters with this thing had unfolded were all merely bad planning on his part. At worst, it could lead to something more abysmal than whatever the government had planned. But he was out of options—and this thing might be the best way for him to get out of D.C. in one piece.

He approached the creature, eyes blinking in the glare. Shielding his sight with a cupped hand, he emitted a hoarse cry.

"Hey! Hey, mister! I'll go with you, but you gotta bring this guy, too."

Aaron hooked a thumb back at Job. The guy was as good as dead if left to fend for himself. Aaron was the prize, and whatever the military wanted this guy for, he would be so much chattel with their main guy gone. They would probably torture him, searching for information he couldn't provide. Aaron didn't even know the guy, but at the same time he didn't want that on his conscience either. He also didn't want to be left alone with the creature.

Aaron stared for a few moments, peering at a creature that stood stock still, its vision trained on Aaron, who in fact could not even tell where the thing was looking. Those weird eyes threw him off. Abruptly, the creature bounded up into the truck and strode over to Job. It stopped short, looking down at Job's limp form. A few tense moments passed, and then it scooped him up, tossed him over its shoulder, and headed for the doorway. Striding right past Aaron, it dismounted in a profoundly unnerving move that was too smooth and unnatural for anything organic. There was no jarring drop, it merely changed levels in one fluid motion and kept on going. Turning on a dime, it headed toward the front of the vehicle. Aaron paused for a moment and marveled at the unfathomable *flow* of the thing. Then he snapped back into focus and scurried out of the truck. Unlike that thing, his knees jarred roughly as he landed, and he clipped around the corner. He was all in a rush until he saw what awaited him.

Spread out beyond the truck were the remnants of a multitude of Humvees. The tires had buckled on a few, the rims curving into the wheel wells under whatever tremendous blows had caved in their front ends. One was on fire, the center buried under a thick blanket of coiling smoke. Curling orange flame licked up from the front tire. Bodies were strewn about like chattel, the remains of some nearly unrecognizable puddles of pinkish organs that were spilling out over blood-stained rags. Others were little more than mangled torsos, a few of them retaining the remnants of a head or limb. A number were complete shells, only with a corpse so badly burned that the stiff figures resembled melted sculptures of stone, their darkened sockets marking what had once been eyes and a mouth. Rivulets of brown ash webbed over the blackened remains of everything, the cloth and the flesh so fused together they formed a continuation of the same charcoal shell. Pinkish chunks were scattered about, some of the bulbous bits crushed and smeared into a thick stain.

One of the Humvees was on its side and the tailgate was missing, revealing a darkened mishmash of an interior. Glistening strands trailed across the gloomy maw. On the top a glimmering array wound down from its coiled perch around the rooftop antenna. Aaron tried to figure out what he was looking at. Then, with a surge of revulsion, he realized they were the unwound cords of a human brain.

He seized up, convulsed and unable to move. Bent over, he tried to retch. Ropy strings of stomach acid were all that made it out, escaping from the corners of his mouth in slimy yellow strings. Although there was nothing in his stomach, he kept dry-heaving. Spasms wracked his chest, and his abdomen felt impossibly tight. He managed to calm himself and have a moment of clarity when the smell of burnt cloth and plastic clogged his lungs. An undertone of cooking gristle crept in and pushed him over the edge, and he could do little more than rock unsteadily as he tried to retch again on an empty stomach. His eyes were squeezed closed, his thoughts clouded in fog, but he knew. He *knew* what this was. He had seen the same slaughter at the cabin. People were simply meat to that thing, grist for the mill. Whatever this was, the intensity of it was breathtaking. So gritty and horrifying. He had to get away. He didn't even feel like he should be seeing this, like it might infect his brain like a virus. Then he realized that he might be the cause. That maybe this thing was massacring for the sake of him, or for possession of him, and if he ran again, this would happen all over again, as many times as it needed to, until he finally was trapped or expired. It was suddenly all so depressing, a dark road with no end he that could see.

Aaron didn't know how long he was immobilized. When he looked up, he could see in the distance the form of that thing with the limp body of Job over its shoulder. It was beckoning to him from across a wide expanse of horrors, the terrain separating them littered with the shredded remnants of bodies and burning vehicles. Smog wafted across the landscape in choking waves, the stench of human innards and the chemical odor of burning rubber a companion. Aaron felt a sense of vertigo, and found that he couldn't stand up straight. He rose slowly, but he couldn't get his bearings. The lightheadedness was so thick he was sure he'd topple at any moment. He managed to make it to his feet, every inch a struggle, but everything was top heavy, and he knew it was only a matter of time before he came crashing down. As he was about to reach an apex, his body almost upright, he started to fall. More like a waking dream than anything real, he lost control of his legs as he collapsed.

As he fell, something hooked under his shoulders. He tried to recognize, to somehow respond, but everything faded to black.

THE FUCK OUT OF DODGE

Maryland sucks. Long roads of nothing, lanes of asphalt barreling through a nighttime tunnel of tree-lined walls—thin walls that shield boring suburbs and industrial warehouses at that, the flora a vain attempt to pretend otherwise.

Maybe I'm biased from having lived nearby, although it's not like Virginia was much better. It did give the impression of having a little more flavor, though. Especially Southern Virginia, once you got away from the stultifying yuppie America of Beltway existence.

I'm so removed from that aspect of my life, it all seems like a long-ago dream. I've traversed the country, hiked the Amazon, and even ventured out into space. I've seen extraterrestrial life and interacted with it firsthand, a reality I barely dreamed was possible. Even when I knew there was life out there, after working for the government had opened my eyes, the physical encounter was still a shock. At the beginning, I figured we were trailing after scraps with the little bit we managed to recover. But now I'm in an alien body, and it looks like I've started some sort of interstellar war. The U.S. I knew is falling apart, and nothing is the same. Yet even with that vast divide in my history, this revulsion to the area still remains.

It feels like I left the region only yesterday. It's funny how I filed away all the grimy details until I'm physically back. The little thoughts that play off all my insecurities and make me second-guess everything. I'm nothing like the man I once was. So much has changed. My senses have expanded. I can see wavelengths, magnetic field lines, thermal imagining. Things no human could imagine. I can sense the time and temperature. Navigation. Everything is clear to me in this body. I can instantly reference anything in my memory. My wits have grown sharper. Nothing about me is remotely human—so why is this still affecting me? At most it should be a passive file of a bygone era.

Yet the experience feels crisp, flooding me with a rush of memories and their associated emotions.

Consciousness being so complex, not to mention the factor of chemical inputs that help make up the receptors, I was terrified that I was losing what made me... me. I don't eat or breathe, and the chemical compositions that feed into responses and actions are no longer a factor, so how could I possibly be the same person? Humans feel better after a good meal, more energetic after a cup of coffee, more clear and invigorated after a good night's sleep. Without that rollercoaster of inputs, do I simply have a more steady conscious state, or have I evolved into a completely different creature? Come to think of it, though, every new input evolves the brain. There is no static consciousness. Maybe I'm pining over something that isn't even there.

I try to shake out of it, to clear the detritus from my head. What's done is done, and there is no going back. Thoughts keep flooding in, and I yearn for a way to prioritize them. When I was on the run, the singularity of my goal kept everything in line. Now everything is scattered, and I don't know what is happening. Maybe all of this is a feature of this body. It was made to be inhabited in the short term for information gathering, paying close attention to minutia more important than evaluating the overall picture. Except that an explorer might need to complete a long-term goal, so that might not be it. I have no idea how any of this plays out, and all I've received so far are deceptions and half-truths. This shell wasn't built for humans, so the effects might be completely unpredictable. The Al'lak hinted at as much.

I clear my thoughts and try to focus on the road.

The gears of the M35 whine, and the sleeping kid in the seat next to me emits a nasal snore. A twin column of light stretches out before me but fails to illuminate the endless stretch of road. The metal slab of the dash below is alive with a swarm of gauges and levers, the soft red glow of the fuel meter a constantly falling gas needle. This truck is as interminably slow as it is a gas guzzler. The canvas shell ruffles in the wind, its steady patter a background to the hum of the engine and whine of the gears. Occasionally the canvas snaps sharply, the sharp noise a piercing break in the drone. Trucks intermittently pass by, one of the only signs of a society that is otherwise obscure to me. I have no idea what the current political situation is. Interstate travel might be complicated, and the Northern states were always more cohesive as a unit. I roll down the window. As a human, I felt it put me in touch with the road.

Now the glass is a barrier I no longer need. The wind rushes in, and although I register the drop in temperature, it doesn't affect me. I focus on my hearing, scaling down the frequencies the M35 emanates so I can get a better sense of my surroundings.

I detect a hum in the distance. It sounds like it's up high and has a deep, pulsing frequency. It steadily grows louder, as if the source is approaching. I try to isolate the noise, to close off the other sounds that are buffeting me, and run a comparison in my memory banks. Only I don't have time. As I start to discern a pale red glow in the sky, a deluge of brilliance drowns out everything. If my vision didn't adjust so quickly, I'd be blinded, which something tells me is the intent. I bring the truck to a halt.

The only people likely to be flying right now are military or paramilitary. Either that group in D.C. has found me or some militia has stumbled upon what they are about to find out is a serious mistake. My trek across this country the first time was a swath of violence. I remained unscathed, even if my transportation rarely lasted long. But this will require a more surgical approach as I'll need to keep both this vehicle and its occupants intact. I doubt they are in a "shoot first and ask questions later" mindset. If that were the case, they would have already lashed out. They want something, and it has something to do with that kid, I'm sure.

I sit in the driver's seat with the engine running and the transmission shifted into neutral. The engine emits a steady rumble, causing the red glow of the dash panel to vibrate. The helicopter blades thump steadily overhead, its spotlight cascade enveloping the truck. That's a disorientation trick, which tells me they have no idea what they are dealing with. I augment my hearing and pick out the reassuring nasal exhalations of the kid and his friend in the back. Nothing happens at first, the helicopter hovering somewhere above the brilliance. Then I pick up the vibration of approaching vehicles. They sound heavy, too, probably some HMMVWs, perhaps a Stryker as well. The guys in D.C. might have tapped into some local reserve group, although I might not be on their agenda anymore and this might not be about the kid. It feels like it's been a year since I left, although there's been some kind of time distortion.

Everything appears fresh, as if it happened recently.

The pounding of footsteps brings me to attention. It shouldn't be long now.

Troops emerge from the darkness and swarm around the truck. A legion of barely visible silhouettes, the intense light casting them into stark angles of washed-out contours. They are definitely military, and more heavy duty than reserve troops. I try to sharpen my outlook, only I can't. My vision is strangely disturbed. This is a first. I attempt to concentrate again, but it's no use, my thoughts in a fog. No, not quite that. I just don't feel up to speed, as if I was just a human, stripped of all my advanced functions. This is screwing up the plan. I can't stay in this truck and operate blindly. If I get out into the forefront, it should kick-start whatever this is. I'll need to take them out before they get to the M35 or its occupants, but that shouldn't be a problem.

I crack the door and drop down. When I hit the concrete, the impact takes a moment to register, like I'm on a time delay. I lurch forward, angling for the nearest form. Although his outline is blurred, I chalk it up to the intense light and my inability to control my vision. I'd be able to filter the disruption under normal circumstances and this must be some aberration. I feel the pressure on my chest as I'm bathed in bullets, the muzzle flashes yellow bursts in a deluge of brilliance. I'm within steps of the closest soldier, his form still a haze. I aim for the center and take a flying leap.

Everything blurs even more once I'm in motion. The rustle of clothing whizzes me by, and I plow headfirst into pavement. Asphalt shreds as I crater the road. It's all still a woolly maelstrom, and I feel like I'm watching from inside an armored shell I can't control. I struggle to my feet and twist around, my vantage even further degraded. What I assume is a soldier consists of a cloud of overlapping shadows. Bursts erupt, and I behold an impossible throng of trailing flashes. Bullets impact against my body, pushing me back, my feet gouging grooves in the pavement. More gunfire joins in, the multitude deluging me and scrambling my already shaky perception. I'm convinced a legion of troops is firing at me, but I'm seeing even more than could possibly be there, the trace of every projectile scrambled into a horde of incoming missiles. The light slowly dims, the pounding airwaves of the helicopter drawing away. I stumble to my feet against the swarm of bullets, but the light dies out and the onslaught draws down into a staccato of shorter blasts. The haze of shredded asphalt wafts across, glimmers of muzzle flashes peppering the steady glare of headlights. I try to focus on a single soldier or vehicle, but it's all a jumbled disarray. I'm seeing three of everything, a smoky filter of rock and gunpowder obfuscating the view, and I can't adjust to all of the inputs.

The gunfire dies down. It's only enough to keep winging me every few minutes and nudging me off balance. The vehicles are retreating in the distance, and everything slowly fades away. The whistling of the wind the only accompaniment to the glowing orb of the sole remaining headlight on my truck, its lone gleam burrowing through a thinning wisp of smog. The stupor in my head is gone.

I clamber to my feet and dart back to the cab. The kid is gone. I head to the tail of the M35. The tailgate was left down, and the canvas rear door flaps cut loose. I hoist myself up and view an empty cargo bed. My fury mounts as I realize that this was planned. My presence was anticipated and nullified, which tells me the kid was the real target. If this was the military, they must know a lot more than they did previously. Maybe they knew it all along and it took this long to trickle down to the local levels, but they apparently have something that can deal with me. I'm not sure what this has to do with the other party I met on the road earlier, the older guy who treated me like I was not worth his time. I don't know if one is in bed with the other or if they are playing some sort of game. That guy cropped up later with a change of heart, but even that could have been a ruse. He was the first one with the technology to easily disable me, and if he is not working with this paramilitary group, I don't know where they acquired their ability. Then again, I don't even know how many players are on this field, or what the real story is. But I do know that they've convinced me what my next target should be.

SOMEWHERE IN DELAWARE

Hours pass, the wind a steady whistle through the holes in the windshield. I trek down an abandoned highway, one I'd passed ages ago when I was still human and the country in one piece. The roads had been filled with a steady stream of traffic, the taillights a ribbon of crimson in the dark. That was then. Now four abandoned lanes stretch out before me in the glare of my single headlight. Warped and pale, the rocky surface looks worn and ancient, like the vestiges of a long-dead civilization. A thin barrier of trees walls the sides, giving the illusion that the remnants of humanity aren't thronged just beyond. It's funny, this modern society of social media and long commutes to soul-numbing jobs actually eroded people's connection to their neighbors. Acting as social groups being the evolutionary advantage that helped Homo sapiens win the extinction race with the Neanderthals, it's typical of the species that they abandon their genetic advantage at the very moment when they need it most.

The night is clear and bright, a legion of stars visible now that the artificial lights of humanity have been extinguished. A few dark clouds roll through, their gossamer wisps trailing from dense central masses. The Delaware Bridge should be coming up soon. It's a straight shot from there to Maine, about nine hours at my current speed, provided there are no more hiccups. That place in Maine has to be where they are taking him. I remember hearsay about it being a naval base that was officially closed in 2005. Only it was never really shut down. All the conspiracy nuts were crazy about it. Maine in general was supposed to be a hotbed of UFO activity, and if things are as dire as I'm being led to believe, there might be something to it. The highways are emptier than I would expect. Even since the collapse of society, I've seen an occasional vehicle on the roads, but everything out here looks utterly abandoned. The overarching road lights are out, the rest stations are desolate, and not even the slightest glimmer can be seen through the trees.

I duck my head and peer out the window. The bulk of the atmosphere blocks out the ambient starlight. Only the shaft of my headlight pierces through the mist. I stomp on the high-beams switch and slow down to forty. This is not good. The Deuce is slow enough as is, and all this extra traveling is a waste of time. I have the sneaking suspicion that whatever is going on with the kid is time sensitive.

The smothering isolation I'm embroiled in does not bode well. I try extending the range of my hearing, listening for the slightest vibration. There's the rustle of leaves and underbrush in the wind, the scamper of rodents in the woods, but nothing else.

After another mile I see a metal skeleton on the left. It's only a few glimmering beams contorted at odd angles. The twisted shafts jut out of a low-lying smog. I switch to infrared, but instead of everything growing clearer there's a foggy distortion.

That's strange.

I switch back and focus my vision. The beams look like crossed metal frame rails, their hidden origins buried deep within the dark recesses of a central structure. It has the look of a utilitarian vehicle, possibly military. As I close in, I notice clumps of rubbery black where the wheels would be. The tires have melted away, the slop of deformed rubber smothering the jutting silver edges of the rims. I slow to a rolling stop as I close in.

It's definitely military, and looks like an HMMWV. The shell of the roll cage is now apparent, as is the slender column of an antenna. I crank down the window and switch to infrared. The area looks foggier than usual. There's no static distortion like there was last time when that military unit showed up, yet everything is slightly out of focus. It's as if every crevice is emanating a smoky brume. I crack open the door and hop down. It's a few feet to the wreck, and I cross over to it stealthily. Feeling a little less impervious after my last encounter, I have the suspicion that I might be walking into a trap. As I draw in, I see that the darkened shell contains nothing other than a jumble of scorched metal and ash. There's no top left, and no trace of anything organic. I can't even be sure there were troops in this thing when it got hit. If there were any organic remains, they have been removed.

I get the sense that none of this was recent. It might even date back to the beginning of the conflict. I switch to thermal imaging but pick up nothing. There must be some factor I'm not aware of that's playing tricks with my infrared—unless this body is finally starting to break down. I don't know how much of the control over it is me, how much is the body, or how long the two can continue to sync. I was told that I am the only one who has remained coherent in this suit for an extended period, and although I'm likely the first human who has inhabited it, anything else told to me is suspect. Who knows if the creatures that supposedly made the suit were telling the truth? It might be a relic from a more advanced civilization and they are as mystified by its workings as I am.

I pick up a faint creaking in the direction of the bridge, and I swivel my head. My headlights are reflecting off the pillars. They look like gleaming strips of white in the fog-shrouded distance. Drooping beyond them are metal support cables. They look slightly askew, like some of the cables have ruptured and twisted the supporting joints. I climb back in the M35 and roll forward. The front end suddenly drops and I fly into the dashboard. My face tears into the flat surface, ripping through as I grind to a halt, half-buried in a rat's nest of black wires. I place my palms against the metal and push out. The cab is now pitched at a downward angle. My hand has broken off a portion of the steering wheel, smashed through the windshield, and is inches from touching the rough edges of a torn asunder asphalt highway. The road has risen to eye level, and I rotate my head from side to side for a minute, thinking I might have fallen into a trap. I let a moment pass and nothing happens. I didn't take down a pitfall cover, and no one is rushing in to take advantage. I must have fallen into a pothole. I probably just overlooked it with all my concentration on the bridge.

Hoisting myself upright on what's left of the wheel, I reach for the door. The remainder tears off and I drop chest first into the steering column. My hand is still clinging to a chunk of the steering wheel as it sails through a gap in the broken windshield. The horn blares loudly, and I instinctively bounce back up. Balancing my palm on the dash, I feel around with my toes until they reach the edge of the doorframe. I reach over and attempt to open the door, but it's jammed. I punch at it and my fist flies through the metal. Aside from a slight bend, the door stays much the same as it was, only with my hand now stuck through it. Enraged, I furiously extract my arm. Then a realization flashes over me.

Anger is mostly a chemical reaction. An inanimate object is making me furious. That kind of gut reaction is completely nonsensical. I calm down and smoothly push out the hinges. Tapping on the handle, the door flies free, skipping a few times across the pavement before gliding to a rest in the bushes beyond. I let a moment pass, survey the rubble, and climb out.

The blackness is almost absolute. I glance back at the sunken truck. The headlight beams on the rim of a crater, the reflected glow faintly illuminating the front. Clouds having smothered the ambient starlight. I scroll over to night vision and the view becomes downright comical. The vehicle is pitched at a 45-degree angle, the front end buried in a pothole. The more I look, the more I am convinced that this is military. First the Humvee and now cratered roadblocks. I scan the ground, first around my truck, then toward the nearby Humvee, steadily circling out until I am viewing the rest of the road. That's when I notice why the support cables on the bridge looked off. The ones on the left entail a frayed jumble of silvery strands. Some have snapped, the tension on the remaining cords having slackened so quickly they rebounded into kinked tangles of wire. Others have managed to hold on, the overextended cords clinging for dear life. The bridge itself has dropped in places on the left, its highway a dramatic slope that varies up and down like speed bumps under the tension of the remaining supports. About a hundred feet out it comes to a jagged end. On the other side of a two-hundred-foot watery gap, a rough edge of concrete resurrects into a road. I scan the ground around me. There are no shells, indicating this wasn't a firefight. Am I so important that such a measure was taken to impede my progress? Maybe. Or maybe the politics of everything are more complex than I'm aware of. I think if they could kill me outright they would have done so, although I might be overestimating my importance. It's more likely I'm being used, and neither side has clear motives. The one that has communicated with me is giving me part of the story. Either they don't want to elaborate or they don't know how, and the closest thing I have to an answer might be in Maine.

I approach the front end of the truck and peer down into the hole. Cracked concrete descends into a hollow of packed soil, the edges of the rubble burying the mangled front end. The hood of the truck is heavily dented on the left, the lip closest to the wall rippled into grooves of cracked paint and stressed metal. The grille is wedged into the sidewall a few feet above the bottom, and it's all keeping the truck aloft from a bottom that is a few feet lower still.

I edge to the rim, reach in through the gap that was once a door, and hold down on the clutch. Stretching farther, I push the shifter into neutral.

Withdrawing, I grasp the edge of the doorframe and slide down into the pit. My feet move blindly and kick broken chunks of dirt free as I descend the narrow gap. I twist and duck my right arm under the front axle. With a push, I hoist it up, the front complaining with a nails-on-chalkboard screech. The thing smoothly ascends at first until it jars to an abrupt stop a few feet from the top. The PTO winch is probably caught on the underside of the pavement. I re-adjust and torque it a little more. The lip of the crater holds for a minute, then dramatically bursts, chunks of asphalt flying free as they bounce across the pavement. Still holding the vehicle aloft, I shove it backward. With a whine of gears it rolls a few inches and grinds to a halt. I leap out of the pit and back up onto the roadway.

I think I caught sight of a side road in my peripheral vision as I approached. If I'm lucky it leads to another bridge spanning this same river. I climb back into the truck and try to start the engine. It takes a few turns but finally fires up. I put it in reverse, circle around in a wide loop, and head back the way I came. If nothing comes up, I would hate to sacrifice this vehicle, but I can always come back and cross that river on foot.

A Slight Detour

The night sky is blanching into the pale of early morn, the overhead stars dying a slow death as the hazy morning mist steadily drowns out their light. Wind tears in through the gaping hole that was once a windshield, the engine emitting a steady rattle. The sun has yet to surface, although the lower reaches of the horizon have already illumined into a pale line of blue.

After about a mile, a trail pops up on the right. It's connected to the main thoroughfare in a worn-out affair of tar-besieged rocks and sandy asphalt, the skeletal limbs of yellowed roots edging out into the pavement. Dipping down through a small field, it levels out and delves into a throng of trees.

As I swivel what's left of the wheel, the truck jolts over the connecting bump, the front end dropping jarringly as it descends into the sand. The fall into the pothole damaged something in the vehicle, and now it's clattering loudly as it bounces along the trail and into the woods. Loose branches scrape the metal frame, the wiry tendrils snapping into the windshield gap. The stiff suspension and uneven road buffet the truck about, the turmoil of the lashing branches an endless barrage.

Once immersed in the woods, I can see that the trees haven't quite thickened into a forest. The trunks are a little scattered, their openings revealing the glittering surfaces of waterlogged meadows. Streaks of early morning sunlight arc down through the tree limbs. Dead logs and leaves float in the swampy morasses, their shimmering edges entangling with the pole-like stalks of the cattail weeds.

A little farther, and the woods swallow me up to the point

I can no longer see the road behind me. A misty smog is rising out of the swampy quagmires all about. This resembles more of a Louisiana bayou than anything in the Northern woods. Even though I can't feel the temperature, I register it as fifty degrees, which is on the cool side for this time of year.

The haze in front of the truck parts enough for me to spot the wooden rails of a narrow bridge. It must traverse a creek, although the low-lying fog remains impenetrable. As the front tires roll onto the bridge, the timbers creak and droop, the rickety expanse giving the impression that it will give at any moment. I don't think this thing was built to hold the weight of a military transport or anything close to it, but I make it across and continue into the wooded abyss, my wounded truck clattering as it scales the sandy path.

An hour passes, and nothing changes, the trail still buried in fog. The roughness of the ride tells me it was abandoned long ago. The swarm of overhanging tree limbs have thickened, their wiry tips jumping out at odd angles in the prevailing mist. I detect a high concentration of MVOCs and ammonia. If I had a sense of smell, this area would register as pretty rank. I scan the periphery, but can barely see past my pockmarked hood. Cottony tendrils of smog drift in through my broken windshield. The ropy haze verges on a physical thing, the rolling tendrils overwhelming the floorboards and burying my feet. My skin is registering a slight pressure as well. The fog has some mass behind it. Then a raindrop catches me, quickly followed by another. Big, thick drops, the precursor of a thunderstorm. A minute later it comes, the downpour so intense that the streams of rainwater are pounding the hood like incoming projectiles and rebounding off in tiny geysers.

Rain flows in through the shattered windshield, pelting me in an ever-escalating torrent. A watery sheath runs down my extended arm, rivulets dribbling off in undulating streams. The floor beneath my feet quickly becomes a pool, the water rising until it is level with the doorframe. Wisps of peeled bark and clumps of leaves float in the gathering basin, cluttering in about my ankles. Then it starts to trickle out of the door wells, amplifying into mini waterfalls every time I hit a bump. The darker forms of stone pillars materialize on the distant corners of the road, their silhouettes barely visible in the deluge. As I try to focus on them, the contours fade from view in the watery brume. They are mirages, tricks of the light, and if I were still human, that is what I would think they were. Only my memory has sharpened since then, and I know I saw something.

The rain picks up even more, the skies pouring down in true biblical fashion. The tires slip in the wet soil. These NDT military tires were never that good on wet roads. A loud clap echoes, like a gunshot has hit the undercarriage, and the truck drops a few inches and starts shaking ferociously. The tires must have blown out. I roll to a stop and shut off the engine. Sitting absolutely still, I pan through the wavelengths that compose my hearing.

Aside from the constant pounding on the roof, there is no other sound. If someone laid a trap, they aren't around to see its outcome. Grabbing the metal edge of the windshield, my fingers crunching through shards of glass, I pull myself up and swing out of the vehicle.

The roadway is completely blanketed by the deluge, transforming it into a muddy coursing stream several inches deep. Its sheen a pale tan from all the kicked-up soil, the currents gush and twist in convoluted streams like some living thing. Tiny waterspouts from the barrage of incoming drops burst forth from the currents, the torrential downpour feeding the frenzy. Wading through it, I circle around the front of the truck and bend down. Only the top halves of the tires are visible above the water, but it is enough for me to see they are shredded. Both tires have the same pattern, the cuts too clean and similar in appearance to be accidental. I circle through the current and head toward the back of the truck, the blistering downpour limiting visibility to only a few feet. Not far beyond the rear wheel, I see a dark mass under the water. Squatting down, I run my fingers along the ground. Sure enough, they hit metal. I grip an edge and pull up a chain of road spikes.

Holding aloft a dripping string of corroded spikes, I debate whether this was intended for me. There was little chance anyone knew which way I would head or the detours I would encounter, so the real question is whether this was meant to prevent intruders or to ambush them. If it was meant to ambush them, was something being hidden? Was it for protection? Did the current climate of instability instigate it, or was it pre-existing? Regardless, the vehicle is toast. I rise to my feet and look around.

The rain refuses to abate, as does the fog. I glance one more time at the beaten silhouette of the truck, then walk past it and into the heart of darkness.

Oh, What a Tangled Web We Weave

I am scanning with all my receptors and picking up nothing. It makes me feel naked and vulnerable, a situation I have recently found myself in all too frequently. The atmosphere is so distorted in the storm that I can barely see the hulking shafts of tree trunks. Branches appear out of nowhere, their boughs whipping furiously at me as I pass. There's a faint glimmer in the distance. The source is hard to isolate, the ferocious downpour occluding my sensory inputs and cutting off my connection to everything but my immediate surroundings. I'm not even sure if I am still on the trail. Even though I've avoided the trees so far, it's too dim and the torrent is too thick to be sure.

The ground feels fairly even beneath my tread, so I assume I am still on the road or at least a nearby footpath. The wispy traces of a rectangular pillar materialize out of the fog. I draw a little closer and see that it is a waist-high pedestal of piled rocks. It might be a trail marker, although it doesn't look modern. Its watery sheen and the blinding rainstorm obscure most of the details, but judging by the pitted and mossy condition of the stones, it must be ancient. I straighten up and continue down the trail.

The rain lets up into a sprinkle, and as I stumble across heavy debris it becomes clear that I'm not on a main road anymore. I crouch down and try to take a closer look through the low-lying fog. It's a narrow and slightly concave path of muddy dirt, the soil glistening with moisture but no longer a small river. Waist-high embankments rise on the sides, specks of mica glimmering in the loam. The tendrils of roots and sharp edges of rocks jut out of the packed soil. This route is far too narrow for any vehicle. As I follow the path, more of those strange pillars materialize out of the mist, lining the sides in a spotty queue whenever the earthen embankments level with the ground.

Thunder resounds in the distance and flashes split the stormy sky, throwing the woods into brief fits of stark contrast. A dangling shade in the distance catches my eye in one of the flashes. The lighting strikes again and I get a better look. It appears to be the skinned remnants of a human body, and an older one at that. The muscles are grayed and wrinkled, thick rivulets of black blood are pooled in the crevices. Movement on my left snags my attention and I snap around. Closer to the road, there is another hanging corpse, this one with its skin intact. It appears to be a young male, the body only a few days old. It's naked, the flabby skin a sickly bluish-gray, the hair a matted tangle of brown clumps atop a swollen face. Pale blue irises stare vacantly into the distance, the eyes bulging out of a constraining lip of skin. The mouth is agape, a dried trickle of blood trailing from the lower lip and dangling off the chin. Has society has sunk so low that this is now the new norm? Every man for himself, the more isolated the environs the more severe the barbarity? A humming starts in my head, growing more intense by the second. I try to shake it loose but it holds fast, the intensity growing until it is physically pummeling my cranium. It's hard to focus, and everything becomes an uncontrollable blur. In a choked string of thoughts, I realize that this has only happened when someone has directly fucked with me. I don't know if that is the case now, or if this is something more generic, but whatever the source of that signal, it's nearby. First the roadblock, and now this... all of it might be no detour after all.

A dangling shade in the distance catches my eye

While the pounding in my head doesn't let up, I grow more accustomed to it as I stamp through the fog. An hour goes by—an hour of shambling in steadily dimming light, my head filled with wool. As I stumble down the trail, I see more bodies hanging from trees, some of them wearing military uniforms. I was never an expert, and the limited view makes me unable to ascertain the branch. From the waterlogged olive BDUS and black combat boots, they look like grunts. Low-level ground troops.

The trail slants upward, the hanging rope-like appendages of vines dangling down into a tunneling path. Wide, contorted trunks close in on the sides, their thickness warping the trail into a dark tunnel. The sensation of my feet notice that the dirt path comes to an abrupt end in a pitted, mossy stone stairwell. I can't see much in the haze and darkness, but the steps appear to sweep up and off to the left, the huge trunks of misshapen trees cloistering in on both sides. I ascend the stairs slowly, my feet slipping on the coarse blocks. The right side of the stairwell becomes an uneven wall of packed soil and jutting roots, the left opening up and falling away into a sheer drop that descends into a shadowy abyss. I can only assume a forest lies at the bottom, the depths too dim for me to make out anything.

The stairwell curves, and the leathery bulwark of distorted trunks takes over, crushing in on the sides until it all becomes a dark, twisting tunnel once again. As I climb, the glow steadily grows until I finally pass through a circular portal of vines and up onto a better maintained flight of steps. A pale mist dampens the air, the blue light of a coming dawn now cresting the upper echelons of the trees. *Was I in there that long?* My senses remain dulled, but I'm getting used to this state and beginning to cope. The pounding in my head has sharpened, though, and it adds a piercing edge to everything.

I pass through the portal and out into the grounds of a weed-strewn, dilapidated courtyard of red brick. The mist has stopped now, much of the fog has dissipated, and sprawled out in a darkened niche at the end of the courtyard are the L-shaped remnants of a two-story house. No, more of a building than a house, the foundation formed of off-sized blocks of fitted stone. It's reminiscent of ancient Mayan buildings in Mexico, only the stones are smaller and of the dark, northern variety. Thick spreads of green moss cover everything, fanning out and augmenting the breaks in furry clusters.

Stranger still, an enormous tree rises out of the middle, its trunk as wide as a room, a swarming flurry of thick roots spilling down the shingled, mossy roofs and drooping into the courtyard below. The closer I draw toward it, the worse the pounding in my head grows. By the looks of it, the place was abandoned long ago, although most of those hanging bodies couldn't be more than a few weeks old. Then again, they were around the base, at the bottom of the stairs. I can't even be sure they are associated with this, or for that matter, what their connection is. Whatever is in that building is affecting me, although it might not be directed at me per se. I would imagine this area has been extensively explored, and none of this could have escaped scrutiny, but none of that matters right now. There's some weird shit going down, and not having full control of my senses is throwing me off on tangents that have nothing to do with my current agenda, which would be finding that kid and getting to Maine. I'm not even sure I should be wasting my time with this.

Then again, considering I have no vehicle, I'm in the middle of nowhere, and this might be the same weakness that was exploited to take that kid from me in the first place, maybe I can find some way to deal with whatever this is since I'm stuck here anyway.

I step out of the tunneled stairwell and into the courtyard. Weeds jut out of the cracks in the brick amid pools of dark soil. The sky has lightened, and the bricks of the courtyard have no pools of water, even though it just rained, and there is no way they dried out this fast. As I step in, the pounding in my head intensifies. It's almost a physical thing, and the sensation throws me off, narrowing my ability to focus. The building before me appears dark and damp, but beyond that I can't control my vision enough to get a good look into the interior. I glance around the courtyard. The reddish bricks terminate in overgrowths of weeds and bushes. The whole scene is far too silent. I reason that maybe animals are sensitive to the same vibration that is affecting me, and it's scaring them away. As I cross the plaza, the roots of that massive tree in the center draw ever closer, their ropy tendrils sprawling across the cobblestone and cracking the surface as they burrow into it. I step over a knotty dark gray outgrowth and into the dark archway of the door.

As I pass the threshold, the pounding magnifies into a searing agony. Grabbing my head, I drop to my knees, my environs reduced to a mindless throb, my surroundings registering only as flickering flashes amid intense waves of pain. I think I hear a scraping, but it's hard to make out anything with the jackhammer in the base of my skull. Then, in a snap, everything goes blank.

So Much for Blacksburg

Dana wasn't sure how she felt about having Tommy tag along. She had a pretty good read on him, better than any of the guys, but things were getting tight.

She didn't want anything bad to happen to him. He was a lost cause sort of kid, the one with a sarcastic edge that was more clever than the other guys. It didn't hurt that he wasn't bad to look at, and he was the only one in on the joke. The joke that the rest of the guys bought hook, line, and sinker—the whole machismo, "I'm a hunter-gather, only I really mooch off my parents" deal. All the guys pretended to be tough, strutting around wearing their cut-off band shirts and boots, traces of gothic jewelry festooned about their wrists and neck, all of it cheap Renaissance Fair type stuff that they took way too seriously. What was hysterical was they all made a big fuss about the cheap weapons they had, which were mostly low-quality knives and fancied-up items like baseball bats.

Tommy had normal-length black hair, not the Mohawk or dreadlocks of all the other guys, and it was always covered by a plain black leather baseball cap. Even his jacket, a light, European-looking thing, avoided being the "punk rock" standard. He had real stubble that he kept shaved, and a gloomy, young Johnny Depp face. All the girls liked him, and he'd bedded more than a few. He never worked at it, it just happened. He and Dana had made out, but it hadn't gone any further than that. She knew what he was all about, and the minute he slept with someone he treated them like less of a person. The weird thing about him was that he approached everything as if he couldn't be bothered, which made him a great foil for all the strutting machismo and bursting male hormones of the other guys. But the same charm might prove an impediment if some real shit went down.

Right as it all hit the fan, he had tossed out some comments that the rest had dismissed as his normal craziness. Only Dana could swear they held more weight. The "they let us go" bit hadn't escaped her, nor had the coincidence that he and that friend of his had shown up moments before everything got seriously crazy. They might even have brought it with them. Or some part of it.

Dana craned her head slightly so she could still see the road and Tommy at the same time, and asked, "Hey, Tommy? Do you know anything about those people that just stormed the house?"

He didn't answer. With his typical pale-faced indifference, he stared out the window and shrugged. Although she had expected as much from him now was not the time.

"Tommy! What the fuck! This is serious. Do you know what this is about?"

"No."

"Why did you say they let us go?"

He looked out the window and mumbled, "It's obvious, isn't it?"

Dana was now pissed off. She raised her voice and demanded, "Well, do us all a favor and enlighten us, won't you?"

Tommy sighed, and after a few moments he said, "This is the fucking Army. You think a bunch of teenagers could outsmart them and get away unless they wanted it to happen?"

"Tommy, you know you're always welcome, but it's not cool if you brought trouble down on us," Dana said. "Things were getting weird, but they didn't tee off until you arrived. Do you know something or not?"

Tommy sighed again, still staring out the window. It was driving Dana crazy, and she was about to explode. As she started to speak, Tommy responded.

"I don't know. Shit just got crazy and I decided to come down here. I only have my grandparents up in Fairfax, and they are useless. As I was about to leave, these guys show up at the house. I hear them bossing around my grandparents, and then what sounds like them being forcibly restrained. Then Aaron shows up, they flip out, I grab a gun, and—"

"Where did you get a gun from?"

"I just had it, okay? I went out there, my grandma is out cold, my granddad is all tied and it looks like he'd been roughed up. There was some jackbooted thug there, and I shot the guy."

"Was he with the government? Did you shoot a government guy! Is he dead?"

Dana was freaking out, whipping her head back to stare at him and barely watching where she was going.

Chris's face was pale, his eyes were glued to the road, and he hysterically barked, "You're gonna crash the car!"

"Fuck, Tommy, did you kill someone?"

"Yeah. Sorta."

"Sorta? You killed him! You killed him and now we're all involved!"

There was a tremendous jolt, and the 4Runner's right tire bounced up a curb and onto the sidewalk. The kid in the passenger seat yelled, "Watch out! You're gonna get us all killed!"

Flipping back around, Dana's eyes were so wide they were popping out. Every nerve on end, sweat trickled down her temple. She could feel the truck vibrating, like she'd bent the rim, only she didn't dare take her eyes off the road. Without looking back, she yelled, "Tommy! What the fuck! What's going on?"

Tommy said nothing and simply stared out the window.

"Tommy, I'll stop the fucking car! I'll park it right here and we can all wait until you answer me!"

Panicked, Chris snapped, "No, Dana! Don't fucking do that! We'll all die! We have to get out town ASAP. We'll try to figure this shit out later. Tommy can wait. What's done is done."

Speeding down a two-lane street and past an eerily vacant spread of conservatively manicured lawns fronting the darkened façades of small businesses, they raced through a red light, narrowly missing an oncoming car. It blared its horn, the sound fading quickly as they continued picking up speed. Flying down the streets, the vehicle thumping with the vibration of the bent rim, the whipping, bass-heavy sound of a helicopter broke through.

Tommy and Chris craned their heads and peered out. The highway hit another intersection, this one a circular turnaround, and Dana jerked the wheel, attempting to arc around the grassy plot in the center. Two wheels left the ground, and Chris and Tommy both yelled in panic. Running on adrenaline, Dana snapped back.

"Shut the fuck up! I'm doing my best!"

She was at the breaking point with both Tommy and Chris. It wasn't like they had stepped up to do anything. They were acting like little kids, and as usual she was expected to be the mom. If it were up to these guys they'd still be back at the Fort licking their asses and talking shit.

The truck bounded out of the circle and onto Main Street. All she had to do was get to Prices Fork Road, then on Highway 460, and from there it was a straight shot into the mountains. Provided they had no pursuit, and the vehicle survived, they could chill out there and figure out a game plan.

KATAHDIN, MAINE

They had been in the air for hours. Aaron was strapped into some sort of plastic folding seat, in a weird-looking flying craft that was unlike anything he had seen before. He didn't know whether to think of it as a plane, a helicopter, or some combination of both. He knew from the brief glimpse he had gotten outside that it had wings like a plane. Only they were burdened with large turbines and propellers that were angled upward, like on a helicopter. The craft was long and thin, like some experimental military aircraft. Even though he had never been in a helicopter before, the inside of this thing didn't look anything like what he had pictured. Rows of folding seats lined both walls, a crazy, complex array of steel beams encircling the interior as some sort of heavy-duty structural support. The spaces between were interspersed with depressed pockets filled with bundles of wires and metal pipes. A few bright yellow stickers were plastered on the beams, blocks of black lettering commingling with arrows like job sites Aaron had seen.

Jackbooted soldiers sat bolt upright next to him and Job. Wearing heavy black gear, like some urban assault squad, their faces were buried under visor-fronted helmets, and each was casually holding aloft an M16. Every one of them had an impassive, blank stare.

Aaron shivered in the cold bite of the ambient air. His nose was running and he sniffled, dabbing at it with his sleeve. The cabin was heavy with the scent of sterile metal and grease, a slight tang of gunpowder underlying it all. His feet dangled over the edge of the chair and barely touched the floor, and it was making his thighs grow numb. He looked down at a labyrinthine tangle of metal blocks and rubber mats. A few weird circular depressions fostering large metal rings blossomed out of the floor. Aaron figured they were probably the entrance to a hidden compartment. This had to be military, or some specialized agency linked to the military. He wanted to ask what was happening, but was too nervous, and the soldiers looked deadly serious. He heard a groan, and swiveled his head. Harnessed in a seat across from him, Job appeared to be waking up.

"Kid...what's...what's going on..."

He was mumbling, his eyes barely open, his head rolling from side to side. He jerked his chest forward, and moaned.

"My back...it's on fire..."

Then he sunk back into a slouch and cradled his bruised head. "Fuck...everything hurts..."

Aaron stared wide-eyed. He didn't know what to say. This guy was in pretty bad shape. First that animal in the parking garage had mauled him, then that car crash had knocked him out. He definitely had a concussion, and maybe even some internal damage. Those claw marks on his back might be infected as well. Aaron realized that he might not make it, but he was too terrified to say anything. He didn't think the soldiers knew the extent of the guy's wounds. If they wanted him dead they would have finished him off a long time ago. Over the rush of the wind and buzz of the motor he mumbled, "*Hey!*"

There was no response. "Hey!" he said, louder this time. Still nothing. The soldiers didn't even acknowledge him.

"He's going to die!" The guy to his right arced his head slightly. "Did you hear me?"

"We are almost there. He'll be taken care of," the soldier said in a monotone, and turned his head back.

Aaron was scared, and a little shocked the guy had responded. Not only that, he looked pissed off. Any more might be pushing it. Aaron sat, mouth agape, trying to think of something, anything to say that wouldn't make matters worse. His ears popped and he realized they were descending. The interior was dimly lit by a few overhead phosphorescent lights. Nestled in their shell, Aaron heard a whirring noise, and the thumping of the propellers grew in prominence. There was a startling jolt, and everything suddenly felt more solid. A moment later, the rear hatch dropped open. The misty light of a cold dawn poured in, the frozen smell of woods in the winter flowing in with a gust of cool air. The soldiers immediately came to life, releasing the safety belts and standing as upright as the low ceiling would allow. All but two filed out of the cabin. Aaron crossed his arms and shivered. His nose was running again, and the snap of cold air had jolted him to trembling, bleary eyed attention. The soldiers next to him and Job rose after the rest had finished exiting, reached over to loosen the straps, dug hands into their armpits, and pulled them upright. Angling them toward the door, they drove them forward.

Outside of the craft, a gale kicked in, and Aaron's ears started burning. The air nippy and misty, Aaron realized his legs were asleep when he tried to walk straight. The tingling limbs refused to cooperate, and he stumbled down the ramp and onto a wide concrete expanse. His cheeks flushed, and he tried to compress his neck into the collar of his leather jacket. Behind him, Job was in way worse shape. Barely short of toppling over, he looked a wreck as he staggered down the ramp. A strong gust hit Aaron, and with numb arms he hugged himself closer. Strands of his Mohawk fluttered off to the side, the chill biting into his exposed temples.

As they rounded the airship, the gaping maw of a vast tunnel stretched out before them. It protruded a few feet out of a rocky mountainside in a tube formed of thick concrete blocks. The base of the tube melded into a furrowed rock cliff that scaled up into the clouds, the entrance gilded with a metallic lip that had the words "Katahdin Mountain Complex" stamped on it in white block letters. They were still a few feet away, the lot narrowing into a smaller road walled by a chain-link fence topped by a coiling network of razor wire.

A few empty Humvees abutted the fence, large gray lampposts poking out between them, their illumination dim in the early morning light. A white sign plastered on one of the poles set the speed limit at 15 miles an hour, the sign below admonishing drivers to keep the lights low. Aaron's eyes felt swollen, his head filled with gauze, and it was hard to pay attention in the constant windy mist. Despite all that, he could still see that all of this looked way too serious, like some hardcore black ops type shit. Wasn't there a structure like this in Cheyenne Mountain? Some Cold War nuclear bunker intended for the top brass?

Aaron heard a thud and glanced back. Job had collapsed. Two soldiers picked him up and dragged him along, the trooper behind Aaron giving him a shove. Aaron twisted his head around and gave him a hard look, but the soldier didn't even meet his gaze. Eyes forward, he pointed at the entrance.

They passed through the gate and entered the tunnel. Overhead, corrugated ribs of metal took over, funneling inward with a string of hanging phosphorescent lights trailing along. Knee-high walls of concrete shadowed the road into the black chasm, two parallel metal pipes flowing above them. It was cold and terrifying, and Aaron felt like he was going past the point of no return. The soldier shoved him again, more roughly this time, and he stumbled forward, nearly tripping. He looked up in exasperation. The soldier was as inscrutable as ever. He hated this guy. In fact, he hated them all.

The New World Order

When I woke up, it was like a switch had been flipped. There was none of that human sense of being grudgingly drawn from a dreamlike state into consciousness. One minute there was nothing, and the next I was turned on like a machine. It was disconcerting to say the least. Sure, humans are basically organic machines, and rising from sleep is essentially an inefficient ripple of evolution, but rationalizing it doesn't make it any less uncomfortable.

I find myself in a very strange room. It resembles an ancient study, the kind in which a gentleman of means may have ended his day at the end of the previous century. I'm propped up on a delicate-looking Victorian chair, its wooden framework ornately carved in floral patterns. A mandala-pattern carpet lies at my feet, the walls darkly stained slabs of wood covered with mounted trophy heads. Behind me, a large door-less entryway leads into a room that is walled by a heavily latticed dome of glass, the panes so numerous that it resembles the eye of some giant insect. The desiccated remnants of several tall plants encircle the base, their withered trunks poking out of porcelain vases. On my right, astride a short pedestal of ornately carved wood, is a full suit of Samurai armor. Black swaddled hands and feet tuck into sleeves of red, the mask a wooden pantomime of a warrior's face topped by a crimson helmet with golden horns. At the base of the figure, a loose pile of very old-looking books fans out, their covers worn leather, the pages gilded in gold.

I don't know how long I've been out or where I am. The roar in my head has dwindled to a dull oscillation now, but it's still throwing me off from my normal heightened state. My thoughts are taking too long to gel, and everything feels askew, as if I'm on a time delay.

The thick arabesque doors in front of me swing open, and an old man walks in. He must be eighty, his face a wrinkled map of pale, spotty skin. His jowls droop, the eyes reduced to dark slits that peer out through swollen eyelids.

Tufts of white hair arc above as fearsome eyebrows. Solitary white strands poke out from under his charcoal bowler's cap. His clothes are simple yet elegant: a charcoal-colored trench coat and matching pants. There is a momentary blip in my perception, a slight line of static that arcs across the old man, and I realize this must be a projection. Is the entire room a projection as well?

Focusing in on my tensile receptors tells me that whatever I'm sitting on is rougher and stiffer than the plush crimson cushion I see beneath me should be. I try to narrow my sensory input to see what else rings false, only the distortion in my head won't abate, and I am bombarded with conflicting sensations. Objects subtly change character when I try to zero in on them, and the outlines remain hazy. I give up and return my attention to the old man.

Crossing the doorway, he stops. He appears to look at me, although I can't quite tell as my vision doesn't permit me a clear view of his eyes. He is fully aware of my presence, yet he doesn't seem anxious to engage and I get the feeling that some elaborate game is being played here.

"Ah, the man of the hour." He cracks a smile, displaying a row of yellowed teeth. His dark eyes widen. "You've proven to be quite bothersome, and I'll bet you don't even know why."

He absently looks around for a moment, seemingly oblivious to my thoughts. He returns his focus to me, and in an even tone says, "You'll have to speak up."

What does he mean by that? I can't communicate verbally— he must not know it. Matter of fact, he might know less than I thought. This projection made me assume I was dealing with something advanced, like the people, or things, or whatever they were that could previously read my thoughts, but that might not be the case. Then everything slows down and draws out in a weird pause, like a temporal ripple effect.

The old man gazes at me with a fixed glower, the unwavering intensity surpassing any degree of normalcy. I try to concentrate my vision and look past, but I have no control. Then, as if play was hit on an invisible remote, the old man's face comes to life, his eyes focus more directly at me, and he speaks.

"I can hear you, this distortion just makes it difficult. If you want to say something, project your thoughts more." His smile widens into a disturbing grin that shows off a row of stained, uneven teeth. "I don't really expect you to say anything relevant. You're merely an ordinary human who stumbled across something far beyond his ability to comprehend. It's a twist of fate that you are in that body at all."

"Who are you? Al'lak?"

"No, no, nothing like that. I'm human. I just had some assistance in getting here."

"So what are you?"

"It really doesn't matter. What does matter is that you reign yourself in. If you keep acting like an uncontrollable brute, we'll be forced to dispose of you."

That seems to be a repeating motif. I think if they could do that, it already would have happened. Every side is playing games, and I'm not sure how many sides there are or what the game even is. If I can keep him talking, maybe I can start to figure out all this.

"What do you think I'm doing?"

"It's that human kid, David. That's what you're spending all your energy on."

That's my human name! How do they know that?

"Leave him alone. You have no idea what is going on. The government won't pursue you anymore. You are free to do whatever you want, provided you stay away from this. Someone has filled your head with lies, and they are using you. Just walk away. You don't have a dog in this fight."

More twists to this story. So someone on this planet must be involved. If they want me out, they better show me something pretty convincing. So far, I only see them trying to hide whatever is going on, and they appear willing to go to extremes to do so.

"Why should I give you more credence than anyone else? So far, everyone has fed me conflicting accounts. I come across some Al'lak suit, and suddenly everyone is trying to get me to do their bidding. I need to see something more concrete than these vague hints and gestures."

"Oh, you think that suit came from the Al'lak?" I respond quicker than I should have with:

"Who then?"

Immediately I regret tipping my card. The old man pauses, and like a rat who's stumbled across a treat his grin widens. I found this form on a crashed Al'lak ship when I was a military technician, but it's entirely possible they didn't make it. When I encountered the Al'lak they called it a "failed experiment." They never specifically said they created it. Then again, no one I've yet encountered has told me the complete story, either through a lack of willingness or an inability to communicate. This body was my ticket out of a frail human frame. Beyond that, my whole story since then has been improvised.

"No one knows. It's one of a kind, and it has been here for as long as anyone can remember. If you are told differently it's a lie. That thing has been used countless times, and whatever inhabits it eventually goes mad. In fact, that might be happening to you right now. Do you think you're some knight in shining armor, on a quest to save humanity? You're a lost child, and much bigger forces are at work here."

I know he's fucking with me, although what is actually going on is a good question. There is some galactic-level event in play, and I'm feeling like a small fish in a very big pond. I don't even know this kid they want me to protect, but he's part of some vast military conspiracy, and strange people are trying to sell me alternate versions of the same reality. I'm seeing and hearing things, and I'm experiencing things that should no longer be possible. Frail human things. At my most paranoid I reason that these are the failing sparks of some artificial reality created by my brain, and I died back in that bunker in North Carolina when I first tried to get into this suit.

The glamour of the room is fading, the man is already gone, and the atmosphere is gradually draining away before my eyes, like a mirage dissolving as I draw closer. I'm now sitting on an ancient wooden chair, the weathered planks pitted with rot. Light streams in through the windows, motes of dust lazily drifting in the beams. All is dim and gloomy. The walls are antediluvian slats of dark wood, the ground a dusky slab of rubble-strewn concrete. My limbs feel like iron weights—my whole body, in fact. I can barely find the will to move, and every moment it gets worse. My thoughts are cloudy, as if I'm in the mental fog of extreme exhaustion, and in my mind

I find it hard to piece words together into whole sentences. Is this how it ends? With a whimper? Without me learning a single truth?

THE BUNKER IN THE MOUNTAINS

They had thrown Aaron into a crude room resembling a cell. The walls and ceiling were rough slabs made of concrete blocks, the floor a polished stretch of pavement. A single unshielded light bulb dangled from the ceiling, the lines of two metal pipes missing narrowly as they shimmied by. Other than that, the room was bare. No windows, no decoration, only a narrow wooden bed nestled in a corner. It was military neat, a black blanket stretched tautly across with a single pillow resting at the headboard. A plain, boxy-looking wooden armoire hugged the other corner. The center of the room was taken up by a low, square table made of the same light wood. Two crates were nestled on either side, stand-ins for chairs. The room smelled like old concrete and fresh lumber. The soldiers had locked the door behind them and time slowed to a crawl. Aaron paced the room, too wound up to sleep. With nothing to read or watch, there was nothing to focus his attention on. Nervous energy coursed through his body, alternating with flashes of a cool, numb sensation. Usually that meant a cold was coming on, or that he needed sleep. In either case, he didn't dare rest. In fact, he felt drained, just not tired, and there was no way he was letting his guard down right now.

Minutes ticked by, and Aaron finally took a seat on a crate. He spread his arms on the surface of the table, and rested his cheek on its cool, unpolished surface. He closed his eyes for a moment and started to drift. Then recent events, with all their bloody carnage, came flooding in. Images of severed heads, with intestines spilling out of torn bellies and sheared appendages slung across tarmac. His eyes popped open and he bolted upright. Nervously blinking his eyes and shaking his head, he debated whether or not he wanted a smoke. He bit his lower lip, drummed his fingers on the table, and bided his time. He craved the nicotine, and the lack of it put him more on edge, but now wasn't the right time.

Another twenty minutes passed, and he heard the click of approaching footsteps. Straightening up, he prepared for a sudden change in his situation, namely one for the worse. The sound grew louder and then abruptly stopped. All was quiet, and then tumblers fell with a loud thunk and the door swung open. To Aaron's surprise, an oddly non-military-looking man walked in.

Although he was flanked on either side by normally attired soldiers in camo uniforms, this guy looked like an office worker. No, a little more sinister than that. He was wearing a conservative black suit, or maybe it was navy blue—Aaron couldn't tell in the dim light—with a simple black tie tucked over a starched white shirt. His face was stern and square jawed, but the confidence of his pose told Aaron he was someone important. Looking up, Aaron realized how unusually intense his eyes were. He wasn't sure if they were closer together than normal, or the brow proceeded too far over the eyes, but it all looked abnormally fierce. His salt-and-pepper hair was cropped shorter than any civilian, and when he started talking, his words sounded a little too crisp.

"So, Aaron, you've proven hard to get to. I have to apologize for the rough treatment. I assure you it was local authorities overreacting and did not come from us. Follow me to a more appropriate room and we'll discuss the situation."

He uttered the words like they were having a casual conversation, but the whole time that odd intensity burned in his eyes. His behavior rang false, and Aaron recognized it instantly. The guy had simply taken one look at Aaron's punk rock garb and started stereotyping. Aaron knew that it was only a matter of getting a read on who this guy was and what he wanted. Then he'd promise him just enough that they'd loosen his constraints. These people were currently playing nice, which meant they must want something, and that gave Aaron leverage. All he had to do was figure out how to use it to his advantage. The main issue was that he was in the wilderness, surrounded by an overwhelming military presence. And he was trying to one-up men who had a history of breaking people. He didn't even want to think of what the consequences of a misstep might be.

The man motioned to Aaron, wheeled around, and walked back into the hallway. Aaron rose and followed.

Outside the room the walls transformed into a slick veneer of white. Aaron couldn't tell if the glimmering walls were metal or coated drywall. A series of florescent lights ran along a central beam overhead, its blinding light bleaching out everything and reflecting in glistening blobs off the polished stone floor. Aaron glanced up, and between the burn flashes of the overhead bulbs he noticed sunken compartments. It looked severely industrial and was several degrees colder than the room, making Aaron feel small and famished. He ground his jaw and tensed, trying to hold in warmth. His nose was running again and he dabbed at it with the back of his hand, sniffling and breathing in a cool gust of air. It carried with it a scent of grease and chemicals.

They passed a few alcoves, their slight depressions dropping in on red doors. At least he assumed they were doors. There were no windows or markings on the crimson slabs, making them appear all the more menacing. After they had passed by several, the man turned into one and opened it into a white-walled room.

A single large box overhead provided the only light in the form of a set of glowing florescent tubes. A large rectangular table took up most of the middle, its white surface highly polished and with metal folding chairs positioned on either side. The man settled into one, motioning for Aaron to take the other. Aaron paused at the head of the table, glancing back at the door just as the guards were shutting it in front of them.

"It's just you and me, Aaron. Take a seat."

Aaron pulled the chair out, slid into the seat, and scooted it up to the table. He rested his elbows on the slick top and buried his head in his hands. A headache was starting to kick in, and he pressed his palms against the sides of his head in an attempt to alleviate the throbbing. The room was warmer than the hall, with more of a neutral smell. He could feel it counteracting the bite of the headache, a migraine that was probably triggered by the chemical fumes of the hallway and exacerbated by his lack of sleep and food. He stared at his reflection in the glossy tabletop, unsure of protocol and hesitant to make eye contact.

"It's natural for this to all seem a bit overwhelming, Aaron."

Without raising his head, Aaron angled his vision upward. The harsh lighting wasn't doing the man any favors. Aaron could see the pockmarks of teenage acne on his cheeks, his face a bleached-out whitish-blue under the unforgiving overhead lamps. His sunken eyes had an animal intensity, the beady pupils gazing out from under thick salt-and-pepper eyebrows. Liver spots dotted a face canvassed with deep wrinkles. His voice sounded almost normal, but the monotone vibe and serious edge infused it with a dark undercurrent.

"Look, you don't have to like this. It wasn't the intent of anyone to cause you harm. I think there was a breakdown in communication with the authorities closest to you. The current atmosphere is so tumultuous, and some officials overreacted. Again, I apologize. Your government needs you, Aaron. You're in a unique position."

Aaron didn't raise his head. In a thin voice that sounded weaker than he intended, he replied, "Do what? I'm a nobody. I don't know what you think I can do."

The man's face remained a mask of stone, but his eyes seemed to burn all the brighter. Sitting bolt upright with his hands hidden below the tabletop, he looked more machine than man, and Aaron was starting to feel the burn. The air smelled funny, too, stale and dry and with a chemical aftertaste lingering in the background. Nauseous and thick-headed, he wondered if they had released some sort of "truth gas." He tried to get a good look at the man's nostrils, without giving it away, to see if there was a filter stuffed up in there, but it was no use. The light bleached out everything. The man's face was the same black, immobile slate it had been from the beginning, and his mouth moved like it was a separate entity. His tone was different now, too, some of the warmth gone. It was as if he had given up the pretense of being friendly.

"You know that's not true, Aaron. Let's not play games. I'll talk to you straight, but you need to talk to me straight."

Aaron looked on with his mouth slightly agape. Thoughts kept racing through his head and he felt oily and tired. He was so out of his element that he wasn't even sure what the appropriate response was. He knew weird things had happened to him recently, such as starting in one place and arriving in another, with no idea how it happened or even what was going on. He was sure of one thing, though, which was that if he opened up to this stranger, it would all be downhill from there. He'd seen the movies and heard the conspiracy theories. From what he had managed to glean from his military intelligence father, even that was the prettied-up version that had been leaked to the public.

Aaron had always been treated as less than a person. Just by looking different, by being a young skateboarding punk in the South. If there was a real reason to bring out the big guns, he could only imagine how severe it would get. He kept his head nestled between his hands, raising his face so that his eyes were level with the man across the table.

"I don't know who you think I am, or what I can do, but seriously, you have the wrong guy. I'm just a kid. I ran away from my parents, saw some bad shit in New York years ago, and ended up in the hospital. That's it. Everything went sideways recently, and I went to a friend's house so we could ride this out together."

"Tommy, yes. You're referring to Tommy. He'll be here soon."

"What do you mean he'll be here soon?"

"I told you we're not here to play games. We could take different measures if we had the luxury of time, but unfortunately that's not the case. Things have come to a head and the situation has gotten out of hand. You've seen it for yourself. We are your government. We are not the bad guys. There is some very serious shit going down right now, and we are doing our best to stabilize it."

There was an awkward silence while the man looked on blankly. *How much could they possibly know?* Aaron wasn't stupid, and that bit about "we are your government... we are not the bad guys" sent chills down his spine. He knew this game. The government was the last thing he'd trust. They wanted something, and they were assuming he could deliver it. He was traveling between strange places and hearing people's thoughts, but it was totally random and he knew better than to tell them any of that. Doing so would turn him into their guinea pig, and he'd probably be locked away and experimented on. If he claimed he could do whatever they wanted, they'd start demanding demonstrations, and his bluff would be called. His best bet was to profess ignorance. With a wink and a nod that let him drag it out while he tried to figure something out. That guy looked pretty serious, though, and Aaron wasn't sure what he could pull off.

"Aaron, I'm going to leave you here so you can think about the situation we find ourselves in and your part in it. You probably don't trust us. That's to be expected for your age and demographic, but we don't have the time it would normally take to let you grow up and mature. If that was the case, we would wait it out and approach you as an adult. Unfortunately, you need to grow up fast and face the world head on. I'm here to help, but you have to work with us."

Aaron could swear that even though the man's lips moved, nothing else did. He couldn't even say for sure whether the guy blinked. This entire time, those eyes bore down on him from a mask of stone. Nothing about this was normal and all he wanted was out, which probably wasn't an option. He had to come up with something that would pacify them, and come up with it fast. Some kind of trickery. Some way that could get him out.

Abruptly, the man rose, swiveled toward the doorway, and walked out, the steel door giving away its massive size as it shut behind him.

THE TANGLED WEB

The military interrogator now sat in a room that was a clone of the previous one. The room was darker, and the whitish tone had shifted toward pale blue under a single overhead box. The man had lost some of his domineering look, if none of his intensity. He was a little more anxious now, the bad cop act off the table for the moment. Across the table sat a bespectacled man in a lab coat. Thinner of face and body, the man sported a wild shock of white hair.

Looking slightly more at ease, he was peering down at some papers spread out before him.

Without lifting his head, he inquired, "What does he know and what did he reveal?"

"He seems to know very little. I don't think he knows what he is doing, but he knows he is doing something, and he's hiding whatever that is. Stalling for time and playing dumb, in my opinion."

"Do you think he has any control with regard to what he is doing?"

"I don't know. He won't admit anything unusual is occurring. I would say that the more he acts ignorant, the more control he has."

"Maybe he's just a confused kid?"

"Highly unlikely. He's hiding something. And we need to find out what it is and deal with it before it becomes a threat."

"You soldier types are always so quick to jump to extremes. Not everything is a conspiracy. A scared kid is going to deny everything as a matter of course. He's probably embarrassed it's happening and is acting out of a blind survival instinct."

"If he knows less and we overestimate, we lose nothing. If he knows more and we give him the benefit of the doubt, everything could be jeopardized."

"He's just a boy. A skinny adolescent in a disenfranchised subculture. His psyche is fragile. We want him to work with us voluntarily. That way will be so much easier. We need to foster trust. He didn't have that with his parents, so we need to become his surrogate parents."

"He might be stringing you along. Another party could have gotten to him, and he could be trying to play some sort of game. The Viet Cong used children to do their dirty work. So does nearly every terrorist or underground cell. We have to anticipate the worst-case scenario in eventualities like this."

"He's not stringing us along, and I seriously doubt he's even told anyone about this. We've been watching him since day one."

"This subterfuge could have started years ago, long before you began keeping tabs. Teenagers his age lie. It's like second nature to them."

"Oh, I have no doubt he is fabricating something, but he's just doing it so he can get through this the best way he knows how. We've been watching him his whole life."

"What do you mean his whole life?"

"Oh, you didn't know? We made him."

New River Junction

Dusk was settling in by the time they pulled into New River Junction State Park. The highway had narrowed into a series of dramatic bends through ever-darkening woods. Dana seemed to know where they were going and didn't slow down even if some of the hairpin turns had the car swaying and Tommy grinding his teeth. But Tommy knew he was in a sensitive position here, so he stared out the window and kept silent. The road narrowed into a trail of half-buried sand as it burrowed through the woods, and even at their reduced speed the 4Runner bounced over an endless series of potholes and cracks. As trees engulfed them on all sides, the scent of fresh soil and the burnt-oak aroma of autumn poured in through the windows. Branches and debris lay strewn across the path, adding more jolts to a ride that was already too rough for Tommy's liking, yet he knew he was here by the good graces of Dana alone.

The truck bounced over a particularly rough patch, and Tommy grunted. He straightened up from his slouch and peered out the window. The gargantuan trunks of trees crisscrossed the trail in a puddle of shadows, the bright glare of the setting sun filtering down through the leaves. As they crested a hill, the trees dropped and the shimmering expanse of a large body of water, its far reaches dimming into the faded blue of distant hills, came into sight. Feathery clouds, their bellies tinted bright orange, rolled across a wide expanse of sallow purple overhead.

Dana turned off the trail and cruised to a stop in a clearing. All about them, dying grass fought a losing battle with the soil. A few rocks dotted the plot, their smooth surfaces streaked with moss and lichen. The guys popped the doors and stepped out, immediately looking about suspiciously. Tommy remained in the back seat a moment, grudgingly joining the party in a slightly delinquent "too cool for school" fashion.

The guys were already acting like they were on a secret mission, strutting around as they vigorously tossed about supplies. Tommy figured this whole scenario was pretty serious, but they still looked ridiculous. The guys pulled out the folded shell of a tan dome tent and unrolled a few bundled sleeping bags. Tommy leaned against the truck and watched. He waited until they had formed a pile and one of the guys had wandered off before shambling over and grabbing the cooler and one of the bags.

Dana was digging a fire pit with a shovel. The tent was partially aloft. It seemed they only had one plastic stake, but one of the guys had scavenged up a few medium-sized branches and was busy whittling them into stakes.

Although the shelter itself looked roomy, Tommy only saw two sleeping bags and wondered where he would fit. Dana had brought along her boyfriend, meaning he'd have a real hard go at conning a space with her. He didn't see any blankets, and that thin plastic floor didn't look the least bit comfortable.

Even with sleeping bags you could feel every root and twig. He wished he had an air mattress, but beggars can't be choosers, so he decided to let it go for the moment and popped open the lid of the cooler.

Three steaks, some hamburger patties, a bag of buns, and five beers. Tommy grabbed a Sam Adams and settled the cooler top back in place. He pulled out his keys, popped the lid, and took a swig. This scenario wouldn't last, and Tommy glanced around skeptically. These kids weren't outdoor types. They'd probably make a pathetic attempt at recovering some nuts and berries, and maybe even some game, but things would get desperate pretty fast. He'd have to figure what to do before it came to that.

Darkness settled in, the sky dimming into a deep slate blue. The treetops dimmed into a tangle of black shafts, the air crisp with the scent of approaching winter. Tommy shivered and pulled up the collar of his leather jacket. A yellow flicker caught his eye and he strolled toward it. The guys had managed to get the fire pit going. A knot of flames licked at a skeleton of branches configured like a tepee. One of them was kneeling, rubbing his hands over the flames and blowing. Chris muttered to Dana and then veered off for the cooler. He gave Tommy a sidelong glance as he bent over and lifted the lid. Grabbing one of the beers, he shot another look Tommy's way and headed back to the campfire. Tommy didn't know whether that look was because he had taken one of the beers or because he was there in the first place. The guys huddled around Dana, but Tommy didn't feel like joining in.

He took another swig and scanned the sky. It was completely dark now. Funny how bright the stars were in the isolation of the woods. The clouds had mostly dispersed, the dusty purple strands of a few pulling apart across the heavens. It was too homey, too still and peaceful. Something horrible would happen before long. It always did. They'd run low on food, there would be arguments and sides chosen, other people would show up and add to the volatile mix, and who knew if there were any police or government to keep things from getting crazy? He didn't know if this was safer than being in a city. Then he heard a muted noise, a far-off, whipping sound. He thought it might be the treetops swaying in the wind. Only there was no wind, and the sound was too regular. He tried to focus. It was rhythmic, and definitely getting louder. There was a snap, followed by a metal click, and the woods came alive.

Black-garbed soldiers erupted from the trees. They looked like some special forces operation one would see on TV, their faces buried beneath black helmets and visors that reflected the light of the campfire. They held aloft H&K submachine guns, blinding glares spewing from the barrel-mounted lights. Dana and her two friends froze, their eyes wide. Tommy stayed close to the cooler and tried to look behind the tent without being too obvious. He felt stupid for not recognizing the sound of an approaching helicopter sooner. They were fucked, and he had as yet formulated no plan. Maybe if they were preoccupied with Dana and her friends they wouldn't see him and he could slip away. Then he heard a branch snap and spun around to see one of the soldiers right behind him. It was pointless.

"Fuck..." he mumbled.

A few of the men had reached Dana and her friends, and were pushing them face down into the dirt and zip-tying their hands. One of the men strode over confidently, raising his visor a few inches as he approached.

"John, tie him up."

The soldier behind Tommy stepped forward and roughly grabbed his arms, pulling them back and binding his wrists. Tommy didn't see the point of saying anything. He would find out soon enough. Everything was going to shit. That Aaron kid had brought down whatever this was, and now he was tangled up in it.

MORE THAN MEETS THE EYE

The mountaintop bunker was buried under a rocky cliff. Hulking walls enshrouded bulkhead doors that sealed off the compartments. The gates at the entrance were 25-ton blast doors built to withstand a nuclear attack. The interior doors were not quite as thick and resembled those of a bank vault.

A single wide road led into the complex. Climbing up an isolated mountain, it crested one of its lower perches and entered through a razor-wire fence.

Beyond the entrance, an enormous tube tunneled into the mountain, beginning as a divided roadway and then spreading out into a vast underground hangar. A multitude of vehicles were parked along the curving rock walls. HMMWVs, Strikers, M1117s, and a couple of civilian cars. At the end was another set of blast doors, leading to a labyrinthine complex of multi-use rooms. Deeper still in the bedrock, through a series of increasingly complex security barriers, were the conference centers and the war room. Narrow corridors trailed off from these and led down into a warren of labs and storage rooms. Even much of the top brass had only limited clearance there.

Nestled in the base of one of those buried zones, three figures in white hazmat suits were bent over a circular rim of controls. Its satin metal base was garnished with a complex series of screens and dials, a glass tube of green liquid rising out of the center. Cables snaked out from the base, splitting up as they wove across the floor in a myriad of twisted and gnarled roots. Inside the cylinder an old man floated completely naked, a long black pipe twisting down his throat. A steady stream of bubbles floated up, under lighting throwing the suspended form into a pall of wrinkled flesh and harsh shadows, its luminescence throwing a green glare across the visors of the attending scientists. Atop the tube, a snarl of metal spouts erupted, their narrowing tops twisting into a rat's nest of crossing lines before melding into the metal grates of the ceiling. The sole entry door swung open, the blinding light of the hallway pouring in. One of the scientists craned his neck to see who had entered. An old man, the exquisite sharpness of his designer gray suit only making him look older, lumbered forward. The green light reflected in a sheen on his bald head.

Inside the cylinder, an old man floated

As he drew closer, the green light revealed a warren of wrinkles and the liver spots, his eyelids drooping with the obsolescence of time. His mouth was cracked open in a stilted leer, every breath hoarse and cumbersome.

"Can you bring him back to life?"

One of the men in a hazmat suit stepped away from the console and walked toward the gentleman. Only it wasn't a man at all. Three beady eyes gleamed behind the visor, peering out of an ashen gray face that was slick with moisture. When it spoke, the lisp of phlegm slurred the words.

"Maybe. We caught him…at the moment of death…halted most of the deterioration. The human brain is…complex. Soon the old ones will be back. You will never face this…problem again."

The words were more staccato spurts than fluid dialogue, a strange accent distorting their delivery. The old man nodded, the corners of his mouth drawing back in a weary grimace. He turned and ambled out of the room. The creature gazed after him, watching his frail movements with a cool, affectless stare. Then it loped back and resumed its work.

THE SEMBLANCE OF NORMALITY

They had been real harsh when the soldiers tied Tommy and shuffled him into some overbuilt helicopter that was all black and bulked up, the wings jutting out the sides like some airplane from hell. He could swear he had seen a craft like that before, on an underground conspiracy website. They stuffed him into a dark cargo bay, crammed between armed soldiers who wouldn't even look at him, and then proceeded to fly for hours in absolute silence. If that wasn't bad enough, the soldiers had sat bolt upright and stared at the wall the entire time. Once they had arrived, amid snow flurries on some desolate mountaintop, they cut off his zip-ties and shoved him forward like abrasive assholes. They had ordered him out of the helicopter and marched him into the gaping maw of an apocalyptic-looking bunker.

Inside, soldiers swarmed throughout it as if they were in some combat zone. Tommy followed some of that Coast to Coast, Alex Jones stuff, and he bought most of their premises—eugenics experiments, Lee Harvey Oswald, New World Order, all that stuff. This looked like their worst nightmares come to life, but, in a strange twist, the troops had softened up after he was inside. They didn't manhandle him, and they used commands that were more like actual sentences than single words. To top it off, he wasn't escorted to a jail cell, but instead to a sparse yet fairly comfortable room. A stripped-down, all concrete and raw wood room affair that smelled musty, but at least it had a bed and table. No TV, and nothing to read, but at least he didn't feel like a common criminal and that was something.

They had left him there for less than an hour before a

middle-aged military guy opened the door. He was sporting a black beret, camouflage BDUs, and had a clean-cut, square face like a stereotypical high school jock. Not the kind of guy Tommy usually liked or trusted, although this guy seemed amenable enough.

"Tommy, you must be hungry. I'm here to escort you to the mess hall."

He wasn't hungry, although being in a mess hall sounded better than being in a solitary room. He rose to his feet and followed, the guy leading the way as four armed soldiers brought up the rear. With their cloth caps and camo BDUs, they didn't look like the thugs who had captured him in the woods, even if their M16s and ultra-stiff posture still set off warning bells. The bunker was a few degrees too cold, and it smelled like fresh laundry detergent and gun oil, casting everything in a somber air. None of the soldiers smiled or made eye contact.

The narrow cement hallway he was being led down was crude and utilitarian. It made a few twists, passed through a set of double doors, and opened into a mostly empty large room. Two tables stretched across the middle, the tops a heavily lacquered white circle anchored by a black post. Stainless steel arms stretched out from the post to hold aloft black ceramic chairs. Dark gray beams bastioned a latticed roof enswathed with pipes, rows of florescent light boxes dangling from the ceiling in clusters of steel cables. At the far left, hunched over a table and pecking at a plate of food, was a disheveled guy in black hospital scrubs. His head was wound with fresh bandages, and he looked to be more moving the food about with his fork than actually eating it. Tommy glanced around at the other empty tables. The place looked so strange, like it was set up for a crowd, not just for the miserable guy in the far corner. The soldier in front motioned for Tommy to join the occupied table.

"This is Job," he said. "You'll find that you have a mutual friend in a moment."

Tommy reluctantly trudged over. The troops didn't follow him, and Job barely raised his head, his eyes peering at him in an upward slant. He put down his fork, picked up the mug next to him, and in a gravelly voice inquired, "Who are you?"

Tommy took the seat opposite him. "I could ask you the same question."

Job smirked, did not improve his eye contact, and mumbled, "You guys with your games."

Tommy was looking at Job intensely, and after a few moments with no response he spit out: "What, you think I'm with them? I'm here against my will."

"Sure you are."

The dude was definitely giving him attitude and he didn't have the patience for it. Sitting back in his chair, Tommy muttered, "Believe whatever you want."

Minutes ticked by slowly, Job looking miserable the entire time. He swirled his coffee, poked at his food, and occasionally scratched his bandages. The room had a stale, pumped-in smell, the area augmented with the bite of industrial cleaning chemicals. Tommy was starting to detect the scent of dried blood and body sweat drifting over from Job. He scrunched his nose, yawned, and stretched his legs. Trying to lean back in the chair, the ceramic proved too stiff for comfort and he kept squirming around until he was upright again.

Time crawled by, and Tommy was about to attempt conversation again when he heard the click of boot heels. A man emerged from a door on the left and strode over holding a mug and plate of food. He was sporting white chef's attire, conical hat, the works. Without saying a word he laid it in front of Tommy, pulled a white napkin wrapped set of silverware from his apron, set it down neatly next to the plate, and turned to leave.

Tommy glanced up at him and asked, "What is this?"

"Roast beef, potatoes, salad, and coffee. Do you need anything else?"

"Water."

Without a word, the guy pivoted around and walked out. "Fucking dick," Tommy muttered.

"Going all out with this acting thing, huh?" Job muttered.

"Whatever, man."

They sat in silence for what felt like an eternity. Tommy drank his coffee and picked at his food, looking around the room gloomily and telling himself this was all Aaron's fault. Finally a different door opened, and a spry, if slightly disheveled, Aaron walked in. Job's head drooped, but his eyes tilted toward the door. Tommy twisted around.

Aaron spurted out:

"*Tommy?*"

He recognized the other guy from D.C. He looked a little rough, although he had apparently been patched up. Aaron didn't know if this changed his opinion of these people, but it was a mark in their favor.

"What bullshit have you gotten me into now?" Tommy asked.

Aaron strode over and sat next to him. Looking as sincere as he could muster, he said,

"Dude, I don't know who these people are or what is happening."

Tommy gave a muffled grunt in response, looking at the floor and shaking his head.

"It's the New World Order," Job mumbled.

Aaron took all this conspiracy theory, tinfoil hat stuff with a grain of salt. He knew that Tommy bought into it more than he did, though, and it wasn't much of a surprise that he was now focusing on Job. The expression on his face had shifted from resentment to fascination.

"You know what's going on?"

"No, but I know who is involved. At least I think I do. And we are fucked."

"So who is it?"

"I told you, the New World Order. The same power elites that have controlled everything since day one."

Aaron snorted derisively. "Oh, come on. That's right out of Alex Jones. There is some civil disobedience going on with the country, and the assholes in power are just using it as an excuse to establish martial law. They may even be behind it. It's nothing new."

"Shut up, Aaron," Tommy snapped. "I want to hear this."

"I work for a government watchdog group," Job said. He kept looking down at the table, all the while holding up his hands and gesturing emphatically while he spoke. "Well, I used to work for them. Who knows now? There's some serious shit you guys probably don't know."

Aaron looked at him evenly, still a little skeptical. Tommy, on the other hand, was absorbed.

"The government is huge. You guys have no idea how big. You think that six hundred and forty dollars for toilet seats and seven thousand six hundred and twenty-two dollars for coffee makers scandal was bad? *Billions* disappear all the time, and it's only under random scrutiny that it any of it ever gets covered up. Then accidents happen, like the financial records for two point three trillion dollars disappearing with the 9/11 Pentagon attacks. Where do you think all that money really goes?"

He paused and rubbed his eyes, and then dropped his hands so his elbows were resting on the table. Looking at Tommy and Aaron directly for the first time, he continued.

"This shit has been going on for quite a while. The government has these secret projects buried in bunkers and safe houses throughout the country. They even have them in foreign countries. And the government is not really the government like you think it is. The people elected are just public figureheads. I'm not sure when it all changed, maybe around the time they had JFK assassinated, but there's something going on here. I'm not sure what, but something has been pulling the strings for a long time."

Tommy reached over with his hand extended. "Tommy."

Job looked at him for a moment and then shook his hand. "Job."

Then Job looked at Aaron, who kept his hands in his pockets but grudgingly offered up his name.

"Aaron."

There was a moment of silence, and then without looking back at Aaron, Tommy said, "So now you believe me, huh?"

Aaron shrugged and tried to look indifferent. "I didn't say that, although Job here helps your case."

Tommy looked up at the ceiling in a dramatic show of indignation.

"I don't know who I should trust," Job said. "I barely know

Aaron. I didn't even know his name until now. He saved my life in the chaos of D.C., only to get me taken hostage moments later by the fucking military. Who knows what they want, and who the fuck knows why this kid? Something big is going down. Something that was in the works way before all this civil unrest stuff. There are FEMA death camps—*death camps*—with hundreds of stacks of plastic coffins. There's all sorts of weird shit going on at the Denver airport, and there's all these weird bases, including some that fuck with the atmosphere. I mean, just look around you! You think this hasn't been here for a long time? This isn't the famous Cheyenne Mountain bunker everyone knows about. This is at least as big and nobody knew shit about it until we ended up here!" He threw up his hands in vexation.

Tommy glanced at Aaron and muttered, "Fucking Aaron."

Job brought his hands to rest on the tabletop, a raspy whine cutting through as he talked. "I'd probably be dead if it wasn't for this kid. I'm not blaming him for all this, I'm just wondering why he is so important to them."

"Well, Aaron?" Tommy said. "What do they want? You didn't save *my* fucking life."

Put on the spot, Aaron was not sure what he should say or how he should phrase it. As a matter of fact, he wasn't sure he could say *anything* that didn't make him sound crazy. He knew that weird shit had been happening lately and he had no control over it, and that was the extent of it.

"I...I don't know..."

Tommy sneered. "It figures. We are all about to die, and you're still holding secrets."

"Weird stuff has been happening lately," Aaron said. "Like, weirder than normal stuff. That's all I know."

Job and Tommy were both eyeing him intently now.

"I...I've been hearing stuff. Like people's thoughts..." He paused, quickly glancing between Tommy and Job. Both were still staring at him, and not in disbelief. "And I've been...I don't know how to say it...traveling. Like starting in one place, but when I arrive, it's somewhere else."

He glanced up again, scanning for signs of amusement or

skepticism. Both were still captivated.

"That's how I got from Blacksburg to D.C. I went down a hallway in that house we were in, Tommy, and ended up in a tenement in D.C. Not only that, but it was the old D.C., back when the hip areas were still rough and there were abandoned buildings all over."

He was sure Tommy was going to interrupt, tell him he was full of it, dismiss him out of hand. Only Job and Tommy were still giving him that same steady stare. Aaron felt hot, nervous electricity running through his body, and took a deep breath. The odor of dried sweat and that cheap aftershave Tommy was always wearing greeted him. Sweat began trickling down his forehead. "They said something about needing me. About how this country was in a crisis and I could help. They seem to think I have control over things, but I don't. It's random."

"Who's your dad?" Job asked. "Is he military?"

"Uh…yeah. Ex-military. Why?"

"Were you born in a military hospital?"

"Yeah."

Tommy kicked in.

"You know they've been doing some eugenics experiments for decades, right? They got it from the Germans. From the scientists they stole after the fall of the Third Reich."

"Uh, yeah, okay…"

"Don't you see? They probably gave your mom something! This shit was planned!"

"I…I don't see—"

"It all makes sense now. That's why they want you so bad!"

"Want me for what? That theory doesn't even make sense. None of this came up until recently. It would have kicked in a long time ago or at least I would have been watched if it was a government experiment."

"Dude, you don't think they could've been monitoring you since birth? Don't you watch movies? None of that shit kicks in until you're a teenager."

Aaron's head was swimming. It did make sense if you went out on a limb and played Hollywood for a moment. Still, it was a huge stretch. He didn't know what to believe, who to trust, or what the real story was. Things were tough enough as it was, and it probably wasn't even true. Not in the calculated, government conspiracy way.

Tommy leaned his head against his palm and in a calmer voice said, "This whole place is bugged anyways. I'll bet that was what this meet-up was about, to get you talking. You wouldn't tell them what they wanted to know, so they just used us as patsies." He shook his head and looked down in disgust.

The War Room

Oversized screens encircled a dark room in an elevated digital panorama. Byzantine maps of the world, all sketchy blue landmasses against a sea of black, were interspersed with brightly glimmering news reports. A ring of fluorescent globes dangled from cables anchored high above the large round table in the center, throwing an oppressive deluge of brilliance over the small group assembled. Although forty chairs encircled the table, only five people were present. Three were huddled together, conferring nervously in low tones, two water glasses were haphazardly spread amongst them, commingling with a sprawl of notepads and a closed briefcase. Two of the men were octogenarians. They were dressed in expensive charcoal suits, as if going to a formal ball they had been sidetracked by this minor inconvenience. Knowing looks splayed across their faces as they lounged back in the chairs. Next to them was a four-star general in his dress formals, all his badges and metals on display, the national security director beside in navy-blue civilian dress attire, and an out-of-place-looking Asian guy. He wore a decent quality dark suit, if wrinkled and a bit scruffy. The guy looked like Albert Einstein, with a shock of white, shoulder-length hair. He was also the most animated, speaking in soft, rapid tones and punctuating what he had to say with wild gestures. The two military men looked on edge, in direct contrast to the octogenarians, who appeared so relaxed it was as if they were in their own little world. The other three huddled together, the government officials sweating and tense, while the Asian man looked lost in thought.

Out of nowhere, the Asian guy kicked in. "This hasn't

been done before, and I urge caution. Not to say that it can't be done, but we have no idea what the unforeseen consequences could be. You are talking about disturbing the fabric of reality. Breaking a barrier we know nothing about. It could be completely destabilizing. I'm not talking about discomfort, I'm talking about an end to everything as we know it."

One of the older men leaned in. It was the man from the lab, the oily sheen on his liver-spotted forehead gleaming under the lights. Sagging jowls puckered his lips as he spoke.

"Oh, don't be so melodramatic. This has been done before, just not by us."

The Asian guy looked over at them, a nervous anxiety distressing his otherwise youthful appearance. "By whom? By these...these things? These creatures that are assisting us? Out of the goodness of their hearts? I don't think we have the full story. We should run tests and examine all the angles first before we step into something and find ourselves past the point of no return."

The older man cast a sidelong glance at his fellow octogenarian, and then looked back. "Frankly, we don't have the time." He made a point of giving each of the participants a meaningful look. "This world is coming to a climax. Certainly you can see that with the U.S., but it's only the beginning. The population of the world is too large, and it's only increasing. There simply won't be enough resources to sustain us all, and we are rapidly destroying the ones we have now. The core temperature of the planet is increasing, deforestation and other factors are accelerating the process, and the entire planet will descend into a state of nature not seen since the end of the last ice age."

"People have been predicting that for the last hundred years," the Asian said, outstretching his hands and shaking them dramatically as he talked. "Technology always finds a way. More people live comfortably on this planet now than could have been foreseen in the wildest of dreams one hundred years ago. And we haven't even spread beyond this planet yet. There is a whole universe out there. Right now we are wasting our resources, spending over half of our intake on the military alone. You know what the science budget is and has been for years? Almost nothing. Even during the Cold War, when the threat of world communism propelled us to make astonishing advances, we spent a fraction of what we spent on the military. We don't have to make a deal with the proverbial devil, this is something we can do ourselves."

The old man smirked. "Our own solar system is still a mystery to us. Colonizing anything is a wild dream at this point, and in case you haven't noticed, funding NASA is the last thing on anyone's mind. As I said before, we don't have the time. For all we know, the Earth is about to rotate on its axis and we'll all be screwed. It's way past time for that, and no amount of NASA funding is going to change how devastating that would be."

"Even if it is within our technological grasp, opening a gateway to who knows what with no prior testing is a tremendous risk. We don't understand how this is done, where it leads to, or anything involved. Creatures that we barely know are making unsubstantiated claims that we are taking at face value. This is not a wise course of action."

"We've been assured it will benefit all of us."

"All of us? Who is this 'us'? And why do we trust any of this? We don't know enough to make an educated decision."

"You are overthinking this and looking for problems where none have ever appeared. So far everything we have been promised has come to pass. If you sleep on this because you are skeptical, nothing will ever be accomplished."

"With this kid? Is that what you are talking about? That's hearsay! Yes, we've heard secondhand what he can do, though we have no actual witnesses. Further still, let's accept that he can somehow open a portal into another world. Where is that world? Even assuming that the multidimensional theory is correct, an alien dimension might be very hostile to us. It could operate on a whole different set of physical laws, or be composed of antimatter. I don't think you understand how far down the rabbit hole this goes."

The general spoke then, his voice deep and gravelly. "These...things, they contacted us. They could have contacted the Chinese or the Russians, but they contacted us. Even with all this chaos, we still have the largest and most advanced military in the world. And we have the best scientists, which is why you are here. Your role is to give us advice and offer a guiding hand, not to hinder the process."

The scientist rolled his eyes and looked away with a dramatic gesture of his hands.

"Does the president know?" he asked. "Congress? The Senate? Are they even viable anymore? All I see are a few men around a table deciding the fate of the world."

The old man leaned in and smiled. "You'll notice the president isn't here. It's irrelevant."

That ruffled the feathers of the general, and he said, "What Jacob means to say is that this isn't really a political issue."

Abruptly, a few of the screens became a frenzy of movement, the maps of various continents panning out to reveal the entire globe. The planet and the grid overlaying it were shown in shades of blues, a plethora of red dots now swarming in around the periphery.

A door cracked, light poured through, and a young man in naval dress blues stepped in. "We've got a problem."

ACROSS THE REACHES
OF SPACE AND TIME

Everything snapped into focus and I jerked upright. The room around me was the gloomy ruin I remembered it devolving into. Only my body was at full capacity. I felt a clarity that I hadn't realized had been so completely degraded until I had it back, stronger than ever. I could now see how truly decrepit were the pitted and stained graying timbers of the wall. Soil and dead leaves piled into the corners, their crumbling remnants scattering out across worn slats of floorboard. Light filtered in through gaps between the wall planks, their thin shafts of luminescence breaking apart in the disturbed dusk. My hearing isolated the tiniest pin drops of noise: a mammal scurrying through the underbrush outside, the swish of leaves in the wind, the old timbers of the building creaking against the gale, the sticky slurping of... I twisted around in my chair and found myself confronted by the strangest creature. It was slate gray, with a head that craned up on a curved stalk until it coalesced into a face sporting two large eyes. A wide, flat face with a multitude of openings where a nose or mouth should be. Four long appendages, their tips tapered toward the ends, twisted and curled in the forefront. The thing was head height, and it rested on four limbs. I couldn't tell if it was squatting and would be much taller if it stood up or if that was a natural position. The front two tentacles were long and wiry, ending in a trifecta of lumpy claws. The back limbs were splayed out and bent like those of an animal, the bottom half bending again at an unnatural angle and continuing down into a set of nubs that functioned as feet. I couldn't make out much of the chest because of the dim light and with the writhing appendages in front of it, but what I could make out looked barrel-like and striated by what may have been a great many ribs. The creature was coated in a mucus membrane, the glistening residue trailing into the room behind it. Its thoughts erupted in my mind in a strange, deep, solemn tone.

"You must go. They are trying to stop you."

I had seen a lot recently, but this took the cake. It wasn't even humanoid. In fact, it looked vastly different than anything I had ever encountered. Yet it seemed to find conversing with me easy enough.

"Who are you?"

It continued writhing and moving, the slime flashing glimmers of reflection as strange textures puffed out or pulled away from the light. The stalk of a neck drifted back and forth slowly, the multitude of openings on its face blowing open and fluttering closed at random intervals. A slick layer akin to a membrane flicked across the eyes.

"I've been communicating with you the whole time. I tried...over the reaches of space...but it wasn't enough...."

"That turn-of-the-century guy? You said you couldn't get here. At least you implied that."

"This is a one-way trip. But this can't happen. You have to stop..." The words grew unintelligible.

"Who or what do I have to stop? You haven't told me anything. I never ran into all of this trouble before you, and that kid is disrupting my life."

"This has been coming, and it will affect you. Things are being summoned...you can't imagine how bad the universe can get. How bad it was. Varieties of your species have been around much longer than you think, and you've been almost wiped out and restarted so many times that your race doesn't remember."

"Even if that is so, what does any of this have to do with me?"

"I don't have long. I am giving my life for this. But life doesn't matter, only survival. Once you were incapacitated we couldn't risk *the outcome. I traveled here to set you free."*

"Why should I step back into the fire? You are one of many telling me things, and the last few have all lied. Maybe it's bad for you. How is it bad for me?"

"You...maybe not...no one knows what you are. But your world is in danger. There were different strains...different...I think you call them hominids. Only humans survived. These things, they are subject to different forces than we have in our universe. Different laws. They are more powerful here."

I stare at him, if it is a him. It's so bizarre. Little ticks in its glistening skin tell me it's alive, even if all the communication is non-verbal. Only you think in the language you are accustomed to, not in some universal thought dialect. So how does it even know English? Come to think of it, how can it even make sense of my language? None of this adds up.

"You can see the truth of what I am saying in your myths and religions. There is a darkness there, a history of primitive humans struggling against powerful forces."

"You are feeding me a line of bullshit. You are saying all the right things, but you slipped up. You speak my language too well."

There is a pause, and the thing just looks at me. Actually it's hard to say. The eyes appear intent on me, the transparent membrane steadily scraping them clean. It reminds me of a wiper on a car windshield. An idea pops up, and I debate whether this is a manifestation courtesy of the Al'lak, crafted for my benefit. For who knows what agenda. Or it might be some completely different alien race. I have no way of knowing and no clues as to what to trust. That thing interrupts my reverie.

"You don't understand. Your consciousness is in a thing not made by human hands, yet it has seamlessly melded with you. Language is a surface manifestation of an underlying system. We are a very ancient race that has been watching for millions of years. The universe is always growing and changing, and we are so far away now, it is hard for us to interact. The structural laws that influence the universe have altered to the point where communication and travel is difficult. In the early universe, when the fabric of reality was compressed, it operated

differently and these things were able to cross a dimensional barrier. They overwhelmed everything in our universe. When they were finally expelled, they left behind a disenfranchised few who worked ceaselessly for their return. A few who will finally succeed unless you stop them." The picture beginning to take shape in my head is like nothing I've ever considered before, and in this new light some wild theories that have been around for centuries might have relevance. There were various hominid species in pre-history. Neanderthals, that hobbit-sized species, Homo floresiensis, I think, and probably more. I'm not too familiar with ancient anthropology. People like Graham Hancock have been speculating about advanced ancient civilizations for decades, and recent findings like that 11,000-year-old city in Turkey have strengthened his argument. Still, it's hard to tell what is real. This is all so deeply buried in time.

I refocus on my immediate surroundings. The creature before me is falling apart, the edges fluttering away as they dissolve into the shadows. Only the core remains solid, and even that is disintegrating.

"What is happening?"

"I told you...I can't stay...this is a one-way trip..."

The communications have become less clear, everything associated with this creature increasingly more slippery and ethereal.

"You are stronger than you think. You can get past anything they throw at you if you will yourself past it."

"Who is this 'they'?"

"Loyalists...lesser creatures, they have been enthralled with empty promises. Save the child if you can, but kill him if you must..."

The thing is almost gone now, little more than a ghost-like outline. I can barely decipher its words.

"They are the biggest threat...to everything...even you..."

Bright light washes over, the intensity drowning out everything. I feel displaced, like I'm adrift in an intangible, hazy whiteout. Then, in a flash, I'm falling. I barely have time to catch a glimpse before I crash into an asphalt roadway. My limb craters the pavement, chunks of black pelting me in a grainy deluge as I flop over into a clumsy roll. I tumble once, and immediately sprawl my limbs like a spider in an effort to gain my footing. Everything is crisp. I feel reinvigorated and ready to take on anything. I look around and notice I am in the middle of a two-lane highway. The road tilts to the left as it trails down a slight decline and disappears into the trees. All is wet—it must have rained recently—and I'm registering a cool forty-five degrees. The woods circling around me are on fire with the yellows and oranges of autumn, their dead leaves choking the roadside grass and venturing out onto the asphalt in wet clumps. A hazy mist wafts through, reducing the landscape into a smog of yellows and greens. Surmounting the distant forest, the blue silhouette of a mountain rises out of the murk. I concentrate my hearing and pick up the rustle of animals—the cawing of birds, the dripping patter of waterlogged plants—but nothing human. That thing sent me here for a reason, and as usual I am operating without instructions, so I don't even know which way I should go. Picking the mountain at random, I head toward it.

THE LITTLE BLUE PLANET

Three giant, beetle-like Al'lak warships hung back, the tiny pinpricks of a thousand lights dotting their glossy black shells. A legion of disc-shaped fighters swarmed about them, zipping in and out like drones around a queen. Flitting dots of light commingled with tail flashes of blue, the nimble craft weaving between one another as they coalesced into a web over the planet.

The Al'lak didn't usually intervene in the development of primitive planets. It had been millennia since the barbaric old days, when it was every species for itself and a wild frontier attitude dominated. Entire planets had been enslaved. Wars had been fought, empires had crumbled and risen from the ashes, and crumbled yet again. Genocide and savagery on a galactic scale.

Things were different now, more secure. Feisty, troublesome segments like the K'Kl were kept in check, and developing planets were left untouched. The fragile alliance had held for thousands of years, but all that was in danger now. Things had grown more tense, and although petty squabbles had coarsened the ground, something had popped up amidst the maelstrom.

Something ancient. Few had any memory of it, but the Al'lak kept scrupulous documentation. There was a blip in their primordial past of a horrendous presence, and while the information was mostly recorded hearsay, it all pointed to something so dire that it could not be ignored.

The Al'lak were contacted by entities they had long since relegated to the realm of mythology. Beings that existed on the edge of the known universe, and possibly not even in the four-dimensional world. The Al'lak had no time for anything transcendental or religious, but this...this was something else.

They barely picked up the contact. It was a shift in wave patterns that only a species as OCD as the Al'lak would recognize. Even then the signal was brief, and transmitted in scrambled spurts. They refined their tuning, zoned in, and within a few key words the immense scope of what they were facing was apparent.

Buried in their records was a prehistoric recounting of some immense threat. According to legend, it was only the banishment of this "great evil" that had allowed them to progress from a more primitive species. It was an otherworldly awfulness that had torn through the known universe, reducing the inhabitants to dribbling slaves and easily mowing down what little traces of civilization they had managed to achieve. What had banished this terror was lost to the threads of time, and the gradual evolving of the universe had changed the fabric of reality such that a barrier to re-entry was established.

Still, the universe was vast and full of secrets. Acolytes of this ancient menace had survived and thrived. Living in secluded enclaves, often wallowing in a self-induced illusion of victimization, they had fantasized that bringing back this hoary scourge would change the balance of power and place them back where they belonged.

All of this was a revelation to the Al'lak, and they triple-checked every possibility. It seemed farfetched, but if nothing else the Al'lak were logical to a fault. In the end, it was a numbers game. If any of the ancient text were true, the structure of the universe as they knew it would crumble. Once the decision to accept the threat as real was made, desperation quickly set in. The coddling of primitive species and adherence to normal laws be damned. They wouldn't risk the official channels. This was too dicey and it was too late to take a delicate approach. Drastic measures were called for, and this cancer had to be cut out at its root. The Earth had to be taken out before this went any further.

The Heart of Darkness

The sun was setting in the distance, a glowing orb of white, its rays rippling through the walls of trees in shafts of yellow. Rocky cliffs shouldered the road, their tops blossoming into verdant hills of leaf-strewn grass that led up into forests of pine and golden-leaved oak. I trudged down the highway, into the blinding gleam of the setting sun.

Over an hour passed, the road curving as it steadily scaled upward. The trees fell away as the landscape rose into increasingly severe slopes. The light had mostly faded, but I could still make out the furrowed mass of wooded hills far below. As I rounded a turn, the road drew to a close in a large, empty lot.

Beyond it a huge tunnel bored into the mountain. Skirting the entrance of the lot was station that had "MILITARY" written all over it. A razor-wire fence shouldered it, blocking off all entry. It'll bet this is where they took that kid.

It was no big secret that the military had secret bunkers in the mountains. Well-stocked relics of the Cold War that were outfitted to withstand a nuclear Armageddon. Or any other world-ending scenario.

About thirty minutes pass, and I draw closer. The last vestiges of light fall behind the mountaintop, only a faint bluish glow holding on. I calculate one more round of the bend and I'll be in sight, and whoever is in that booth will see me. There were no lamps that I could see, but the glow of the well-lit entrance illuminates the lot. There doesn't appear to be a stealthy approach option, the area too cleanly partitioned to sneak in. My best bet is probably to be quick and surgical in my approach. I'll dart in, and as they are still trying to neutralize me with conventional firearms, I'll grab the kid. Clearly they want him alive, so that should forestall the weaponized barrage. The challenge will be figuring out where he is before they have a chance to shuttle him away. Even if the grunts know, it's not like I can talk to them, and the layout of that bunker is likely a maze. I have no real plan, but time being a key factor, I decide to bulldog my way through and improvise.

I'm within steps of rounding the final corner when a projectile smacks into the side of my head. From the velocity registered, it's a high-impact sniper round. I reach up and nab the lead wad as it's falling from my temple. Nice shot—and apparently they aren't taking any chances. Two more slugs smack into my head, mushrooming and immediately sliding off. I train my hearing and detect a distant rustle. They must be 200 yards away. Everything grows deathly silent and in that jarring calm I round the last bend. The brightly lit kiosk at the front gate comes into full view. The guard inside is talking on a receiver and looking in the opposite direction, but if snipers hit me, they know I'm approaching. Maybe he's calling in a visual confirmation. A few yards behind the kiosk, distorted by the brilliant lights, is the entrance tunnel. I'm within fifty feet of the guard when a large projectile slams into my chest, tossing me airborne and engulfing me in flames. I crater the pavement, furrowing out a trough as I tear backward through the asphalt. My knockback grinds to a halt and I'm left sitting upright. A torrent of rocks pelt me like rain as the licks of fire trailing back toward me die a slow death.

I wonder if they know what they are dealing with. Last time they had a device that scrambled my senses. I don't think they knew I was coming this time, which would make all this a preliminary front while they get something ready. As if on cue, whatever they have kicks in, and I start to feel a pulsing in my head. It's merely a hum, yet the intensity swells quickly until soon it is an unbearable hammering. I grip my head and start to curl over. Then I remember what that thing said to me about how I am stronger than I think.

Maybe whatever they are using attacks some of the properties left behind by my organic brain. Pain is an organic sensation, a nervous response the human body creates to prevent damage. That makes it only one of many sensory inputs, and I should be able to shut it out. I open my receptors and try to locate any trace of my Homo sapiens nervous system. Maybe that is what is holding me back. My head is raw and anything but clear, and I start to fear that if I let go of whatever this is, maybe I'll forever lose my last remaining human aspect. After all, how the human body responds to sensory input may be at the core of what it means to be human. Love, death, pain, euphoria...I don't know, and I can't think clearly enough to make such a choice...

The dilemma repeats itself like a broken record in my head, and it's only after a few minutes of stumbling forward in a torrent of bullets and smoke that my attention breaks and I snap back to the situation at hand. Second thoughts like this couldn't come at a worse time. I'm in a warzone, on a mission that involves the fate of the entire world, and I'm at a loss for what to do. *I didn't sign up for any of this shit!* I just wanted out of a frail human form, and now I'm being dragged into a galactic conspiracy that I'm not sure I even believe. My knees start to buckle. I can't take much more of this. If I had teeth I would grit them. All that matters is finding a way to make this stop. I want to clench my eyes shut, but I can't even do that. And then I realize, like a shot through the head, that I want to elicit human responses because whatever this is, it's attacking what's left of my human faculties. All I need to do is let it all go. Be like those martyrs in the dark ages when they were being tortured and transcend it.

THE GAMES OF OLD MEN

The circle of screens was alight, the map of Earth clustered with hundreds of red dots. The technicians below were conversing and moving about excitedly, their expressions dramatized by the lights of the control boards. The officials in the war room were leaning in unison on the central table, tossing around ideas and derailing others, a tone of hysteria belying their words. Only the two elderly men seemed calm.

"Don't worry," one of them said. "This will all be taken care of."

"What are you talking about? This is a disaster. We can't even respond to something of this magnitude!"

The old man reclined farther, his face slinking into a satisfied grin. "Don't worry, we have friends."

A figure stepped out of the shadowed doorway and tapped the old man on the shoulder. In his mid-forties, he had closely cropped, if slightly graying, brown hair, and was sporting a conservative navy-blue suit. Leaning over, he whispered in the old man's ear, backed away, his hands hanging at his sides, and stared off into nothing. The old man made a dismissive gesture. The intruder took a step backward, spun around, and walked out, a nictitating membrane whisking across his eyes as he left.

WAR IN SPACE

The Al'lak had encircled a third of the planet. Three of their motherships released a horde of fighters. One harbored a weapon. A horrible weapon from the height of the old days whose very existence had prompted a move toward the present era of peace. Only all of that was in danger now, and the Al'lak rationalized there was little choice. It was a weapon that could destroy a planet, scorching its surface in a burst so powerful that it would strip off the atmosphere in one fell swoop, incinerating everything with a flame so intense only the extremophiles would survive. It was an apocalyptic weapon from which a planet would never recover. But if things were as drastic as the Al'lak believed, the sacrifice of one planet could save thousands.

The motherships drew in, the fighters flitting about them in carefully planned trajectories that emulated a shield. They only needed a brief window. The weapon would shoot into the heart of the planet and set off a destructive chain reaction. One would probably do it, so they brought three just in case.

This was an all-or-nothing affair, and they couldn't afford to miscalculate.

Once they reached a comfortable distance, the network of swarming fighters tightened about them. The firing chambers in the mothership were aligning when the blips of incoming craft appeared all around. A few were oval, resembling the K'Kl, but there were four they had never seen before. They were familiar with this quadrant of space, but these new ones looked like the husks of Earth insects. The outer sheaths were a patchwork of black plate that absorbed light, while the holes along the sides revealed an underbelly of convoluted ridges, glowing dots interspersed therein. Antenna-like prongs jutted out from the fore, and clusters of machinery suspended from the belly on thick cords. Despite the fact this was totally foreign to the Al'lak, its appearance probably was no coincidence.

An executive decision was made to ignore the intruders for the time being. If the fighters kept them at bay long enough, it would all work out. Living wasn't important. Saving the galaxy was, and that would only take moments.

The tip of one of the strange ships glowed, and something that resembled an intense flash of lightning lashed out. It crackled into a hundred fighters and a moment later they imploded, folding into a ball and then bursting outward in a shower of debris. The tips of the other ships glowed, and the Al'lak were down to a third of their fighters in a flash. They were so close but there wasn't enough time. If the drone wasn't aimed perfectly, or if it was intercepted en route, they might lose the only chance they had. There weren't extras lying around, and creating new copies would take time. The motherships backed off, unsure of how to proceed. Most of the rest of the fighters imploded, and they engaged in a full-blown retreat. Although the few fighters that were left had no chance of survival without the motherships, this was a matter of numbers. Destroying the planet was a priority, and the Al'lak weren't sure how to deal with this new threat. Warping space and time, the motherships retreated to a safe distance past the Oort Cloud and conversed with those back home.

A Deal with the Devil

The technicians started to freak out when the number of objects encircling the planet increased, the under lighting of the controls heightening their flurries of desperation. The general and the National Security director leaned toward each other and whispered in anxious tones, the scientist maintaining his distance and staring at the overhead screens for a minute before joining in. Then the red dots started to wink out. At first few in number, the frequency drastically increased until only a few remained. The larger motherships pulled back, and then zipped off the screen. The small ones that remained slowly followed. Only the new craft remained, their cluster maintaining a copious distance.

The old man spoke. "See? Friends."

The general cupped his head and muttered, "What have we made a deal with?"

A door snapped open, and a soldier leaned in. "Sir, we have a problem."

The old man raised his eyebrows and looked over with a sardonic expression. "The kid. They are here for the kid."

CHAOS

Soldiers looked on in horror as a strange creature that couldn't possibly exist strode toward them. Bullets flicked off it like so much chaff. A few came forward with RPGs and bathed the creature in a torrent of flame, yet even as the smoke was still dissipating they could see they were having no effect. The noise was deafening, the pounding bolstered by a swarm of soldiers dashing to the forefront and setting up heavy-duty tripods. The asphalt all around the creature was riddled with craters, the smoke that engulfed it choking with the aroma of gunpowder. Yet every time the mass of smoke cleared, the thing was closer.

The middle-aged man in the navy-blue suit watched from behind the front line. He stood solemnly still, the look on his face inscrutable.

One of the soldiers, his face smeared in grease, ran up to him and shouted, "Sir! You better get inside."

"I'll be fine."

The soldier looked exasperated. He ducked, gripped his head as another RPG explosion rocked the area, and scurried back to the front.

As the creature neared the front line, the soldiers pulled back. Holding their weapons aloft, they maintained a steady barrage of fire. A few of the rounds ricocheted off the creature and dug into the exposed arms and legs of the men. They cried out as they fell, teeth gritting as they collapsed into a writhing clump. Indifferent to the squirming bodies all about him, the creature strode forward.

The man watched for a moment, then headed back inside. He had almost reached the titanic door when the creature broke into a sprint. A moment later it was on him, plucking the man aloft by his armpits and pinning him against the wall. Stock still, the man dangled several feet above the floor in bemused silence. The creature craned its neck from side to side as its eyes scored over him.

At a distance, the soldiers had stopped firing and one yelled into his handset, "It's taken a hostage. How do we proceed?"

Unaffected, the man looked down at the creature, the nictitating membrane fluttering across its eyes.

THESE FUCKING CREATURES

This was one of them. I had no idea what race it belonged to, but it wasn't human, and it most likely knew where the kid was. I just had to make it communicate. Projecting my thoughts forcefully, I demanded, *"Where is the kid?"* Its only response was the same dispassionate stare. Holding the thing aloft, it exuded a weird, inhuman aura. The body temperature was much lower than normal, and it seemed remarkably unfazed by my presence. Not that any of this told me what it was, or how much it knew. I wasn't sure how to threaten it, as I had no idea what it might respond to. I didn't even know what team it was playing on, if any.

"I could kill you now, squash your head into the wall."

It smirked at that, a telling sign that it could hear my thoughts. Then it spoke, exuding a smooth, slithering confidence that came off as completely alien to what I had pressed against the wall.

"What do you think you're accomplishing? This isn't your fight." There was a pause, and I sensed a thick wave of condescension. "You are allowing yourself to be used like a pawn."

Whatever this was, it was trying to confuse me. And it was working. I had one agenda, and it was pretty clear that if what little had been made clear to me was even close to the truth, quitting at this point could be a catastrophic event. Not only that, it didn't feel right. On one side was a misfit kid, and on the other was a vast military conspiracy, and I'd worked for the military. I knew how devious it could be. I focused my attention back on the thing.

"The kid. Where is the kid?"

"Do with me as you like. It matters little. There are things afoot here that surpass you and I."

"What do you need the child for?"

A metal clatter followed by the stomping of boots resounded from beyond the wall. A nearby door folded inward and a hoarse voice called out, "Hey! We have the kid!"

Craning my neck sideways, I observed the growing cluster swarming out. A squad of soldiers, all wearing cloth hats and simple military uniforms.

Grunts, not the special forces I'd encountered out front. Nestled between them was the kid, looking grumpy and disheveled. His vision was trained on the floor tiles, but when they stopped he raised his head and his eyes widened. Coming up behind the squad was a square-jawed man whose demeanor broadcast that he was in charge. Short and stout, he had lines etched across a face harboring deep-set pools of darkness.

"Put the man down and back away."

The crew drew into a loose semicircle around me. I assumed that if I didn't react they'd get closer still, and that was all I would need. No weapons were drawn, although fingertips hovered next to holstered guns, and the rifles strung over more than a few shoulders were tilted forward. Two of the men had the child by the arms. The man I was holding finally registered a hint of worry. Barely noticeable, it was enough to serve as the tipping point.

Kicking into gear, I slammed his face into the wall. His skull squashed like a melon, a yellowish, lumpy gore splattering across the concrete wall.

Releasing his carcass at the moment of impact, I hurtled toward the first soldier, decapitating him with my left hand as I punched the other guard beside the kid with my right. His sternum collapsed inward and he gurgled blood as he fell back, releasing the kid as his hands jolted open in an involuntary nervous response. My left hand made a steady arc, missed the kid by inches, and knifed free the head of the other guard as he was doubling over. I plowed forward into more soldiers, whipping my hands like a whirlwind, each balled fist a skull-shattering attack. Within moments the kid was one of the few left standing, his meek frame surrounded by the shrapnel of a dozen crumpled soldiers. Only the general, judging from the stars on his lapel, remained. He backed away in shocked silence, his hands extended in a plea of mercy. With a quick dart forward my forefinger tunneled through his forehead, and his lifeless body crumpled to the ground. The kid had bent down and was throwing up again. Well, he was trying, his chest contracting spasmodically as drool trailed from his mouth. He wiped his lips with a clumsy brush of the sleeve and raised his head with a look that mixed resignation and relief.

Taking a deep breath, he spit out a phlegmy wad and spoke. "Look, I don't know what you want, but I won't resist as long as you rescue my friends."

I extended my hand in a gesture of "lead the way." He looked at me for a moment, nodded, and headed back toward the door.

IT ALL COMES FULL CIRCLE

Aaron led him down the entrance hallway, looking over his shoulder occasionally to make sure the creature was following. As best as he could make out, this thing was an improvement on the military. It might have done horrific things, but they had never been aimed at him. Actually it had been fairly gentle with him, and who knew the story with all the others involved? They were the same militarized peons that had been causing everyone trouble lately. Maybe Aaron was jumping to conclusions. In horror movies, the creature was often the misunderstood one, its violence simply a reaction to a hostile world. It was his cultural programming that had prompted him to jump to stereotypes when confronted with real life. Not that this thing was entirely copacetic, but at the very least it appeared to be the lesser of his evil options. He had already escaped from it when things got sketchy, and that was partially because it hadn't restrained him, which was another mark in its favor. For all he knew, it might have been rescuing him from this military thing, whatever it was. At the very least, he was probably safer in its company than anything related to the government.

Aaron took a winding path, passing through a rat's nest of slick, white-paneled tunnels until he finally opened a door, where instead of another tunnel he was confronted with a dank-smelling stairwell of stained concrete that spiraled downward. Descending it and after a few twists and turns, the stairwell ended abruptly at another door. Twisting the handle and leaning to press it open, Aaron staggered out into yet another white-paneled hall. He held the door and turned for the creature to finish making its descent, but it was behind him. Practically jumping, he felt his ears prickle and his skin grow tight. Something struck him as very unnatural about all of this. How had things gotten so out of hand? It seemed only yesterday he was riding his BMX and building tree forts. Now he was in the thick of some serious adult shit and everything was life or death. Aaron let the door go and walked down the corridor, following its twists and turns as it led ever deeper into the labyrinth. His stomach had constricted into a tight ball of gnawing hunger, his mouth felt dry, and his legs were aching, all of which was minor. He could get past it. If nothing else, being a broke punk rock kid in the South had taught him how to tough through hard times.

The hall ascended some more stairs and split into an intersection. He paused and looked back to make sure that thing was following him. When it rounded the bend he couldn't help but shiver. The tunnel was already so creepy, with its monotonous walls and unearthly bluish lighting, and this creature pushed everything over the edge. It was completely unlike anything he had seen before. Its black contours didn't reflect the phosphorescent light, they absorbed it. And the way it walked... Its legs had this weird way of moving. The hips didn't sway, and it made no noise as it tracked across the tile. The weird, lens-like eyes were the only feature on an otherwise blank face and the only break in a strangely amorphous body. The whole thing was monstrous and otherworldly. Aaron tried to push past what he told himself were religious and social beliefs that had been inculcated since childhood. This was the real world, there was some serious shit going down, and none of that old-school fairytale nonsense applied. Yet he couldn't help a slight apprehension. He breathed in deeply and climbed the steps that led to the room he was kept in.

He tried rotating the knob to no avail. When he looked back he saw the creature was right behind and involuntarily shrank back. He quickly regained composure, but he noticed there was no response from that creature. It stood stock still, unwavering and immobile, like a machine waiting for some input. Aaron pointed at the doorknob, timidly reached over, and demonstrated that he couldn't turn it. He retracted his arm and looked up at the creature, wondering if it understood. The overhead fluorescent lighting bleached out the corners of everything, giving Aaron a headache. He shuddered, feeling weak and sick. Should he try again? Did that thing understand English?

Then it abruptly reached over, snapped the knob off, and pushed the door open.

Tommy and Job were sitting across from each other at the table, and both looked over in wide eyed surprise.

"What the fuck...?" Tommy murmured.

Job said nothing for a moment, then he held up his hand accusingly, stammering out, "Y-You...you're real..."

THE END OF THE LINE

The creature stepped aside and Aaron slid through the door. "Tommy! Job! We have to go! Now!"

Job's hand was still raised, his stare concentrated on the brute behind Aaron. "That thing! I've seen it before!"

Tommy looked skeptical. "What are you talking about?"

Job paused for a moment, mouth ajar, and in a nervous, high-pitched spasm he said, "There are etchings and stories about that thing. Early culture, beginning of mankind stuff. There is no good way to translate any of that ancient text and we always assumed it was a myth. Like gods of fire or water, that sort of thing."

He stopped, his eyes rolling from side to side as he tried to collect his thoughts, then continued at a frenzied pace.

"We got a more definite idea of it in some early cave drawings, but we took them as animated spirit bullshit. Only then some kids reported seeing the exact same thing that was in all that old mythology stuff. We assumed it had to be some sort of hoax, only we wondered what could have given them the idea in the first place. It's so obscure."

Sweat was beading at his hairline, his forehead gleaming in an oily sheen. He paused and tapped his lip, struggling to find some connection.

Tommy looked a little more interested now, toggling his head between Job and the creature. "That thing? What's it supposed to be?"

Job looked seriously unsettled, his eyes almost popping out of their sockets, and he spread his fingers wide in exasperation. "I don't know. It's all pre-history, ancient civilization. No one does.

Like I said, etchings and cave paintings. All that antediluvian shit is indecipherable. What the Catholic Church didn't destroy was burned up in the Library of Alexandria. There's no Rosetta Stone for it, no written record." He was wondering aloud now, his words spreading further apart as his hands fidgeted and he tried to give voice to some scheme that put all the pieces together.

Aaron had grown wide-eyed and desperate. He shook his hands maniacally and hissed, "We have to go! I don't know what this thing is either. It plowed through a dozen soldiers and killed some general. It's going to rescue us, but we need to get out *NOW!*"

Job looked on for a moment, then kicked back his chair and stood up. Nonchalantly, Tommy muttered, "Well, let's go then."

Natural Born Killers

The creature stepped aside so Tommy and Job could file out. Aaron seemed a little unsure of where to go and looked up at the thing, then immediately chided himself. What did he expect? The creature didn't move, didn't respond. It just steadily looked at him like some cold, mechanical thing.

Aaron knew that the way out would entail them reprising the same route they had taken coming in. The halls would probably be swarming with troops by now, but he didn't know where else to go. He scrunched his eyes and tried to focus. The intense light of the hall was drumming in his head and making him feel queasy, and the nauseating chemical smell didn't help. He needed to do something, only his mind felt like rubber and he kept drawing a blank.

Then a door clicked and a tube was rolled in from the far end of the hall. It took only a moment for Aaron to realize it was some sort of grenade. A fresh jolt of nervous energy tore through him and he took off running. Tommy and Job followed, a sudden look of desperation taking form as they rushed out of the room. To Aaron's surprise the creature headed straight for the grenade. It went off before the thing reached it, hazy tendrils of ocher smoke wrapping around and consuming the creature. Aaron and his friends bolted the other way. The corridor T-boned at the end of the short hallway, splitting into two identical white-paneled pathways. Aaron stopped short, face aghast with indecision.

Armed troops rounded the bend to their right, making the decision for him. He darted left, Job and Tommy already bypassing him as he sprang into action. There was the crackle of gunfire, and slugs tore into the paneling on either side. Aaron had gone to the range with his dad. He was used to a firing gun, but he was always on the shooter side and always wearing earmuffs. He couldn't believe how much louder and more terrifying it was when bullets went screaming by mere inches away from you. They impacted with a force that seemed almost surreal. Aaron gasped for air and ran as fast as he could, but he knew it wasn't nearly fast enough. His stomach was a tight knot, his legs were sluggish, and the sole that had been slowly tearing loose on his combat boot now flapped comically as he ran.

Ahead of him Tommy was repeating "Oh shit, oh shit, oh shit," his hand holding his cap in place as he sprinted forward. Job was loping behind Tommy, an awkward scramble the best he could muster given his condition. Aaron didn't think Job would make it. Then Job's head jerked forward, a spurt of blood flying back and pelting Aaron in the face. Job's limp body flew forward in a rapidly descending trajectory. Aaron could taste the fresh blood, imagined he could smell the gore amid the gunpowder, and lost it. Vomiting as he ran, syrupy liquid trailed from his gaping mouth while he pawed at his face with his coat sleeve in an attempt to wipe it clean. He couldn't catch his breath and was falling into a loping stumble as he neared the far corner.

Tommy had already rounded the bend and was out of sight.

Behind Aaron there was yelling and the raucous sounds of a scuffle. He tripped when he tried to look back, falling into a tumble that sent him straight into the wall.

He was stunned for a moment. His head rang and he felt dizzy as he struggled to regain some composure. Grasping his head with both hands, he sat up and struggled to look up at the troops he felt certain must be almost upon him.

Only they weren't.

Apparently that creature had rejoined the scene and was tearing through the soldiers. Amid the mash of blood and body parts, Aaron guessed at least five were dead. Bits of pinkish brain matter and the darker sliminess of intestines were rampant. And blood. Gallons of blood. Aaron had no idea the human body could hold that much. Whatever was left of the squad had retreated around the bend, that thing on its heels. Aaron could still hear gunfire and cries of desperation, only now they were muffled and distant. The air was thick with smoke and the floating remnants of wall paneling, the smell a pungent mix of bile and gunpowder.

Fluorescent light beamed down in an unrelenting pall, drenching the whole scene with a sickening, bleached-out hue. Aaron crawled to his feet and loped down the corridor Tommy had taken. As he was about to leave the scene of the massacre behind, he glanced over at Job's lifeless form.

Glossy eyes stared at the ceiling, the body tilted to one side while the head was twisted backward at an unnatural angle. The mouth was partially open, the face frozen in a look of disbelief. The jaw had cracked in the fall and was hanging down limply, the body below stretched forward like that of a stranded fish. The arms were tucked down by the sides, the brown shirt puffed out with the cotton bandages the medics had applied to his back. For a moment, Aaron wondered why they had bothered, if they only intended to kill him hours later. None of it mattered, though. He didn't know Job personally. He certainly didn't want him dead, especially not like this. It was all too cavalier, like he was just a piece of meat. Those soldiers, the military, they were all evil. It struck Aaron that he was glad they were all dead. He didn't care if that thing was good or bad any longer. This death had made up his mind for him.

Turning to face the new hallway, a new resolution burned through him as he took off after Tommy.

DEEPER DOWN THE RABBIT HOLE

"That was bad. That was very bad," one of the old men in the war room said, his face drooping in disappointment. The general leaned forward, the harsh lighting of the overhead lamp rendering his features as all the more serious. "It was an accident. Friendly fire. The soldiers were ordered to scare the kids, not injure them."

"They didn't injure him. They shot him in the fucking head!"

"That Aaron kid. He's the important one, right? He's fine. You said the rest were expendable. We just scooped them up on the off chance they might prove useful."

"They were expendable in the field. There was no reason for anything to have happened here. This is supposed to be a controlled environment."

"It was an accident, and the soldier who did it is already dead. Your monster took care of that."

"It's not *my* monster. We had nothing to do with it. It was your sloppy netting of the kid that led it to us."

His features drawn back in a mask of repressed fury, the general was about to speak when the man in the corner stepped forward and whispered to the old man. Staring at the table, an inquisitive finger on his lips, the old man bent his head and listened.

"Don't worry," the older gentleman replied. "We'll take care of it."

His confidant emitted a weird, insect-like noise, his throat going through the convulsions of swallowing before he replied. "You can't take care of it."

"Oh?" The old man faced his comrade, looking slightly

amused. "I thought you had a way to deal with this thing? Something that's worked for you in the past?"

"It's managed to overcome that."

"So what are you saying? That we give up? Is that really what you are recommending?"

"No. Fool that thing. Trap it."

"Okay. How?"

"In another continuum."

"What?"

"In what you would refer to as another dimension."

The old man turned to look directly at the person beside him. His features warped in disbelief, he muttered, "Are you serious?"

"Everything else is expendable. Including that kid and his friend. But that thing has the potential to ruin all of our carefully laid plans. As long as it's anywhere in this continuum it remains a threat."

Appearing stunned and crestfallen the old man said, "How do you even... I don't understand. That kid is everything... There has to be some way to contain...to redirect whatever this...this thing is."

"That child is the strongest case so far, but he's not the only one you have. That thing must be taken care of or all could be for naught."

Eyes wide and face slack, the old man continued to mumble disjointedly, his head shaking as he tried to process the ramifications.

"But...if we start all over, it might take years. The other cases we have are...so much younger... We need adolescence for the anomalies to emerge, and that's *if* they emerge..."

His confidant maintained a cool, unreadable gaze. Staring at him in silence, the nictitating membrane on its eyes flickered. Finally it murmured, "Whatever it takes."

The old man sat in stunned silence. He didn't have years. Even if they could start the project over—and considering the declining state of the country, that was a big if—he wouldn't live to see its conclusion. And he so wanted to live. That was the whole point. He might be betraying the entire human race, but *he* would live, goddammit!

The thing next to him sensed his dilemma and with a knowing glint it whispered, "If this takes longer than your lifespan to accomplish, we'll resurrect you. Your friend passed before we had a chance to take... precautions. If you let that thing keep up its rampage, all your carefully laid plans will come to ruin. Any deal will be off, because there will be no deal left to make."

The old man couldn't shake the feeling that he was being played. This was the highest-stakes game he had ever played. He never did this. He devised schemes, gave orders, had his directives followed to a T. If something didn't work, he pursued a scorched-earth policy and God help whoever stood in the way. But this... this was a game of chance. A risky, uncouth strategy engaged in by a lesser caste of men. If he tried to hold out and chose wrong, all was in vain. Only why would they lie about the risk? What would it accomplish? He knew some grand scheme far beyond his limited understanding was afoot, and that left him more in the dark than he had ever before allowed. Only in this case he was being promised a gift that was so fantastic it might not even be true. But if it held even the smallest chance, he really had no choice.

He raised his eyes again and looked at his confidant. The thing possessed a semblance of humanity, but the old man knew better, and if it had no problem deceiving everyone else, why would it have a problem when it came to him? Then again, age was taking its final toll, the situation had come to a boiling point, and the worst was that an old man died. Something that would happen anyway. He didn't care about the rest of the human race, at least not in any way that mattered, and if this was true, it was too breathtaking to pass up.

A calm resignation settling in, he said, "What do we need to do?"

THE DESCENT

Red warning lights warmed the dim walls of the corridor. Mounted in circular recesses on the darkened ceiling panels, their crimson emissions reflected off the slickly polished floor in a litany of warm spots that receded down a tunnel as it tapered into oblivion. The blaring of a siren pierced the air as Aaron ran in a maniacal frenzy, his body tensing in desperation every time a shrill screech assaulted his hearing. Tommy was way ahead of him, disappearing and re-emerging in every new circle of red light.

Lungs burning, thighs screaming in pain, Aaron loped along as best he could. Past the point of trying to analyze the situation, he was operating on pure instinct, gulping down choking breaths of stale air. Exhaustion would kick in, then the all-too-vivid image of Job being *shot in the fucking head* would scroll before his eyes, and he'd draw from whatever reserves he had left to pour on speed. Only he was winding down. He could feel it, and even though he was at death's door, he didn't care anymore. He slowed, his hoarse intakes of breath all the louder, and tried to convince himself that he was slowing in order to get a better listen. But that was an excuse and he knew it. He was at the exhaustion point, and he didn't know how much longer he could keep this up. There was a clicking sound, and he held his breath. Trying to discern the source, he realized to his horror that it was footfalls. He took a deep breath and scuttled over to the wall, hoping to hide in the shadows there, but just as he reached it, the creature emerged. His body spasmed backward in involuntary shock, and he struggled to regain his composure, but all he could do was gasp for sufficient air and tremble.

He was done. Worn out. Powerless.

The creature stared at him in the darkness, the red glinting off its eyes the only break in an otherwise amorphous black form. As if Aaron were merely a curiosity, it paused only a moment, strolling past him on its way to the nearest circle of red light.

Pausing for a moment, its head twisted to the right as if it were contemplating something. It turned and walked over to the wall, splaying its fingers as it approached. Aaron had no idea what it was doing, but he watched in panting wonder. The creature took a step back, raised both hands, and slammed them into the wall. A door-sized panel flew inward and bounced down a stairwell. The creature glanced back at Aaron, motioning for him to follow. It struck Aaron as a strangely human gesture, and made him wonder again what this thing was. Was it a suit with a person inside? A robot controlled by some external agency? He had no idea how to broach the subject, but now was not the time. Get out of this chamber of death first, ask questions later. He rose to his feet and lumbered over, his movement now ungainly with mounting soreness.

The creature waited until he was beside it, then it raised its right hand and pointed to the portal it had just ripped open. Aaron couldn't make out much and drew closer. A glimmer of light from far below reflected off the stone edges of a spiraling staircase. The pungent odor of what smelled like a slaughterhouse filled Aaron's nose, and he glanced back at the creature. Its raised hands and forearms were covered in dark streaks, thick bits of lumpy gristle accumulated in the thicker rivulets. Suddenly Aaron realized that he was breathing in the fetor of human organs and convulsed in nauseated gags, bending over as he tried to remain standing.

A few blurry moments of dizziness ensued, and when Aaron snapped out of it he realized that the thing remained in the same position, its arm outstretched like it was frozen in time. Everything felt slightly surreal, and Aaron tried to push through the thickness of his thoughts. He hadn't eaten or slept in days, his throat was a dried sinkhole of misery, and every muscle ached. He glanced up at the creature's face again, but there was still no response, so he turned back and stumbled toward the opening. At the edge of the doorframe, he perceived a scene his brain couldn't quite make sense of. Not for a sterile, high-tech military bunker at least.

Solid stairs of stone spiraled down through a tunnel of cave-like rock. Light was rising from somewhere far below, glimmering off the rough-hewn edges. Holding the doorframe tightly, Aaron ventured a foot in. It came to rest on something invisible but solid, and Aaron chanced putting his other foot in. He screwed up his eyes, trying to get a better sense of what lay inside, but it was no use. Letting go of the doorframe, he reached for the silhouette of what he assumed was a railing. His hand didn't quite reach, his foot twisted on the depressed landing, and he stumbled forward, tensing up even as he fell. He slammed against hard metal, the cool solidness of it pounding into his upper arm as he twisted to avoid colliding with it face first. He grimaced and let out a cry of pain, collapsing into a huddle as he rolled against the wall. He nursed his wounded shoulder with his free hand and groaned. The smell of mildew and soil filled his nostrils, making the pain all the sharper.

He was cursing silently and rocking in agony when something solid snaked under him. He started with alarm, throwing back his head to get a look. Then he realized it was that creature. It hoisted him aloft, cradled him in its arms, and descended the staircase.

Aaron's head ached, his stomach was gnarled into a tight ball, and his hands and feet were so cold they felt numb. The newly added stiffness of that thing's arms dug into him, their bite making him tense and queasy. They descended the steps with such mechanical precision Aaron visualized it as a forklift dragging him down into the bowels of who knew what. He had no reason to imagine that things could get worse than they already were, but he couldn't shake the feeling that whatever had come before was just the tip of the iceberg and the true horror was yet to come.

Whatever the source of light was, they passed it, and everything grew dim for Aaron. He felt like he barely moved at first, but now the jolt of each step ground into his backside, and the rubbing soreness was getting to him. He tried to distract himself, to focus on the walls. As they descended, the dark brown stone took on a grimy sheen, as if it were being slowly overtaken by slime. Algae and the thick, heady smell of used grease started to swamp the air, and Aaron could hear the thump of heavy machinery below. A sharp flicker of light occasionally caught his attention, and as he rubbed his eyes in an attempt to clear his vision, he tilted his head up for a better view. A hard crust had accumulated in the corners of his eyes. The moment he realized this and started to palm it out, the creature set him down in a startlingly quick movement and pounced forward.

Aaron registered the bite of rock in his back, the chill of the slab of stone he had been set on, when a blur of motion distracted his attention. The creature's limbs thrust forward, there was a guttural squeal that was more animal than human, and thick, yellowish sludge splattered across the wall. Barked orders followed by the sound of footfalls trickled down from somewhere high overhead, and Aaron recognized the sound of boots descending the staircase. He snapped to full alertness, feverish intensity burning through his skull, and coiled up like an armadillo, peering up the stairs in wide-eyed wonder.

Nothing immediately appeared, and he fought back a pang of fear before mustering up the courage to turn his head and view the room below.

THE GATEWAY

The room below resembled a den in a subterranean cave. Coarse rock walls dropped into a maze of stalactites as they rounded into the corners, the floor beneath an uneven tumult of volcanic rock. A large pool of glistening liquid dominated the center of the den, its churning mass striating the room in languidly revolving patterns of blue. A wide cyclopean ring, its golden surface etched with patterns resembling Sanskrit, encircled the writhing torrent. A tangled heft of corrugated black tubes snaked out from the base, their twisting bulk worming its way across the pitted floor.

Nearly obscured by the brilliance in the middle of the room, a few shapes skulked off to the right. They resembled hazmat suits, only weird ones that were more nuanced and had strange appendages sprouting from the sides. Their egg-shaped heads had strange, wiry protrusions jutting out. Waist-high columns were bunched in front of the men, the shadows hiding all but the edges of rough stone. The smell of ozone permeated the place, reminding Aaron that his head still felt like it was full of cotton. The odor seemed to be coming from that twisting cascade of light, its irregular currents and flashes of light drowning out everything and making his grip on reality all the shakier. Yelling resonated above, followed by the crackle of gunfire, and in a rough jolt that creature barreled into his shoulder, throwing him forward.

The creature wrapped around him mid-roll, its body preventing him from a face-planting as they hit the floor beneath. The stiff angles of its limbs dug into him as they tumbled, and Aaron was bruised and disoriented when he finally rolled free. He careened into the lower rim of that thing, the force pitching him back in a fit of curses. Nursing his sore thigh, he struggled to his feet. The swirling mass leered over him, his eardrums alive with the crackle of electricity as a sonic pulse pounded him in waves. He couldn't take his eyes away from it. The swirling, bluish patterns looked like water, only with edges that were fuzzy, static. It exerted a pulling force. Not strong, but enough that he was careful as he rose. Muffled gunfire resounded behind him, the tinny whine of ricochets bouncing off the walls and down the steps. A round smacked into the floor too close for comfort, and Aaron scooted closer to the rim of that thing, angling to duck around the edge as he backed up.

A heavy boom echoed from beyond the top of the stairs, and the creature sailed into view. It hit the floor and skidded, stopping a few feet before the writhing mass in the center of the room. Aaron had paused for a moment, but he resumed edging toward the side of that thing. A spray of gunfire erupted from the stairwell and bullets bounced off the rocky floor near him, trailing plumes of dust and gravel. He pulled his limbs in and tried to scoot right up next to the rim. He didn't dare break or look behind him, or anywhere for that matter, out of fear that the moment he turned his head a bullet would hit him.

Projectiles sprayed the ground closer to him, and then in a flash that thing was sprawled over him. A host of slugs tore into the creature's back. He balled up more, and the creature pulled the huddled Aaron closer in its arms. Something large pounded the ground near them, followed by a bass-heavy blast and a wallop of force that tossed Aaron and the creature into the air. It was all slow motion after that, and they drifted apart as they flew. Aaron tried to swim in mid-air, quickly getting up to speed and struggling desperately as he tried to reverse the tide, but it was too little too late and he was engulfed.

It was all slow motion after that, and they drifted apart

Thick, ephemeral sheets closed in around him and claustrophobia started to gel. He gasped, but he couldn't seem catch a solid breath. Desperately he tried to will his lungs to move. His hair was on end, his skin felt like it was a separate entity, tingling in some weird, disassociated sensation, and he started to panic. Electricity crackled over, and a substance having the consistency of cotton candy tangled him up into a steadily tighter quagmire. Cool strips of something transient whipped about him, dragging across his exposed flesh.

He pawed fitfully but kept coming away with nothing. The smell of ozone grew stronger, the pungent odor burning through his nostrils. He tried to curl up, to get some bodily control over whatever this was, only nothing seemed to work right.

THE TRUTH OF THE MATTER

The war room was dark and gloomy and, aside from the electronic buzz of the overhead screens, utterly silent. Their faces highlighted under the glow of the monitors, the assembled bureaucrats looked on grimly as a squad of soldiers descended a flight of steps that most of them had never seen before. Tunneled out of solid stone, its raw griminess in striking contrast to the rest of the facility, the troops had opened fire on some strange creature. It was a dead ringer for the same one that had stormed the gate, and it was shielding something. Nothing was clear in the blur of motion and haze of smoke, but it looked like they were driving his huddled form down into some dark basement. Following the soldiers, the cameras briefly panned over what looked like a human corpse slumped on the steps. Only it was all wrong. It was wearing a lab smock and pale gray scrubs, but there was no red, just a gooey yellow splatter that ringed the collar and sprayed across the nearby wall. It was very brief, and the panning focus of the cameras made the feed appear indefinite, and the two military officials were put more on edge.

The video grew chaotic, the camera apparently agitated by the increasing movement. The lens spun around and panned to the back of the soldiers. They were shouting, guns ablaze, pouring a torrent of fire into the darkened burrow below. The feed became blurry, the images jarring patches of brilliance amid the prevailing darkness. In the lower recesses, the pale face of a kid was visible for a moment. Fire zeroed in on it as the camera rotated upward and took in the writhing abyss above the huddled pair.

The general grew visibly shaken and muttered unintelligibly.

The National Security Adviser looked even worse, his eyes wide, his body frozen as he silently mouthed something. The scientist leaned against the table and buried his face in his hands, stroking the widow's peak of his white mane. A loud boom resounded, the bass crackling through speaker drums that were blowing out under the strain, and the screens bleached out in a snap of light. The military men both let out cries and shielded their eyes.

When the blinding glare had diminished, the room was empty except for the strange vortex in its midst, an immense milky pool of blue that whirled within an emblazoned receptacle of gold. Its glistening illumination striped the dark room in eddies of color.

The attendant leaned over to the old man. "It had to be done."

The old man bent forward, burying his head in his hands as he wept in frustration. He had sold out the future of everyone he cared about for a dream that was falling apart before his eyes. A dream that might never have existed in the first place, *but at least it gave him a chance.* Now he was just another old fool falling for an impossible scheme. The young man beside him looked on in silence, a nictitating membrane slipping across its eyes.

Thrown into the Multiverse

The smothering veil broke. A cool wind replaced it in a striking chill that broke sharply across Aaron's face, and with a gasp he snapped his eyes open. He floundered for a moment, wondering where he was and what was going on, and then with a shock he realized he was falling through space. He thrashed about violently in a warm blue sky, the fresh smell of clean mountain air purging his nostrils. Light glared between the gauzy folds of clouds, airborne debris flitting across his vision as he tumbled. Just as he managed to tame his wild contortions he saw a grassy landscape closing in on him way too fast. He tried to curl into a shoulder roll, sure that it wouldn't be enough. He would shatter all his bones, squish his internal organs, and die in agonizing pain. Or, if he was lucky, the impact would send him into unconsciousness almost instantly, the torment a brief, unbearable spec before oblivion. Then, to his shock, just as he was tensing up, he landed softly, as if he had been gently set down in a bed of feathers. Stunned, he popped up, shook the grass and debris from his head, and whirled about.

A wide meadow of overgrown weeds spread all around him, a dark wood line establishing a perimeter on the distant edges. The blades of grass were waist high, and the temperature must have been almost seventy. The air that greeted him was much fresher than the stale rank of chemicals and mold of the military base. Sunlight beat down and he started to feel warm in his leather jacket. His armpits already moist, Aaron unzipped the jacket and took in a deep breath.

Even though he could make out the sandy, warm scent of vegetation, the air lacked that deep woods musk. Aaron was no expert, but he'd been in decent-sized national parks, and this was different. Lighter. And less raw. He could swear he was in a suburb, the aroma of soil and pine muted by the tang of mankind. He peered around in an attempt to get his bearings, and detected a distant buzzing. The sound was on the verge of triggering a memory, but Aaron couldn't quite place it. Whatever it was, a sense of desperation and danger lurked beneath it. He tried to clear his head, hoping to elicit something, but the harder he tried, the more substantial the mental block. He cursed silently, knowing this was important. He picked out a cry that sounded vaguely human, but his perception was still foggy and he couldn't pinpoint the source. The clouds had parted and the intensity of the sunlight bleached out the weed-strewn field, the wooded edges reduced to a mere collection of shadows. Aaron inhaled deeply again and squinted, then a flash of terror shot through him as he remembered.

Bursting into view on the horizon, a silver disc shot straight toward him. The terror of one of the last places he had visited washed over him. It happened during one of his weird, recent travels into what he could only imagine was another world. He had mostly relegated it to the realm of dreams, because that was what made the most sense. That reality was embroiled in a full-on alien invasion. There were corpses, abandoned houses, pockmarked streets, and all the remnants of civilization. A foreign girl dressed in military gear had rescued him. She was like a beautiful heroine, some larger than life movie character. Black dreadlocks falling down over olive skin, she was armed with knives and guns and knew exactly what to do with them. She'd pulled him out of danger and into a safe house. Things were too perfect from there on. She had fed him and seduced him, not that it took much. He wasn't exactly a hit with the ladies, but it was all a mad dream anyway. If it really happened, it was by far the best thing in his young life, but it couldn't possibly be real. In a blur of violence, they had been attacked, separated, and he'd done that weird travel thing where he ended up somewhere else. More weird stuff had occurred, and suddenly he was back home. Well, close to home. It didn't matter. Nothing made sense anymore. Terror snapped him back to reality, and he thought it was just his luck that the absolute worst part of the whole experience was the only part that was real.

He looked at the sky and realized that the silver angel of death was impossibly close now. He would never make it to the tree line in time. His skin crawled, he felt the desperation of so not wanting to die, but also the fatality of knowing he had no choice in the matter. He glanced around, but the weeds were too shallow to hide him. The thing had already spotted him, and even if he had the energy he couldn't outrun it. If he ran, he'd be shot in the back. The last time he was here, people were sprawled out in the grass with half their heads missing. He looked up and it was closer still.

Then it was over him and Aaron tensed, trying his hardest to stand resolute in the face of death. The ship paused, and Aaron wondered what it was waiting for. Then it burst open on one side and fell like a stone. It plowed into the ground with so much force he flew backward, the blades of grass whipping at him with stinging force. The shockwave had forced the air out of his lungs, just as the pungent scent of shredded vegetation bit into his nostrils.

Desperately delving his hand into the grass in an attempt to halt the ride, the friction burn tore into his fingers and he snatched them up with a cry. He finally ground to a halt, intact except for his smarting fingers and uncomfortably warm bottom. The ground shook as another object slammed into it and he looked about desperately. The silver rim of another saucer was half-buried in the grass thirty feet away, a trail of smoke wafting from its side. Behind it, its form hazy in the light, was that creature. Tramping through the haze of smoke and disturbed soil, it seemed oblivious to the carnage.

A whooping cry split the silence, and Aaron turned his head toward the wood line. A small group of people was skulking out of the forest. All Aaron could make out were pinkish dots amid olive-green blurs, but they resembled some military cluster he had seen onscreen. There were none of the hard edges of modern military, like antennas and helmets, which made them what? Rebels? One of them released a guttural, animalistic yelp and started toward him. He recoiled, fearing the worst, but as he looked closer he realized it was the girl! The one from his dream. He scrambled to his feet just as she leapt on him, squeezing his sore frame and swarming his cheek with kisses. He fought hard not to stumble under her embrace, a sudden head rush disorienting him as he smiled and tried to at least pretend that this was all real. He took in the scent of her body odor, the brushing itch of her dreadlocks as they slid across his face. Then she abruptly released him, took a step back, and excitedly pointed to her swollen belly.

His head feeling thick, Aaron realized something that had so far escaped his notice. *She was pregnant!* Was it...was it *his*? *That had all happened months ago. That was all it took, he knew, but still...*

With a big smile, she pointed from her belly to Aaron, and it suddenly didn't matter if it was his. It bonded him to this girl, and that was enough. As a quickly escalating buzzing cut in, her expression morphed into one of terror. Aaron was confused for a moment, until he looked up.

Ten saucers were converging on them, darting through the air in bizarre and unlikely patterns that drew them ever closer. It was just his luck. The highest point he had ever attained in his life, and it was all over before it even began.

Something flitted off the ground, and a moment later one ship after another was rupturing through its sides. There was the popping rend of metal being perforated, followed by a torrent of silver that sprayed out the other side. The punctures blossomed into a spider web of cracks, the silver crafts shattering like an eggshell and falling from the sky. Aaron covered his head and awkwardly tried to shield the girl, pulling her into a huddle as she collapsed into his chest. Tremors rocked the ground, jeopardizing their stability. Ships plowed into the grass all around them, waves of heat pelting them with scraps of torn grass in sandy bursts. It only took moments before suddenly it was all over, the silver husks of broken craft jutting out of the mangled weeds all about them like the decaying skyscrapers of some post-apocalyptic alien planet. Aaron relaxed limbs that were wrapped so tightly around the girl that they were losing feeling, uncoiling himself and raising his head as the creature approached. Blades of grass crunched underfoot as it drew closer, the smoke wafting from the remnants of alien craft drifting across in obscuring gales. Aaron was exhausted, and he couldn't bring himself to summon the smallest reaction.

Passing the last of the half-buried craft, the creature was almost to the small clear circle of soil holding him and the girl when another whistling sound broke through the airspace and the creature reversed course and took off running. A few steps, and it bounded into the air. A blast pelted the thing halfway up, but it seemed to have no effect. The creature plowed into the closest ship, tearing out the other side a moment later and continuing in an upward arc where it tore into the bottom of another ship. More craft swooped in as the two downed ships plunged to the ground. But that thing was on fire, raining silver down into the meadow as it ripped through ship after ship. A whooping started, and Aaron looked back to see that the girl's friends were almost upon them. Most had beards and they all had darker features, the motley crew resembling nothing so much as Aaron's idea of Third World guerrillas. Cheering and hollering, they were throwing up their fists in victory. The lightheartedness and surreal tone was infectious, and Aaron cracked a smile. Maybe this wasn't so bad after all. He had no idea where he was, but he was with the girl of his dreams, and he was a somebody with these people. A warm confidence seeped into him. Everything was going his way for a change. Who knew what tomorrow held? But then again, who cared? He was still a kid. He could ride this wave for a while.

ABOUT THE AUTHOR

Born in 1972, on a small army base in the south, Dan Henk grew up on a diet of science fiction and horror books. At eighteen Dan Henk was kicked out of his house. He spent the next eight months homeless, often living in the woods. Six months later, he was in the passenger seat of a car that flipped and his face broke the windshield. Soon after that, the tendon on his thumb was severed in a fight with a crackhead. He came down with brain cancer in 2001, and his wife died in a hit-and-run in 2007. In 2012, a car shattered his bike, throwing him through the windshield and putting him in a coma for hours. In 2017 he flipped his truck and woke up in the woods. There's a running theory that he is a cyborg.

He's done art for *Madcap Magazine*, *Maximum Rock and Roll Magazine*, *Tattoo Artist Magazine*, *Black Static*, *This is Horror*, *Deaddite Press*, *Skin Deep*, *The Living Corpse*, *Aphrodesia*, *Splatterpunk*, *Tattoo Prodigies*, *Pint Sized Paintings*, *Coalesce*, *Zombie Apocalypse*, *Most Precious Blood*, *Indecision*, *Locked In A Vacancy*, *Shai Hulud*, *Purity Records*, and a slew of Memento books.

2011 saw the release of his first book, *The Black Seas Of Infinity*, care of Anarchy Books. Permuted Press reissued it in 2015, and a few months later released his second novel *Down Highways In The Dark...By Demons Driven*. Splatterpunk issued his short story *"Christmas is Cancelled"* as a signed and numbered chapbook. Now living in Pennsylvania, he owns half of The Abyss Art Studio in New York, and spends what little spare time he has doing Muay Thai and Brazilian Jiujitsu.

Curious about other Crossroad Press books?
Stop by our site:
http://crossroadpress.com
We offer quality writing
in digital, audio, and print formats.

Made in the USA
Las Vegas, NV
07 November 2022

58990371R00164